Back in the Habit

ALICE LOWEECEY

A FALCONE & DRISCOLL INVESTIGATION

Back

in the

Habit

MIDNIGHT INK
WOODBURY, MINNESOTA

FIRST EDITION
First Printing, 2012

Book design and format by Donna Burch
Cover design by Ellen Lawson
Cover art © iStockphoto.com/Giorgio Fochesato

Midnight Ink, an imprint of Llewellyn Worldwide Ltd.

Library of Congress Cataloging-in-Publication Data
Loweecey, Alice.
  Back in the habit : a Falcone & Driscoll investigation / Alice Loweecey. — 1st ed.
     p.   cm.
  ISBN 978-0-7387-2668-7
1. Ex-nuns—Fiction. 2. Ex-police officers—Fiction. 3. Private investigators—Fiction. I. Title.
  PS3612.O8865B33 2012
  813'.6—dc23
                                    2011033090

Midnight Ink
Llewellyn Worldwide Ltd.
2143 Wooddale Drive
Woodbury, MN 55125-2989
www.midnightinkbooks.com

Printed in the United States of America

MY

For my husband, Phil

4/12

ONE

"Good afternoon. may I help you?"

Sidney's always-perky voice faltered when the visitor didn't reply.

The footsteps passed the admin's desk and stopped before Giulia's desk on the far side of the office.

"Your employer, please."

Giulia looked up from the report on her screen, and the world tilted. A moment later, she put on her professional face and rose, hand outstretched.

"Good afternoon, Sister. How may we help you?"

She was surprised at how normal her voice sounded in the face of her former Superior General. Especially considering their last meeting, when the woman had flung Giulia's Vatican-issued dispensation from vows smack in Giulia's face.

Sister Mary Fabian gripped Giulia's hand in that well-remembered "businessman's handshake."

"The Community requires the services of a private investigator. I was informed that such is your new profession."

"Yes, um, if you'll wait just a minute, I'll see if Mr. Driscoll is free."

Giulia skirted her desk and knocked on Frank's door, grateful she chose good, flat sneakers that morning, because her feet wanted to trip over themselves. At Frank's "Come in," she slipped inside, safe.

Frank Driscoll, founder and senior partner of Driscoll Investigations, kept scribbling notes in a handwritten log. "Did I hear someone out there?"

A giggle spluttered through Giulia's lips. "You didn't say that right. Someone—with a capital *S*—is out there."

Frank looked up, running a hand through his short ginger hair, which stood straighter than hair ought to. "Not going back to that barber. Who's out there? Why do you look like Sister Mary Evil's after you?"

Giulia leaned against the door. "Oh, perfect. That's exactly who wants to talk to you." She took a deep, slow breath. "My former Superior General's in the outer office. The Puppet Master."

Frank's hair seemed to rise to attention. "Seriously?"

"Yes. She says the Community needs a PI."

"Seriously? That's great." He smoothed back his hair and stood, buttoning his suit jacket. "Thank God I wore a tie today. Come on and introduce us."

Giulia let herself be carried by his brisk enthusiasm. *Get ahold of yourself. This woman has no power over you anymore. She's just another client.*

She almost lost her composure when she opened the door and saw Sidney's face. Their admin looked exactly like a kid watching her first Fourth of July fireworks: round-eyed and open-mouthed.

The office was narrow enough for Giulia to reach the imposing woman standing by her desk in three steps. *Way too few.*

"Sister Mary Fabian, Frank Driscoll. Mr. Driscoll, Sister Fabian, Superior General of the Sisters of Saint Francis of Greater Pittsburgh."

Frank's handshake appeared more than a match for Sister Fabian's.

"Sister. Pleased to meet you. If you'll step into my office, we'll do our best to help."

Sidney regained her voice the moment Frank's door closed. "Wow. She reminds me of this really strict history teacher I had my freshman year. It must be the outfit that makes her look intimidating. Wait—it's the habit, right?"

"Right. She doesn't look like that just because of the habit. She could give lessons in intimidation." Giulia leaned her burning forehead against the chilled window. *I apologize to every weatherman in Cottonwood, Pennsylvania, for complaining about this record-breaking early cold snap.*

Sidney's voice came closer. "Maybe we should whisper, so our voices don't carry into Mr. Driscoll's office."

"The woman has ears like a bat, but I think she's laying down the law to Frank. We're okay." *This window feels better than air conditioning in July.*

"I bet you looked nicer than that when you were a nun. Did I tell you that Olivier said if you'd been a priest he would've asked you to bless his office? He gets his MSW in December."

"That's very sweet of Olivier. I didn't know he was Catholic."

"His whole family is, something wicked."

"And you're not?"

"Nope. We're just generic Christians. We celebrate all the good holidays without all the guilt."

The snort came out before Giulia could stop it. Then she pushed her face into her sleeve to stifle more laughter. When she opened her eyes, Sidney was staring at her with the "I've said something horrible and Giulia will hate me" look.

Giulia shook her head, sucked in a deep breath, and held up a warning finger. "Sidney, you have yet to say anything offensive to me, so stop looking like you're going to get detention." She snagged the Godzilla coffee mug from her desk and gulped the rest of her lukewarm cappuccino. "One of these days when I'm feeling invincible, I'll tell you so many stories about the convent you'll never want to hear the word again."

Footsteps hit the wooden floor in Frank's office, and the phone rang at the same moment. Sidney made a face, but returned to her desk.

The door opened and, like a gentleman, Frank ushered the Superior General through. "I'll be in touch with you tomorrow morning at ten, Sister."

"Thank you, Mr. Driscoll." She opened the outer door for herself without acknowledging Giulia or Sidney, who was scribbling notes on a bright-pink "While You Were Out" pad.

Frank closed the door without a single click and leaned his back against it. "*Dia trócaire.*"

Giulia raised an eyebrow. "And that means?"

"God have mercy. Don't worry, ma'am, I haven't taken the Lord's name in vain in a month. I think." He pulled at the knot in his tie. "I have to deliver that report to AtlanticEdge by nine tomorrow morning."

"Mr. Driscoll, I can stay and type or read it over for you if you need me," Sidney said. "Oh, and your basketball captain called."

Frank groaned. "That's right. We have a game at six."

"No, you don't, Mr. Driscoll. The other team has three guys down with the flu."

"Poor guys, and hooray. Now that I have tonight …" He squeezed his eyes shut for a moment. "Sidney, can you stay an extra half-hour? Giulia, if I got on my knees to you, would you come back in tonight?"

Giulia grinned. "Sidney, where's your phone? We need a picture."

Frank gave a theatrical sigh and hitched up his trouser legs.

Laughing, Giulia held up a hand. "No, don't ruin that suit. Why don't I just stay?"

"Normally I'd say yes, but I hate making people do busywork just because they have to wait for me. Did you have plans?"

"An intimate session with an elliptical trainer. What time do you want me back?"

"Six-thirty?" When Giulia nodded, Frank turned to Sidney. "I've got most of the report typed, but I need help formatting."

"No problem, Mr. Driscoll, I'm taking a course to upgrade my Office skills. We just finished presentations and PowerPoint." She bounced out of her rolling chair.

Giulia grinned again as Sidney trailed Frank into his office. *I swear, she can make anyone smile. Even Sister Mary Fabian.*

———

Giulia decreased the resistance on the gym's elliptical cross-trainer to finish her third mile. The five o'clock news on the wall-mounted ten-inch TV in front of her ended with a folksy local-interest segment.

Of all people from my past, why did Sister Fabian have to track me down? Does she care that she's one of the top people on my "Die happy without seeing them again" list?

She switched to a national and world news channel. A thin, perky blonde tried to tone down her perpetual smile. "The United States Conference of Catholic Bishops issued a statement on the latest child sexual abuse lawsuit. It urges the faithful to pray for accusers to be healed of the sin of anger."

Giulia punched the TV's *off* button with her right hand and the cross-trainer's resistance button with her left. When the incline hit 15 degrees, she increased her tempo.

I shouldn't want to take a knife to those priests' offending parts, but I do.

Her heart rate ramped up, and sweat ran down the sides of her face.

If they targeted adults, their sin wouldn't be quite so monstrous. Maybe it would. Maybe they'd just fry in a different pit in Hell.

Ten minutes later she climbed off the machine and wiped it down. The buff executive types sweating at the machines on either side of her never took their eyes off *SportsCenter*.

She finished the last of her water bottle as she headed for the showers. *You need to get a clue, Falcone. You're not a representative of the Church anymore. You don't have to try and explain the pedophilia scandal and the Church's sin-of-omission response to eight classes of world-weary teenagers.*

———

Giulia turned up her jacket collar and peered down the street for the bus. "Of course it's windy on the night I don't dry my hair." Her ringtone barely reached her ears through the gusts. *Now I'll have "We Will Rock You" looping through my mind. It may be time to change to a different Queen song.*

"Thanks, Frank."

"Huh? For what? Never mind. Did you eat yet?"

"No, I just got out of the gym."

"Great. Neither did I. I'll get pizza and pop. See you in a few."

She closed the phone. "If my head doesn't turn into a snow-cone first. What's up with this weather? Halloween isn't for another month."

The screech of air brakes interrupted her. The downtown bus was packed with people chattering about the 3-D movie opening that night, about sushi versus burgers, about hooking up with guys at the bars afterward.

I need a date. Not another brainstorming session with my boss masquerading as a date.

Two couples got on at the corner of Euclid and Maple. Giulia watched surreptitiously as they sat in the rows opposite her, kissing and joking.

Suck it up. At least you're not still in the convent.

TWO

"I KNOW THIS IS good, Ms. Pizza Snob, so don't go all connoisseur on me." Frank reached across his desk and handed Giulia a paper plate with two triangular slices on it.

Giulia set down her Mountain Dew and filled her mouth with sausage and peppers. Workouts plus stress had tripled her appetite.

"Mmgph, yefs, it isf." She swallowed. "Where is this place?"

"It took over the sub joint on Oak." He wiped his hands on a recycled-paper napkin. "Did your head nun get her attitude from putting up with everyone singing Fabian songs at her?"

Giulia forced herself to swallow so she wouldn't spray Frank with Dew. "We never did it where she could hear us. When she was younger, she had a vocal range like Julie Andrews. But she had surgery for throat cancer, and it killed her voice."

"Ouch."

"She has trouble being grateful for surviving. It spills over into everything."

Frank started another slice. "Giulia, I thought you gave up sugary nun-speak. Real people don't talk like nineteenth-century prayer books."

She shrugged with one shoulder. "Force of habit, even after more than a year in the real world."

He grinned. "That's why you have me and Sidney to set you an example. Anyway, so Sister Fabian runs the place? No wonder you bailed."

"It was much more complicated than that."

He smiled around a mouthful of crust. "Like a bad divorce, huh?"

Too many replies crowded Giulia's tongue for her to give voice to any of them.

Frank swallowed. "Never mind; you know I'm not serious. Here's the scoop on our new job. First, did you know that four different convents merged last spring?"

"Communities, Frank. A convent is a single building."

"I bow to your superior wisdom. So many nuns called it quits that separately the four Communities couldn't make rent." He finished his Coke. "What did you and your convent-mates think about the merger?"

"We were all for it if it kept us going."

"All mergers should go so smoothly. Apparently everyone felt like that. You done?"

When Giulia nodded, Frank closed the pizza box on the last two slices, and Giulia cleared plates and napkins off the desk. Fire trucks and at least one ambulance sped past their building.

"I'll show you why that's important in a sec." Frank turned his monitor so they could both see it. "This isn't pretty. A Novice—

that's the second year, right?—killed herself eight days ago." He continued over Giulia's gasp, "The higher-ups are positive it was suicide, and the police closed the case. But the parents aren't happy with Sister Fabian's explanation. She claimed the Novice was depressed and unbalanced, and the parents disagree."

"They should. The Community puts us through the entire spectrum of psychological tests before we're cleared to enter."

Frank shrugged this time. "She claims this Novice slipped through the testing cracks. Plus the Novice was from southeast Maryland. She had trouble adjusting with no family nearby as a safety net."

"Did Sister Fabian say whether or not the Novice was watched and hounded and scrutinized every minute she was off the Novices' floor? Did she say that maybe the Maryland Motherhouse was different, and Pittsburgh was the real problem? Did she admit to using her personal brand of humiliation plus intimidation to bring everyone into line?" Giulia snatched her pop can and took a long drink to cut herself off.

Frank whistled. "That bad?"

"Sorry for the rant. Yes, that bad."

"Jesus, Giulia, why'd you stay there so long?"

"Some other time. What does the job entail?" She clipped the words to avoid breaking into another rant.

"Right." He opened a spreadsheet on the monitor. "The parents threatened to sue the convent—Community—for wrongful death. Sister Fabian offered to bring in an impartial third party—namely, us. The parents agreed to abide by the third party's decision, but here's the catch. Some big celebration's on Wednesday, and she wants this dealt with before then."

Giulia rolled her eyes. "Saint Francis Day, Mr. Francis Driscoll."

"Oh, yeah. She said there's also a major reunion starting this week, and the investigation has to be invisible to everyone."

"We'll just use our interdimensional travel beam and psychic powers?"

Frank snorted. "You're watching too many cheesy sci-fi movies."

"I'm serious, Frank. I trashed an invitation to that reunion. The Motherhouse will be wall-to-wall people. You and I don't have a shield of invisibility or supersonic hearing."

A screenshot of the Philadelphia 76ers replaced the spreadsheet. Frank kept his eyes on Giulia. "No, but we have a secret weapon. You."

She stared.

"It's perfect, Giulia. I thought of it the minute Sister Fabian mentioned keeping things invisible." He picked up a pen and drew bullet points on the top of the pizza box. "You won't have to learn how to fit in—you already fit in."

Slam.

Frank jumped. The Dew can crumpled slightly under the force of Giulia's panic.

"Strip me naked, smear my body with honey, and bury me in an anthill first."

Frank dropped the pen onto the cardboard. "What?"

"Go back in the convent? Are you kidding me?" Her heart rate ramped up like she was back on the elliptical machine.

"But it's different now, right?"

"In what possible way do you think a centuries-old institution would be different after a mere fourteen months?" Her hand crushed the pop can into a silvery green hourglass.

"I mean, you know, the nuns. The merger happened while you were getting out, so you probably wouldn't know half the nuns. That's good, right?"

"I'd know even fewer than that. I hadn't been back to the Motherhouse for five years before I left. They had me teaching in the boonies. That doesn't mean—"

"See? Piece of cake. Look at the schedule I worked up." He moved the mouse, and the spreadsheet returned to the screen.

She dragged her hands over her face. "It is not a piece of cake."

"I'll call Sister Fabian tomorrow and ask her to send you a habit—you didn't keep those, right?"

"Of course not."

"You'll need a room of your own." He started typing. "If she has to, she can make someone double up."

"No one gives Sister Fabian orders. Listen—"

"Don't believe her poker face. She's panicking like my mother the night before Thanksgiving."

"Frank."

"I can drive you to Pittsburgh—it'll be smarter than you renting a car and trying to park it somewhere. We can keep in touch by cell."

"Frank."

"You go to Mass every Sunday, right? How does two o'clock sound? I'll clear it with Sister Fabian tomorrow; that'll give her plenty of time. Now, here's what I think your cover should be—"

"Frank!" She clenched her hands in her lap so she wouldn't try to fling the office chair through the window. "Use Plan B."

He stopped simultaneously typing and talking. "There isn't one. This plan is flawless."

"Wrong. It has one big flaw. Me."

"You have a conflict?"

A thin, strained laugh escaped her. "I'll have to cancel my Sunday through Wednesday lineup of dates."

His mouth dropped open a tick, and she laughed for real.

"I wish. Whatever gave you the idea that me going back into the convent would be easy, let alone a good idea?"

"I—but—of course it's easy. You couldn't be more perfect for this."

"Wrong again." She gripped her hands tighter. "I cut all ties when I left, and not only because of multiple nasty fights. I did it because bad things happened, and they're—difficult—to remember. The thought of returning never crossed my mind for an instant."

His expression drooped, changing the pattern of freckles on his face. "Think about it now, okay? Say yes so we can get on the Pittsburgh Diocese's approved vendor list. Think of what it'll mean for the business."

"The business won't benefit by me freaking out in the laundry room down in the cellars."

"Then don't go into the cellars. Oh, wait. You might have to, because that's where the Novice killed herself. But you're strong, Giulia. Look how you testified in court in front of TV cameras to get Don Falke in jail. A few days in one big building won't break you."

Her lip curled. "Fabian could eat Urnu the Snake for breakfast."

She might not want to remember all the details of when Sandra Falke and her brother Don—also known as Urnu the Snake—tried to murder her three months earlier. But she definitely should not remember the ten years of Fabian-spewed crap she'd been inundated with.

She slammed the crumpled pop can into the trash. "For breakfast."

"I don't doubt it. Seriously, Giulia, you're not still under that harridan's thumb. She doesn't have one crumb of power over you."

Her mouth quirked. "That's exactly what I've been telling myself."

"And that's why we make a kick-ass—sorry—team." He hit the *Print* button. "Take home the cover story I wrote for you and her summary of the incident. I'll have her send a habit to your apartment."

"When did I agree to this?"

"Just now, when my flawless reasoning won you over."

"No, it didn't." *He looks like an eager little boy. Does he know it's almost impossible to resist him when he gets that expression?* "I realize getting the Diocese to funnel some of its wealth our way sounds good, but—"

"It doesn't just sound good, it is good. Clients around here don't come much bigger." He grinned wider. "When I started Driscoll Investigations, my fellow cops told me that the cheaper rents in Cottonwood wouldn't make up for all the Pittsburgh business I'd be losing. Hah."

"Jesus, Mary, and Joseph. Maybe I'll get run over by a bus on Saturday."

"Don't be ridiculous." He crossed into the other room and brought back the printouts from the communal printer by Sidney's desk. "What's the address of your new apartment?"

"No. Have two habits delivered here tomorrow." When Frank's eyebrows furrowed, she said, "I don't want her to know where I live. And don't look at me like that. Sensible people don't allow toxic ones access to their lives."

"Point taken. I'll meet you here at one. What's your dress size?"

"So much for a woman's mystique. Twelve." She glanced at her jeans and wool sweater. "You know, the habit's optional in most Communities now."

"Camouflage. You'll be one more anonymous nun in black, especially to the ones from the three other cities. You'd stand out in street clothes, even bland street clothes."

"Are you implying my wardrobe isn't stylish?"

"Well, I mean, compared to, you know …"

"Heh. I don't disagree. Okay, fine. The habit it is." *How fast this discussion progressed from "No way" to a dress fitting.* "Frank, if I end up in psychotherapy because of this, you're paying the bill."

"I'll get a rider on the insurance." He folded the printouts and handed them to her. "And stop putting yourself down. You'll be fine. Strength, intelligence, and charm are the hallmarks of Driscoll Investigations. I'm charm, you're everything else."

"That's not a compliment." She tried to scowl.

"You bet it is. A beauty-queen bimbo would never have suited me."

The scowl worked this time. "No improvement. Time for me to leave anyway. The bus comes in ten minutes."

He returned it. "You're not waiting on a downtown corner alone at night. I'm driving you." He shut down the computer. "Just because you took self-defense training doesn't mean I want to give you an opportunity to use it."

————

Frank pulled his Camry into the minuscule parking lot of Giulia's new apartment building. The wind blew leaves and stray fast-food wrappers across the asphalt. The few people on the street hurried past, raincoats flapping behind them.

Frank unhooked his seat belt. "Are you going to invite me in?"

"A lady needs boundaries, Mr. Driscoll. Besides, I haven't dusted and vacuumed this week yet."

"I'm guessing I could eat off your floors. All right, since your door is barred to me tonight, let's have dinner tomorrow. A last fling before taking the veil."

"Temporarily."

"I should hope so. I have no desire to look for a new partner. Well?"

"I'd love to."

"Giulia," Frank said through laughter, "you need to practice playing hard to get. Make the man wonder if he's worth your time. Make him chase you harder."

So much for reading Cosmo *religiously.* She sat straighter in the passenger seat. "It sounds lovely, Mr. Driscoll, but I'll have to check my calendar."

"Better. Now tell me you'll text me, because that's more impersonal than a phone call."

"And rude in this case." He opened his mouth, but she forestalled him. "All right, I get it." She flipped her hair back with one hand. "I'll text you—sometime."

More laughter filled the car. "Did you learn that coquettish gesture from Sidney?"

"Mingmei. It flopped, didn't it?"

"Uh, well," he cleared his throat. "It needs a little practice."

"I'll reread several *Cosmo*s tonight." She opened her door, and Frank started to open his. "That's all right. I can see myself inside."

"My mother taught me manners. Do you really read *Cosmo*?"

"I have a lot to catch up on. And your brothers taught you how to sneak in a kiss or three."

"I—"

"Uh-huh. Thanks for the ride. I'll see you tomorrow."

Safe behind her own apartment door, Giulia plopped a year's worth of *Cosmo* magazines on the coffee table. "I will learn to do this right if it kills me."

Her conscience whispered that she was avoiding the real issue: her, back in habit, walking through the Motherhouse door on Sunday afternoon. A mere thirty-six hours from now.

"I am not thinking about that tonight. I will let it sink in and dissect it in the sunshine tomorrow."

She flipped pages in the top magazine till she found that month's how-to: "The 'Good Girl's' Guide to Flirting." With a yellow highlighter in one hand, she settled in for an hour of study.

THREE

"I'M WAITING WITH MY camera ready," Frank said from the other side of the office's bathroom door Saturday afternoon.

"Frank, I will call down on you every curse my grandmother taught me if you take my picture in this outfit."

"Curse away. It's worth coming into work on a Saturday to see you in that outfit."

The long, narrow office bathroom wasn't meant to double as a dressing room. Giulia zipped the black A-line dress and adjusted the wrist-length sleeves. The detachable white collar tucked in just as she remembered, a Velcro circle securing it at the back. The two-foot-long veil hung on the back of the door as though it hid a severed head. A narrow ray of sunlight touched it, and the black polyester swallowed like a living shadow.

She grimaced. "All right, that's morbid. Just put the thing on. You haven't forgotten how."

"Giulia, who are you talking to?"

"The habit, Frank." She listened a moment. "Don't laugh. This is your fault."

"I'm not—" he cleared his throat—"laughing. How long does it take to put on two pieces of clothing?"

"Hold your horses." She jammed the veil on her head, hands automatically tucking her brown curls under the narrow white outer band. "I shouldn't remember that trick so easily."

She stood before the mirror over the sink, eyes closed while she adjusted the inner plastic headpiece at the top. A deep breath, and she opened her eyes.

"Oh, crap." Sister Mary Regina Coelis stared back at her—a ghost laid to rest nearly a year and a half earlier.

Frank's voice came from right against the other side of the bathroom door. "Giulia? What's wrong?"

"Everything. Move. I'm coming out." She turned away from the apparition in the mirror and opened the door.

Frank's phone clicked. "*Dia naofa.*"

Giulia tugged the veil farther down over her ears. "An outfit guaranteed to flatter no figure. It makes fat women look like tents and skinny ones like scarecrows. Thus its purpose: an instant turn-off to any man with a pulse."

She rifled through the tissue paper in the delivery box. "Did Fabian remember to send a crucifix?"

Frank snapped another photo. "There's an envelope taped under the lid."

Giulia ripped open the flap on its narrow end. A three-inch-high replica of the San Damiano crucifix fell into her hand. A plain gold wedding band was tangled in the stainless-steel chain.

"Fancy crucifix." Frank's voice tickled her earlobe.

"It's the one that spoke to Saint Francis." Giulia took refuge in ordinary, ignorant Frank. "Seriously, Francis, didn't you ever have to learn about your patron saint?"

He waved it away. "For confirmation, but who remembers that? Put it on so I can get the whole effect."

She worked the chain free of the wedding band and eased it over the veil. As it settled under the collar, the crucifix resting over her camouflaged cleavage, footsteps slapped down the hall.

The door opened so fast it bounced off the printer table.

"Am I too late? Traffic on Saturday is nutso. Oh—oh wow, Giulia, you look just like Maria from *The Sound of Music*!"

Sidney's sneakers squeaked on the linoleum as she circled Giulia. "It's like you're an old-maid librarian or something. All your hair is gone, too." She stuck her nose up to Giulia's chest. "Ew. What a creepy crucifix. The ones in Olivier's parents' house are plain silver or wood. This one's too realistic for me, even with the miniature saints and angels all over it."

Frank was biting his cheek and looked suspiciously innocent. Giulia turned her back on him and stopped Sidney's great white shark impersonation.

"Sidney, what happened to you?"

Her tanned face now looked like a grade-schooler's idea of splotchy polka dots.

Sidney threw her hands in the air. "It's all Olivier's fault. We had our first real argument last night. He said my stir-fried tofu tasted like little soy sponges, and I said he was going to die of a heart attack before he turned forty. He actually eats rare steak." She shuddered. "Then he said I wasn't seeing both sides of the argument because I never ate 'real' food. He said if I ate a Twinkie and admitted it was Heaven with cream filling, he'd eat my tofu-veggie loaf for dinner."

"And the hives?"

Sidney stomped her foot. "I ate the whole thing while he watched—it was disgusting! All that over-processed flour and trans fats and sugar. About five minutes after I swallowed the last bite, I started to itch all over. And my nose stuffed up so bad, I had to irrigate it three times. While I did that, he found an allergy website. We narrowed it down to the yellow dye, of course. Chemicals are evil!"

"You didn't end up in the hospital?"

"No, my throat didn't close up or anything, so as allergies go it's not that bad, but I am so furious! I'm never sick, not even with a cold, and Olivier's messed up my whole immune system because he had to be stubborn."

Giulia wasn't sure how she was keeping a straight face. Sidney looked like a tall, brown version of the famous "mad bluebird" photograph. "You are going to milk this for all it's worth, right?"

Sidney stopped rubbing her arms. "Huh?"

Frank leveraged himself off Giulia's desk. "You took his dare and beat him at it. Olivier will be a walking guilt machine till those hives fade."

Giulia practically saw the light bulb illuminate the top of Sidney's head.

"I never thought of it like that. He already left two messages on my phone, but I ignored them."

"The next time he calls, answer and let him do all the talking. A little groveling will be good for his soul."

Frank *tsk*ed. "Women. You're all manipulators."

"Yet you still chase us."

He pushed through the tissue paper on Giulia's desk and held up the wedding band. "Even though all you're after is one of these."

Sidney's mouth mirrored the *O* of the ring. "What's that for?" she glanced at Frank, then away again.

"It's part of my undercover outfit. All nuns who take final vows wear one. You've heard nuns referred to as Brides of Christ. Final vows are like wedding vows in a sense, so we get a wedding ring."

"I never knew that."

"Since I'm pretending to be my old self, I need to wear it again."

"Ooh, put it on, please! I want a picture."

"So do I." Frank held up his phone. "Smile for the cell phones, please."

The fastest way to get out of this is to play along. Giulia slipped the ring over the proper finger. A little loose, but better than having to spray her finger with cooking spray to remove it when all this was over.

With a big, fake grin on her face, she held up her left hand and waited for the *click*s.

FOUR

FRANK SNAKED THROUGH THE bistro tables that crowded the floor of the Laff It Up comedy club, a Corona in each hand. Every table was full and the bar was standing-room only. On the walls, the framed photos of famous comedians seemed to rattle with the decibel level.

He handed one of the beers to Giulia as he sat down. "They're out of limes. Sorry."

"This is fine." Giulia took a drink. *Thin, but cold. At least it's thirty degrees warmer in here than outside.*

The waiter must have been three steps behind Frank, because he set their enchiladas in front of them while the bottle was still at her lips. Her stomach growled, but she was sure no one else heard it.

Frank swallowed a mouthful of beer. "Forgot to tell you. Blake emailed me with another commission."

Blake, Frank's former schoolmate and the vice president of the AtlanticEdge tech company, had fulfilled Frank's prediction. When Driscoll Investigations saved Blake's life—and high-society marriage—from a crazed stalker, Frank knew that a grateful Blake would talk up Driscoll Investigations to the right people at AtlanticEdge.

"It's better than delivering subpoenas to pay the bills, right?" Giulia cut another forkful of tortillas, meat, and gooey cheese. "I should learn to cook Mexican."

"God, yes. Subpoenas, I mean. No more forced encounters with losers who have more guns than brains. If Blake keeps up this pace, I might have to refuse one of his offers." He looked to the ceiling. "Saint Joseph, patron of hard-working men, I was only joking. I love all this work."

"Hopefully Saint Joseph will read your intention rather than your flippancy." Her eyebrows met. "I'm talking like a maiden great-aunt again."

Frank swallowed his beer too quickly. "At least you recognize it." He gave her the grin that meant *I'm going to get a rise out of Giulia*. "Pretty soon you'll sound young enough for me to take home to meet the family."

The lights dimmed as though Frank had given a cue.

Giulia hissed over the preliminary applause, "I'm younger than you, Mr. Driscoll."

"And tonight you're finally dressed like it."

She kicked his shin—lightly. He grimaced at her and whispered, "I'll get you for that."

Giulia adjusted the sleeves of her faux-silk shirt. *I know I look modern and a little sexy, Frank Driscoll, because Mingmei helped me pick out these clothes.*

When Frank hired Giulia away from the coffee shop below his office, Giulia trained the new barista. Mingmei, Giulia's opposite

25

in practically everything, became something Giulia hadn't had in ten years—a female friend. Close relationships were still frowned on in the convent. At first, Giulia didn't even know how to carry on a light conversation. But then Mingmei caught Giulia reading *Cosmo* magazine at lunch, and Giulia explained her need to catch up on the past decade.

Without Mingmei's fashion advice, Giulia might've worn a beige turtleneck and gray skirt on tonight's date.

This is a real date, too, just Frank and me. Mingmei was right about this burnt-orange shirt and black jeans. I saw it in Frank's eyes when he picked me up. So there, maiden-aunt Giulia. Go tat a doily.

Frank jogged her elbow. "Wake up. The opening act is as good as the headliner."

"I'm awake. What kind of act?"

"Puns and one-liners. If you're not laughing in five minutes, you're dead."

————

Two hours later, Frank's hand came down over Giulia's as she touched the door handle of her apartment building.

"Are you going to ask me in, Ms. Falcone?"

Giulia stiffened, and not because of the sharp wind. "Frank, you're my employer."

"That's an excuse and you know it." He squeezed her hand. "Afraid?"

I can prove to him I'm not an old maid. Boundaries are flexible.

Giulia turned on him as the wind cut between them. "Come in for coffee. Since it's after eleven now, I'll let you corrupt me enough to sleep in and get to ten o'clock Mass tomorrow."

He laughed. "Your concept of sin needs work."

He closed the door after her and she led him to the end of the first floor.

"Remember, Frank, my boundaries are only so flexible."

"Ma'am; yes, ma'am."

She writhed her lips to hide a smile and turned the deadbolt. "I'll start coffee. I don't have cable, so you're stuck with the Saturday night programming for the dateless. Amaretto or caramel or espresso blend?"

"Uh, no thanks on the flavored coffee. Espresso's fine." Frank's footsteps headed toward the living room. "You have to tell my mother how you keep these tomato plants bearing this late in the year."

"Sidney's alpaca fertilizer," she called from inside the refrigerator. She came out with milk and half a chocolate pie. "Have you heard her family's latest radio jingle?"

"Unfortunately. It's the definition of earworm."

The aroma of strong, dark coffee filled the galley kitchen. "If I ever bought one of their scarves, I'd hear that 'spin-tastic' song every time I put it on."

Frank returned to the kitchen. "So much for your Christmas present. That coffee smells good. I get dessert, too?"

"Don't be too flattered. I didn't want the pie to go bad while I'm forced to relive my past." Then she smiled. "Okay; be flattered. I could've frozen this."

"I am duly impressed. Someday I'll charm you into making spaghetti for me, too."

She set cups, milk, and sugar on a tray. "Sorry. When a woman cooks for you, it's a sign she considers the relationship an intimate one." *Good Heavens, you big-mouthed broad, shut up!*

He popped the plastic lid off the pie. "I'll remember that. Got a knife?"

She poured coffee while he sliced. He carried the tray to the coffee table and Giulia turned on the late movie—a Nick and Nora Charles rerun.

At least it isn't a romance. Which is as close as I'm going to get to admitting how much I want Frank to kiss me.

She leaned forward to pick up her coffee. Frank picked up her hand before she touched the handle, pulled her toward him, and kissed her.

Some part of Giulia's brain tried to put together a complete sentence, and failed.

Frank pulled a millimeter away. Giulia remained where she was, eyes closed, and Frank kissed her again.

"I like your flexible boundaries," he murmured.

Before she could answer, he put one hand against the small of her back and the other around her shoulders. Her mouth opened and his tongue touched hers.

Don't sabotage this, old maid Giulia.

She slid her hand into his buzzed hair and initiated the next kiss. His right hand moved around her shoulder and touched her ear, then her neck. It traveled to the top curve of her breast beneath the silk. She breathed in a long, shaky breath. He froze.

Her eyes opened. He leaned away and stared at his hand like it belonged to someone else.

"What?"

He snatched away his hand. "Shit. Boundaries. I'm sorry."

She made a face. "I didn't protest."

He shook his head. "I shouldn't touch you like that. You're a nun."

"What?"

"I'm going to Hell. I can just hear my grandmother now."

"I am an ex-nun. Ex." She sat back against the couch. "I'll show you my discharge papers."

Frank rubbed his face. "You're different. Set apart. There's no way I should be thinking about that lacy bra beneath that soft shirt." He gulped. "Sorry. Shit."

"Maybe I'm okay with it."

His eyes flicked to her cleavage. "Damn it, don't say things like that." He straightened his shoulders. "I apologize. I'll remember how to be a gentleman next time."

"You were perfectly—" She gave it up. An adult male with a be-guiling grin no longer sat next to her. He'd been usurped by a little boy caught with his hand in the cookie jar. *I never thought of my breasts as cookies before.* A giggle spluttered out of her.

She waved away his questioning look. "The coffee's getting cold."

Frank handed Giulia her cup. As she watched him stab the first bite of his pie, she thought, *This isn't over, Frank Driscoll. I'll make you remember I'm a woman, not a plastic statue. As soon as I'm out of the convent . . . again.*

FIVE

After late Mass the next day, Giulia stuffed two pairs of panty-hose into each Godzilla bedroom slipper. "That's too many for less than a week, but the stupid things run if you look at them cross-eyed."

Her beat-up black suitcase was already packed. "Underwear, cell charger, pajamas, toothbrush, wallet, and all that stuff. Got it." On top of everything she set the Day-Timer Frank gave her on her first case and tucked a slipper on each side.

After she zipped her suitcase closed, she gave her plants a final once-over. The (probably) last batches of basil and oregano for the season were drying on paper towels on top of the fridge. The late tomatoes had just a touch of red.

"You'll have to survive without me for a few days, guys." With one finger she stirred the dirt at the base of the tomato. Disintegrating alpaca pellets gave off the faintest odor; in the next breath, it vanished. "Sidney, sales of this fertilizer will put your little brother through college."

The habit hung on her closet door like it was nothing more than an innocent, plain black dress. Giulia stalked over and yanked it from the hanger.

"I refuse to let this thing intimidate me. You hear that, dress? That's all you are: a few yards of double-knit. You're not a real habit because you're not blessed."

She pulled off her T-shirt and stepped out of her jeans. Poised with the habit over her head, she grinned at her reflection in the narrow full-length mirror. *Thank you, imp that sat on my shoulder this morning. If Sister Fabian only knew what lurked under this dress.* The red lace bra revealed hints of nipple; the matching panties covered more, but no respectable nun's anatomy should have been in the same zip code with them.

"Proof positive I'm no longer a nun. Take that, Frank Driscoll." She wriggled into the dress and zipped it. "Someday, Frank, perhaps you will admire this underwear."

Collar, veil, black flats. Now her reflection made her shiver, and she closed in on the mirror till her nose touched it. "You. Will. Not. Beat. Me."

The doorbell rang.

Frank stepped backwards when she opened the front door. "Giulia, every instinct of mine expects you to whap me with a ruler because you're dressed that way."

She raised her eyes to Heaven. "It's a disguise, nothing more. Pretend it's a practice run for Halloween."

He tried to straighten the nonexistent collar on his sweatshirt. "Right. Sure. You all set?"

———

In the passenger seat of Frank's Camry, Giulia maintained correct posture: both feet on the floor, spine straight, hands clasped in her lap. The night before, she'd mended the pocket and shoulder seam in her worn black raincoat.

"I won't be able to call you with updates. The walls between the bedrooms are wicked thin."

Frank merged onto I-79. "I figured as much. We'll stick to texting then."

"If nothing else, it'll improve my texting speed."

"Right. So here's the plan." A Hummer cut them off. Frank cursed and swerved onto the shoulder. "Sorry, Sis—."

"Argh." She banged the back of her head against the headrest. "You're going to drive me to violence. Will you please look past this disguise? I'm still under here."

"Sorry, Giulia. It's too convincing."

If I had no morals, I'd make you pull over and then I'd show you my underwear. In daylight. And in public. That was what she wanted to say. She settled for, "Why don't you watch for renegade SUVs while we talk. That way you can pretend I'm not Sister Mary Intimidation."

Frank bit his lip. "Got it."

They drove in silence for a few miles. Frank muttered at the prevalence of minivans filled with children distracting the driver. Giulia settled deeper into her old self—that is, her character for this assignment.

When the traffic thinned, Frank said, "Texting's the better choice anyway for now. The guy Blake put me on used to be a small-time drug dealer. Jimmy talked to Narcotics, and I'll be working with them for the next few days."

"How is Captain Teddy Bear?"

"Someday you'll call him that to his face. I just hope a dozen cops are there when you do." He merged right and exited onto 376. "He's fine and so are Laura and the new baby."

"Baby?" Giulia's character immersion slipped. "Why didn't you tell me? I'd've made a batch of sauce to give the new mom a break."

"You are not getting within five blocks of Jimmy. He'll try to hire you away again." Frank looked over at her. "I'm not letting you get away from me. That is, from Driscoll Investigations."

Nice Freudian slip, Frank. If only you meant it. "Back on topic: Sister Mary Regina Coelis would have no reason to call a man on a cell phone she's not supposed to have. The texting plan works out."

"Who?"

Giulia laughed. "I forgot you didn't know the name I was given at my Investiture."

"What a mouthful. Is that Latin?"

"You slept through religion classes, didn't you? Yes, it's Latin. I was once named for Mary Queen of Heaven. Fabian and I are going to tell the curious that I petitioned to return."

"What about the cover story I thought up for you?"

"Too complex. I'd've had to remember the name of a fictitious brother, his wife, their imaginary orphaned child, and a weasely insurance company. Instead, I'm re-assimilating after teaching in the farthest places the Community reaches, being gone for a year, and petitioning to re-enter. Simpler and mostly true."

The car idled as Frank waited on the exit ramp from 376 for an opening to turn right. "Is that allowed? Leaving and coming back, I mean. I would've thought once you kicked the habit, it stayed kicked."

"*Tsk.* That expression is juvenile."

Two bicyclists crossed just as the light changed at the next intersection. "You're talking like a nun again."

"Duh, Frank. I'm ten minutes away from being a nun again." The words clogged her throat. "That is, from pretending to be a nun again. I need to talk and think and act like I used to. To answer your question, there's an outside chance re-entering could be allowed because so many nuns are leaving. Few people want to challenge Fabian, so we should be safe playing it that way for several days."

He nodded, his eyebrows meeting. "I bow to your greater experience in matters of the arcane. And I'll contact the Novice's family tonight, get their story without Sister Fabian's filters."

"Sister Bridget. Did you forget already? All the Driscoll charm will be wasted if you don't remember their daughter's name. Not everyone wants to give their child to the Church."

"We're not working for the Church … oh, yeah." He turned left.

The neighborhood became more familiar to Giulia. They passed the high school where she did her first student teaching. Then the consignment shop, tattoo parlor, mom-and-pop grocery, bar. She rolled down the window and inhaled the espresso-flavored breeze from the Double Shot on the corner. "That's wonderful."

That also means we're only two blocks from the Motherhouse.

"Frank, you should pull into a parking space on the next block. That way no one will see you driving me—especially not up to the door."

The Camry parked in the empty lot of a boarded-up travel agency next to a chain drugstore.

"I expected the main convent to be in a better neighborhood."

"Franciscans are supposed to be about poverty. We—they—set up shop where they're needed most." She stared out her window at the Motherhouse's weathered stone wall, visible beyond the prevalent red maples. "We used to sneak sandwiches to the schoolkids whose parents ran out of money between unemployment checks. Beatrice—the Community accountant—knew we did it but didn't know how to tell us not to be charitable." She smiled. "We always wondered if we'd cause her head to explode before she died of old age."

Two motorcycles idled at the stop sign, riders adjusting helmets, before they roared away. When the noise faded, Giulia said, "As soon as I get settled, I'll ask Fabian who Sister Bridget's friends were. If needed, I'll co-opt some of the Driscoll charm to use on them."

"I wish I could watch you in action. Don't get sucked back in there permanently." He popped the trunk and came around to the passenger side with her suitcase. "I'm too busy to train a new partner."

"I can always count on you for an inspiring speech." She took the black bag from him, and he leaned his face down to hers.

For a moment she considered it. Then the wind flapped her veil between them.

"No. You can't kiss a nun."

Dismay flicked across his face. "Sorry. Wasn't thinking."

She touched his arm. "Don't forget that this is a costume now. Underneath it I'm still a free woman."

He averted his eyes from her all-black ensemble. "Right. Text me when you know something."

I'm going to have to seriously deprogram him when this is over. She walked northeast across the parking lot and onto the familiar sidewalk. Frank tapped the horn as he drove away in the opposite direction.

Too soon, she stood at the end of the Motherhouse driveway.

SIX

Like a hallway in a nightmare, the long, curved driveway up to the Motherhouse's front door seemed to stretch as she walked along it. At its end, the century-old five-story building filled the horizon, despite the illusion of distance.

Giulia felt as intimidated as Maria did in *The Sound of Music* when she first saw the von Trapp mansion. Funny, since this experience was the exact opposite. She was coming back to the convent instead of plunging into life on the outside.

The stone walls looked the same as the last time. *It's only been eighteen months since you left the Community, dummy. What did you expect? Graffiti and psychedelic paint?* She'd always liked how the ivy covering the walls shaded from gold to orange to cranberry to maroon in autumn. The farther she walked down the driveway, more present-day details clashed with her memories. That narrow window on the third floor marked her room after temporary vows, the limbo between the Novitiate and a full-fledged Sister of Saint Francis. The cupola should still be decorated with the "all for one and one for all" logo she and her fellow Novices painted on the underside of its roof one midnight. The octagonal window at one corner of the fifth floor would still be the small chapel used solely by the first-year Postulants and second-year Novices.

There was always attrition in the first few months after entering the Community. Giulia's own group lost four Postulants in as many months. But when the rest of them took the veil and became Novices, they'd hung together to survive.

Mostly. She grimaced at the thought of meeting Sister Mary Stephen again. All those fights. All the backstabbing and power grabs. One of the unexpected benefits of jumping the wall had been freedom from Mary Stephen forever. So much for that.

Deep breaths. Keep walking. You're here on a tourist visa. In a few days you'll be back in the office fending off Sidney's endless badgering for convent stories.

She hurried up the stairs and rang the doorbell. It opened a moment later on a plump, smiling, wrinkled old nun. Giulia forced thoughts of raisins from her head.

"Welcome, Sister! We're so happy to have you. Did you carry your bag far? Are you tired? I can't leave my post here, but someone will be along any minute to show you to your room." She took a clipboard off the small table behind her. "If you'll give me your name, I can tell you what room you've been assigned."

"Sister Mary Regina Coelis."

The doorkeeper flipped a page, another, a third. "Here we are. Third floor, south side, room 323." She beamed at Giulia. "We haven't seen this much activity since I was newly professed. Those were such fun days! So many of us at a time—I think there were fourteen in my group. Dinner is at six."

Giulia's attention wandered. *Dinner. Food. That's what's bugging me—this place still smells like doughnuts.*

She snapped back to the doorkeeper's continuing flow of words. "There aren't assigned tables, except for the Novices and Postulants of course, so just fit in wherever you can. Oh—here we are." She waved and called to a young, slim Novice in black habit and white veil. "Sister Bartholomew, could you be an escort?"

The Novice veered toward the vestibule. "Of course, Sister Alphonsus." She smiled at Giulia. "Good afternoon, Sister. Welcome back to the Motherhouse." She craned her head to see the clipboard. "Right. Let me take your bag."

"Thank you, no. I've got it."

Nuns wandered the halls in twos and threes, smiling, talking, sharing photographs. Sister Bartholomew led Giulia up the wide, worn central stairs. She'd forgotten how crowded that huge building could be, but she hadn't forgotten the warped boards on the fifteenth stair. Neither had Sister Bartholomew—she and Giulia took wide steps to the left to avoid the *Crack!*

They grinned at each other.

"Where've you been stationed, Sister Regina Coelis?"

"Nowhere, actually." *Driscoll charm, don't fail me.* "I left a year ago, but I petitioned to return."

"Oh." Her conductor stopped. "Oh, I'm glad. I didn't think that was possible."

"Times have changed. There are so few of us now that they're making exceptions."

They reached the third floor. "It makes sense, especially with the merger. I heard there used to be five hundred of us in this

Community alone. But we're still below that number even with the other three Communities added."

This floor was crowded as well. Sisters of every age went in and out of rooms or sat in chairs grouped around the lamps on the walls. Laughter came from the small library in the west corner. Yet it was subdued, all of it. No word of the many conversations could be distinguished. The laughter's volume was suitable for a sickroom.

"Community Day is always a balancing act between continuing education lectures and a huge high school reunion," Giulia said.

"Last year's was kind of subdued, remember?" Sister Bartholomew said. "We heard it was because the Community could only afford to fly a handful of Sisters back here."

They stood against the wall to make room for three Sisters carrying musical instruments.

Giulia said, "This year it's like Community Day and Christmas and Easter all rolled into one."

"Yeah." Sister Bartholomew opened the door to room 323. "Office is at five-thirty, supper at six. If you need anything, one of us Novices or Postulants should be running around somewhere."

"Thanks."

A tall, gaunt, middle-aged nun appeared at the door frame. "Sister Bartholomew, may we borrow you for a moment?"

Giulia smiled at both of them and closed herself in. The suitcase *thunk*ed to the floor

"I'm stuck in a time warp," she whispered. "If I didn't have a cell phone in my pocket I'd swear I've been here all along."

A twin bed with a white chenille bedspread took up most of the wall to her left. A narrow wardrobe loomed at its foot. A desk and a straight-back wooden chair squeezed themselves against the wall opposite the wardrobe. The off-white paint job hadn't changed, either. For that matter, the 1950s vintage linoleum still held its place as the blandest pattern in the Northeast. An excellent cleaning job didn't hide its age and shabby edges.

She walked to the end of the room and opened the narrow window. The vegetable gardens were cleaned and hoed over for the winter, but mums and asters covered the flower beds.

There's the twins, Sisters Epiphania and ... something more normal ... Gwen ... no, Edwen. Arthritis finally got to them.

A nun in black trousers and a white blouse met the gardener nuns on the flagged walkway and brushed the dirt from their kneepads. Giulia didn't need to read lips to know that they were thanking Sister ... she couldn't remember that one's name, but remembered that she was always the first one to ease the way for the retirees.

She closed the window on the still-cold air as the third nun slipped the padded knee rests off the twins' daring denim workpants.

"Daring" twenty years ago, of course. How the twins loved to whisper the story of Fabian's meltdown the first time those secular clothes appeared. It was one of the few times we laughed that Canonical year.

The room looked smaller and dingier when she turned around. She plopped the suitcase on the bed. Her few pieces of clothing easily fit in the top drawer of the narrow dresser. The spare habit floated like a ghost in the equally narrow wardrobe until she hung her raincoat behind it. With a little effort, she wedged the suitcase under the bed and walked to its foot. Without straining any muscles, she stretched out her arms and placed a hand on either wall.

"I used to think this room design was meant to keep our eyes on poverty and simplicity, but it's a cell. Why did they bother to stop calling these rooms by the true name?"

Not even the feel of her inappropriate underwear comforted her. She opened the wardrobe and stared at her reflection in the small oval mirror, trying to assume the role of Sister Mary Regina Coelis.

"I should've brought a *Cosmo*." She leaned her forehead against the mirror, careful not to knock her veil askew. "In the convent. Right. I could hide it in the Office prayer book and read it during the Litany of the Hours rather than slogging through twenty minutes of rote prayers. Maybe it'll have a useful article like 'The Struggling Nun's Survival Guide: Now with Photos of Our Fave Wanton Underwear.'"

A discreet knock on the door saved her dignity. Model Sisters didn't guffaw.

SEVEN

Sister Bartholomew stood in the doorway. "Sister Fabian would like to see you in her office."

Giulia grinned at her. "Don't look like that. I'm not in trouble."

The Novice's face regained some of its color. "I couldn't imagine what you did between the front door and here to have her gunning for you already." Her mouth snapped shut. "I mean … I beg your … Christ on a crutch."

Giulia yanked her inside and only then burst out laughing—quietly. "If anyone else hears that, you'll be saying fifteen-decade rosaries on your knees for a month."

"You're not angry?" Sister Bartholomew looked just as frightened at Giulia's laughter.

"Why should I be? I'm not perfect either."

Sister Bartholomew landed on the bed so hard it bounced. "You're the first Sister who hasn't lectured me. I mean, I've only slipped a few times since I entered, but man, you'd think some of them came out of a twelfth-century time warp."

"They're trying to mold you to fit the image—"

"Mold! I hate that word. They mold you and mold you and one day they look at you—"

"And say, 'How moldy she is.'" Giulia finished. "That one has whiskers. How many times have you scrubbed the back stairs?"

She groaned. "Don't ask. I see those plastic treads in my nightmares." She frowned at Giulia. "How come you're different? You remind me of my older brother's wife, except she chain smokes and has a Pagan altar in their living room."

Giulia laughed again. "Thank you, I think."

"I love her. She's a riot. One day their corgi—oh, no." She jumped up again. "I'm supposed to bring you to Sister Fabian. She'll have a coronary."

Giulia stood and smoothed her habit. "Let's get it over with."

They went down the opposite stairs that led to the chapel's back corridor and the Superior General's private quarters. The subdued party-chaos of the other side of the building barely penetrated here. At the first-floor landing, the decrepit plastic runners Giulia remembered cleaning during her own Novitiate had been replaced with stick-on carpeting.

Sister Bartholomew whispered, "If we were in the world, I'd take you out for a beer afterward."

"Face-time with Sister Fabian has that effect."

Sister Bartholomew coughed. "Are you sure you're not in trouble?"

They turned left at the bottom of the stairs, away from the chapel. Formal portraits of past Superior Generals still decorated this end of the hallway.

"Ever wonder if their eyes are following you?"

Sister Bartholomew nodded. "I hear it's the worst for your annual spiritual review."

"I'll tell you the story of the grilling I got the first year after temporary vows." She glanced at the Novice. "Maybe not."

A shrug. "Doesn't matter. I've heard plenty from the fourth-years." A gleaming mahogany door stopped their conversation. "Want me to wait?"

Giulia turned her gaze on the dark circles under the Novice's eyes. "Yes, because it'll prevent three more people from sending you on errands." She raised her hand to knock. The flowery print proclaiming "All things come to those who wait" still hung in its frame next to the door.

Giulia murmured, "Welcome to the Puppet Master's realm."

Behind her, Sister Bartholomew made a strangled noise and her footsteps retreated. Giulia forced her face into neutral and knocked.

"Come in."

The room on the other side of the door was not the one Giulia remembered. *Fabian must've won a home makeover contest.*

The vinyl chairs with worn brown slipcovers and the faded tan walls were no more. Off-white textured wallpaper covered three walls of the sitting room. An earth-tone striped couch and two matching chairs surrounded a green glass-topped coffee table. The fourth wall, opposite the windows, had been painted to match the glass tabletop. The hardwood floor—Giulia had to look—still had that "hand-waxed and buffed by minions" glow, but a discreetly flowered area rug reached from the door to the couch.

"Good afternoon ... Sister Regina Coelis."

Fabian, you oughta stop sucking lemons before meeting with me. It'll prevent wrinkles.

Giulia sat in one of the new chairs. "I've begun telling the Sisters that I left, and my petition to re-enter was granted. Because of the merger and the many of us who've left, no one's batted an eye."

The Superior General's frown deepened. "That's not the way I'd planned to explain it, but if the Sisters accept it, then I won't argue." She opened one of the manila folders on the coffee table. "I've typed out everything relevant to Sister Bridget's suicide. How will you conduct your investigation?"

"Who knows the real reason I'm here?"

Sister Fabian's lips thinned. "Only myself and Father Raymond. You must blend in with the Community. I presume you are still a Catholic in good standing and will be able to receive Communion at Mass."

I'd forgotten how easy it is to hate you. Giulia cloaked herself in every atom of "reasonable adult" she could muster. "Driscoll Investigations is always professional. Everything I do will reflect that."

Sister Fabian's earlobes—all that the veil allowed the world to see—reddened like those eyeglasses that get darker when the sun hits them.

"You will come to my rooms every day at four with a detailed progress report."

"Sister, people will certainly take notice if you and I have regular appointments. For an undercover investigation to be successful, it must be invisible. I'm sure you appreciate that."

Sister Fabian's earlobes turned tomato-red.

"Sister. Mary. Regina. Coelis. The Community is paying for this investigation—"

"I'm aware of that. I will conduct it in a way that will bring about a satisfactory conclusion for everyone involved." She stood. "Which Sisters were close to Sister Bridget?"

The Superior General's collar jogged up and down as she swallowed. "Sister Mary Bartholomew, her fellow Novice; and Sister Arnulf. She is on an extended visit from her convent in Göteborg. Sister Bridget spoke Swedish, so she often interpreted for Sister Arnulf."

"Thank you. If you'll excuse me, I'll take these folders to my room to study."

She closed the door, walked straight across the hall, and pressed her forehead below the portrait of the Community's sixth Superior General.

"Sister Regina Coelis? Are you all right?" Sister Bartholomew's whisper sounded in Giulia's ear and a hand touched her shoulder.

"I will be." She straightened and gave Sister Bartholomew a crooked smile. In the same whisper, she said, "When they autopsy that woman's body one day, they'll need a magnifying glass to find her heart."

Sister Bartholomew covered her mouth with both hands this time.

Giulia led them back upstairs. "Talking to her is like playing chess while rollerblading on a freeway."

Sister Bartholomew sucked in a deep breath and took her hands away. "Where do you get the guts to say out loud what everyone's thinking?"

"Not much to lose, I'm afraid. I should let you know that I'm not exactly the best example for young Sisters to follow. What's the schedule for the rest of today?"

She checked her watch. "History of the four Communities at seven-thirty. Tonight's the one from New Jersey."

"Is it mandatory?"

She shook her head. "They're not too bad, though. The one from Indiana showed us all these pictures of when their Motherhouse got overrun by mice back when everyone wore the old habit. One had three climbing her skirt and another was whacking them with a yardstick."

When they opened the door off the third-floor landing, the buzz of multiple discreet conversations enveloped them.

"No, thanks. Before I forget, what time is Mass tomorrow?"

"Office at six-forty, Mass at seven."

"Let me rephrase that. What's your schedule tomorrow?"

"Um, why?"

"Because you're overworked and underfed and not getting enough sleep. What can I do to help?"

Sister Bartholomew stopped walking. "Um, well, um, we have to be available to show new arrivals to their rooms, plus there's choir rehearsal at eleven, and before that we have to buff the chapel floor."

"I used to run a mean buffer. Let me take that one for you."

"Bridget used to—" Sister Bartholomew cut herself off and smiled brightly at Giulia. "That would be great, if you're allowed to."

"You get a little freedom post-vows."

The Novice's expression said, *Tell me another one.*

Giulia smiled. "Not a lot. A little."

"I'll check with Sister Gretchen—she's our Novice Mistress—and see if it's allowed, but, well, don't you want to reconnect with Sisters you haven't seen in a year?"

"I prefer to keep busy."

Two Sisters at once tried to catch Sister Bartholomew's attention as she and Giulia entered the crowded hall.

"Me, too." Her mouth quirked. "Sometimes you should be careful what you pray for." She turned to the waiting nuns with that bright smile.

EIGHT

"FABIAN, DID YOU REALLY think I'd fall for this pile of alpaca crap?"

Giulia flung another page of the "report" behind her. The scattered white printer pages made a random pattern on the faded linoleum. "I'd get better information if I read the floor like tea leaves in the bottom of a cup. She actually expects me to believe that Sister Bridget had been depressed and reclusive since the day she entered—as much as the life of a crazy-busy Postulant and Novice allowed."

She slammed the last page on the polished desk.

"Did Fabian think I'd forgotten the three-day gauntlet of psychological tests? Did she think I'd be suckered into believing that a Community exists that doesn't do testing for prospective entrants?"

She heard her voice getting louder and clenched her teeth.

Communities want outgoing leaders. Even a contemplative Order might've balked at the person described in this "report."

Giulia stared at the puzzle she'd created on the floor.

"Only the strong grapple Formation and win the veil. Something changed Sister Bridget. Before the merger or after?"

She opened her phone and chose the text-message option for Frank's number.

Info not complete. Get all you can from the family.

A moment later, the phone vibrated and the envelope icon appeared.

Got it. Any other news?

She rolled her eyes. *Plenty. I've already committed the sin of wanting to murder Fabian.* Instead, she texted, Not yet. I'll work on the 2 friends next.

The phone went back into her pocket with her driver's license and debit card rubber-banded together. Neither of them were useful in here, but they were another small reminder that she was still Giulia Falcone under this veil. She knelt to pick up the scattered papers.

"Five-thirty. Time's up. Get downstairs and immerse yourself in it all. Make them accept you as one of them. Deal with the repercussions when you're safe in your own apartment again."

———

The refectory at least sounded like a restaurant in the real world. The necessity of making oneself heard over the clatter of dishes and flatware gave Giulia an unexpected sense of relief.

She found one empty seat at a table smack in the middle of the long, crowded dining room. Four other nuns were already seated there: one bouncing lesson-plan ideas off of one reading *The*

Imitation of Christ, one writing a letter, and one leaning against the chairback, looking green around the gills.

"Sister Mary Regina Coelis," Giulia said to the table in general. "Is anyone sitting here?"

The letter-writer shook her head without looking up.

"Sister Eleanor." The greenish one's voice matched her skin tone.

"Are you all right, Sister?"

She opened her eyes. "Our plane landed an hour ago. We hit the worst turbulence in the history of mankind." She winced and closed them again. "Now I know how chicken legs in a Shake and Bake bag feel."

"Eleanor, I told you to drink ginger tea before we left." The letter-writer capped her pen. "A pleasure to meet you, Sister Regina Coelis. I'm Sister Cynthia."

"Your ginger tea was the first thing I vomited on the plane, Cynthia." Sister Eleanor squinted at everyone. "My apologies. I'm only here to collect saltines and ginger ale. Then I'm hiding in my room all evening."

Giulia gave in to her curiosity. "I didn't think there was a Saint Cynthia."

"There isn't. My given name is Cindy. They allowed me to compromise at my Investiture, and I became Sister Mary Cynthia. I could hear my mother's teeth grinding all the way from the back of the church."

The wizened doorkeeper stood, and the room fell silent.

"Good evening, Sisters, and welcome again to today's arrivals. Please bow your heads as we thank Our Father for this meal."

Giulia bowed her head with the rest, but kept her eyes open. The book-reader maintained her spiritual demeanor. The lesson planner at first appeared annoyed by the interruption. Sister Eleanor sank into her chair, the green tinge holding steady.

When the prayer finished, the lesson planner resumed the third week of Advent. Giulia turned to Cynthia. "I'd never have believed they could squeeze thirty-five tables plus two of those restaurant-size steam carts in here."

Cynthia touched the back of her hand to Eleanor's forehead. "This is the first I've seen it. Eleanor and I are from New Jersey."

Sister Fabian's table proceeded to the serving table at their end of the room.

"Do you know the Sisters at Sister Fabian's table?" Giulia said to Sister Cynthia.

"One's our former Superior General, so I'm guessing the others are formers as well."

"I should've guessed from the shared CEO look."

The lesson planner said, "Rank has its privileges."

The *Imitation of Christ* reader primmed her lips. "If it doesn't affect you spiritually, morally, or materially, Susan, then put it aside."

Sister Susan wrinkled her nose at the reader, who closed her book.

"'First keep the peace within yourself, then you can also bring peace to others.' Good evening, Sister Regina Coelis. I'm Sister Mary Elizabeth. Susan and I are from the Indiana branch."

"Did you give the history presentation?" Giulia stood with the rest of the table to get in line for dinner.

Sister Cynthia said. "Eleanor, sit there. I'll get your crackers and soda."

"No, that was our Community's former Postulant Mistress. She was an actress before she entered. The skits she wrote for the Postulants to perform on Saint Francis Day were always clever. She was appointed Postulant Mistress of this Motherhouse after the merger."

Giulia helped herself to baked chicken, potatoes, a roll, and salad. While she added milk to her coffee, Sister Bartholomew and a shorter, plump Novice carried plates to a table filled with retired Sisters. Two Postulants did the same for another full table. A third table with five more obvious retirees watched their servers with avidity.

Right, they're serving. We did the same. But at least there were three of us and only seven retired Sisters. Those girls need a week's vacation.

Eleanor left with her motion-sickness supper. Giulia said to Cynthia, "Are both of you stationed at your old Motherhouse?"

"No, in Tallahassee. No more New Jersey winters, hooray. Eleanor is high school Spanish and I'm Chemistry and Physics." She took a bite of her buttered roll. "What about you?"

"I've been away for a year. This is my re-assimilation."

Susan snorted. "Like the Borg."

Elizabeth set down her fork. "Susan, one day you will say that to the wrong person. Don't forget your review is only a month away."

Susan stabbed her chicken. "Don't worry. I'll behave for the committee. You know I'm always a good example for impressionable young minds. That covers a multitude of sins."

Giulia added sugar to her coffee. "The first one post-vows was the worst. I always rubbed Sister F. the wrong way, and there she sat in judgment on me."

"Our Superior General was easygoing," Susan said. "I knew she'd never win the battle for Combined Overlord."

Elizabeth rapped Susan's hand with the back of her fork.

"Ow. All right, all right. Blame it on menopause." She caught everyone's eyes. "I shall now practice decorum and eat the rest of the meal in silence."

Elizabeth briefly raised her eyes to the ceiling. "Is the rest of your group here, Sister Regina Coelis?"

Giulia surveyed the room. "I haven't seen them, but I just arrived. It was a long trip. My last post was in Pierre."

"South Dakota?" Susan's coffee cup hovered halfway between the table and her mouth. "I guess you really did tick certain people off."

"I didn't realize the Community had convents so far west." Elizabeth shot a pointed look at Susan.

Giulia shrugged. "We do, and I've seen them all. I have a reputation as the nun who won't push girls into Entering."

Susan said, "Ouch. Just as the numbers are dropping like rocks?"

"What's the point of talking up the joys of convent life to girls who anyone could see wouldn't make it past the first round of psychological tests?" Giulia appealed to the table in general.

"You get no argument from me," Susan said. "Four out of the five in my group cut and ran before Investiture, something unusual back in the day. And Eleanor wonders why I'm such a cynical old besom. My solo Novitiate was a never-ending party." She jerked one shoulder. "As I'm sure you've gathered, sarcasm is my major fault."

Elizabeth said to Giulia, "I agree with you in principle, Sister Regina Coelis, but God needs workers, however flawed. Who's to say that with attentive Formation those girls wouldn't have made admirable Sisters?"

There's no polite response to that. Sometimes I wonder how I lasted as long as I did.

Giulia finished dinner and set her dishes in the gray plastic bins on the rolling carts at the back of the room. The institutional dishwasher lurked just down the short hall beyond the carts. Giulia caught a whiff of the powerful soap it required, then gave herself a mental slap. Wrenching her brain out of reminisce mode, she sized up the Superior Generals still drinking coffee at their table. Next, the two Novices and two Postulants. She didn't see the Novice Mistress's bright red hair and quirky smile anywhere. It had been years since they'd met, but she was remembering more and more the longer she breathed Motherhouse air.

She wandered into the nearest of the six rooms that took up most of the first floor, reacquainting herself with the layout of the building.

The first parlor opened into another, then into a telephone room that connected to the main library. No dust marred the books on the built-in shelves, not even the volumes of Canon Law at the very top. If Sister Bartholomew and the others were saddled with the dusting, too, Sister Bridget would've had to work to find the time to get depressed.

Soft muttering from behind her made her jump. In the sagging flowered armchair under the crucifix, a white-haired nun wearing the European version of the modified habit was writing in a spiral notebook.

That habit could kindly be described as "quaint." The gathered ankle-length skirt, cuffed sleeves, and three-inch white plastic crown atop the waist-length veil made Giulia happy to wear a plain, A-line dress.

After what appeared to be each sentence, the little Sister read it aloud. The muttering wasn't in English. Giulia stepped forward, unsure if she could help or if she should try to find someone who understood her language. While she wavered, the elderly nun leveraged herself out of the chair and over to the computer desk. Her arthritic fingers pounded the keys like she was punishing someone.

Giulia sidled through the opposite doorway into the Community Room.

Sister Bartholomew caught her on the main stairs. "Sister Regina Coelis, can you really help with the buffer?"

"Of course I can. What time do you want me there?"

"Right after we finish the breakfast dishes. Sister Gretchen's okay with it. She's being pulled in eight different directions too."

"Are there only two Canonical Novices this year?"

"We had six Postulants enter the four different Motherhouses back in February, but only three of us made it to the new, merged Community."

Giulia kept her voice casual. "Three isn't bad."

"No, there's only two of us now." She shook something off. "I wish they'd emphasized more that 'Canonical' means 'cloistered.' Cabin fever is a bad thing."

"Been there."

Bart gave Giulia that bright smile. "If you can be in the chapel about eight-fifteen tomorrow morning, I'll show you where we keep the supplies."

"I hate to take advantage of you like everyone else, but I don't have a towel in my room." Giulia forced herself not to wince. It wasn't a lie, since her room did lack a towel, but she knew she only asked Sister Bartholomew so she could weasel information out of her.

"No, no, you're not. They're in the linen closet on the second floor. I'll show you."

She led the way to the large bathroom next to the front stairs.

"They're on this shelf … except when they aren't." She closed the door on the empty middle shelf with an apologetic smile. "Sorry. The clean ones must still be in the cellars." She hesitated. "I can get one for you."

"I'll come with you. I need to work off that starchy dinner."

"You will? Thanks." They walked the length of the hall and through the double doors that opened onto the back stairs. Sister Bartholomew appeared oddly relieved to have Giulia accompany her.

"How's the spider situation down there?" Giulia said.

Sister Bartholomew waved a dismissive hand. "They're all over the place, but that's what shoes are for." Her voice smirked. "One got into Sister Beatrice's sheets last month. She tried to take it out on us, but Sister Gretchen told her that since Saint Francis himself isn't going to appear in the cellars to chastise the spiders, Sister Beatrice should practice decorum and leave us Novices to her."

"I remember Sister Gretchen. She became Novice Mistress after I took vows. Does she still do impressions of old movie stars?"

"Oh, yeah. She's added some new ones, too. Her Adam Sandler is great." Sister Bartholomew walked with fast, firm steps.

Giulia's gym routine enabled her to keep up. "Do you still have to hand-starch the veils for the traditional habits?"

"Do we ever." Her voice seemed relaxed but her pace didn't slacken. "At least only five of them still wear it."

"Cooking starch at five-thirty in the morning." Giulia huffed. "No one should touch the antique gas stove at that hour. Unless it's been updated?"

"I wish. Nope. Vivian and I alternate weeks: one collects the laundry, the other cooks the starch. Someday a sleep-deprived Novice will blow up this place."

They passed the gigantic institutional washing machines that looked like UFOs turned on their sides. Formica-topped tables lined one wall. A similar table in the center of the room reserved for the three-foot strips of white linen looked exactly as it did nine years ago. The only change was the addition of two apartment-sized stacked washer-dryer combinations.

"This brings back memories. Once we started singing St. Louis Jesuits songs while we worked, just like we were the Franciscan Seven Dwarfs. Sister Isidora showed up just then to check our ironing job on the veils and lectured us on the virtues of silence."

A floorboard creaked. Sister Bartholomew jumped. "Oh, man, the last batch of towels never got folded." Her voice came fast and jerky. "Do you mind waiting while I tackle these?" She glanced into the dark room beyond the laundry, then dragged her attention back to the pile of clean towels.

"You expect me to stand here and watch you work? Don't be ridiculous." Giulia shook out a towel and folded it, then reached for another. "Do they really expect you to keep up with all your usual responsibilities on top of the extra reunion chores?" She snapped a particularly wrinkled bath towel. "Don't answer that. I already know what you're going to say."

Sister Bartholomew's shoulders slumped. "It's only for this week. Sister Gretchen told us to do everything we could, and she'd run interference for us if someone got on our case."

Water sloshed through one of the washer pipes. Sister Bartholomew gripped her hands together beneath the remaining towels, but not far enough under to hide the gesture from Giulia.

"Last one." Giulia kept her voice brisk. "Where do you want them?"

She pointed and Giulia pushed the two stacks to the end of the table, keeping the top towel for herself. "Did they ever fix that gurgle in the hopper pipes?"

Sister Bartholomew's eyes slewed to the corner where the deep utility sink lurked. "Um, yes, well, they said they fixed it back in June, but last week—"

The pipe hiccupped. She squeaked. Another pipe emitted a low, bubbling moan.

"I'm sorry, Sister, but I have to get back upstairs now. Thanks for helping with the towels."

Giulia stared after Sister Bartholomew as the slaps of her running feet faded upstairs. Then she followed the gurgles to the weepy pipe under the hopper sink—the same source from her time there. Odd that they frightened a Novice who ought to be used to them, what with all the time Novices spent in the cellars.

NINE

At 6:50 Monday morning, Giulia sat in the back of the Mother-house chapel with a borrowed prayer book, and couldn't concentrate on the long prayers to save her soul. Last night's endless, looping nightmare dovetailed too neatly into that morning's reality.

So I dreamed my stress dream: back in the convent, in the habit, wandering the Motherhouse halls saying, "Why am I doing this again?" over and over and over. Her voice joined in the Psalm response. *So what if I'm living it? It's only a job. I didn't retake vows.* She gave the Psalm response again. *I solve this by Wednesday and I'm back in my cozy, plant-filled apartment Wednesday night. Trimming dead tomato leaves never seemed so attractive.*

The Sister leading this morning's prayers finished the last one, and everyone closed their books.

I can receive Communion, too. I pre-Confessed to Father Carlos on Saturday, and he gave me dispensation. This week, I can lie to serve the greater good.

The organist played the opening bars to "Jesus, My Lord, My God, My All." Everyone stood as the priest entered the sanctuary from the vestry on Giulia's left.

He was quite an improvement over the old man who mumbled through Mass in Giulia's years there, even if he looked like Roger Moore gone to seed. He kept his sermon to five minutes flat. Because of that and the two Sisters acting as Extraordinary Ministers for Communion, Mass finished at twenty to eight. Giulia caught herself wondering who strong-armed the Bishop to make him assign this priest here.

———

After breakfast—during which a recovered Eleanor taught everyone at Giulia's table napkin origami—Giulia walked the chapel aisles waiting for Sister Bartholomew.

She'd forgotten, or deliberately blocked—Frank had no concept of the stinking landfill of memories this "undercover in the convent" job had breached—the immensity of the chapel.

The midnight-blue flooring set off the eighty rows of ashwood pews, lit by the morning sun shining through twenty tall, thin, clear glass windows on each side of the building. Four taller, wider stained-glass windows threw faceted prisms of light on the ash-paneled sanctuary. She remembered watching the slow movement of their colors on long days polishing pews. During the summer, that multicolored light painted the bleached-birch, life-size crucifix with colors too lovely for an execution.

The Stations of the Cross have been re-gruesomed, too. Happy reunion, Sisters! Enjoy the realistic torture on all sides! I bet Sister

Francesco got that job. She always was obsessed with the goriness of the Passion. No denying her talent, though. That blood looks real.

The statues flanking the altar hadn't been overlooked. Fresh silver edging framed the Virgin Mary's blue cloak. Opposite her, Saint Joseph's spray of lilies shone like mother of pearl.

A massive C-chord shattered the silence. Giulia spun around. In the choir loft above the last pews, a trumpeter, a flautist, and a violinist—Sister Gretchen—raised their instruments and tuned to the C.

Sister Bartholomew skidded to a stop at the holy water font. She dipped her fingers and crossed herself before walking up to Giulia.

"The buffer's in the closet off the back hall," she said directly into Giulia's ear.

Giulia nodded. The tuning cacophony made normal speech impossible. They passed through the center opening of the Communion rail—so old it was "historical" rather than "outdated"—up three shallow steps, genuflected before the tabernacle, and went through the left-hand door into the vestry.

Another left turn brought them into the hallway that circled behind the sanctuary and on to the Superior General's rooms. Sister Bartholomew opened the door of a large closet that stored the buffer, an upright vacuum, furniture polish paraphernalia, and floral supplies. Giulia wrestled out the buffer while Sister Bartholomew took the vacuum.

"O Sanctissima" saturated the chapel's air when they returned. Sister Bartholomew's vacuum dented the sound by a quarter-decibel. Giulia plugged in the buffer, hit *On*, and promptly crashed it into the wainscoting.

"Oops."

Her muscle memory returned after a few square feet, and shiny overlapping circles covered the left-hand aisle in her wake. When she turned off the buffer to switch the plug to a closer outlet, the other Novice was there, holding the plug out to her.

"Thanks, Sister…"

"Vivian." Her high, soft voice was difficult to hear even over a quieter violin solo.

The vacuum stopped. Giulia and Sister Vivian looked up to the sanctuary. The priest who'd said Mass had enveloped Sister Bartholomew in a bear hug. Just as Giulia thought, *That's a little too touchy-feely between a priest and a Sister*, the priest released her and came toward them.

Sister Vivian's smile maintained an insincere "pose for the camera" look as he chucked her under the chin.

"You're doing a beautiful job, Sisters. The chapel glows." He held out his hand to Giulia. "I don't think you're a new Novice."

She returned his infectious smile. "Not for a long time. I'm Sister Regina Coelis, just helping out."

He shook her hand. "Father Raymond Price, but everyone calls me Father Ray. You're an angel for assisting these hardworking Novices."

"You're quite the charmer, Father Ray."

He winked. "There are too many gloomy faces in the world, Sister. One happy Catholic could start a trend."

Giulia laughed. "That's the best idea I've heard all week."

Sister Fabian strode up the center aisle, several manila folders in her hands.

"Father Ray, if I might borrow you for a few minutes?"

Giulia recognized Sister Fabian's upper-level smile, used when she anticipated agreement from an equal.

"Of course, Sister. Let's go into the vestry." Father Ray's charm shone on all within range before he led Sister Fabian up the sanctuary steps.

Sister Bartholomew's vacuuming had taken her to the opposite side of the altar. Sister Vivian turned her back on everyone and continued to polish the backs of the pews.

Giulia plugged in the buffer. *Charm isn't everything, I suppose. Unless Vivian can't deal with that blemish on his forehead.* She started the buffer to cover a grin. *Or unless she prefers Daniel Craig as Bond.*

TEN

"SISTER REGINA COELIS, WOULD you mind putting the buffer away?" Sister Bartholomew didn't exactly beg, but she'd nailed "plaintive waif." "We have choir practice in about thirty seconds."

"Of course. Go ahead." Giulia restarted the machine and finished the last few squares in front of the Saint Joseph niche. The choir began warm-up exercises. As she wound up the bright orange heavy-duty cord, her cell phone vibrated. She checked her automatic reach for it. Instead, she lugged the buffer up the steps and wheeled it through the empty vestry into its closet. This hall and cutting up the back stairs were the most direct way to her room. Not even Fabian should be in her rooms at this hour. Too much to micro-manage before the big day.

But Fabian was in her room, the door closed. No—open just a crack. Talking to … Father Raymond. Giulia inched nearer to listen, not at all guilty about eavesdropping in the name of duty.

Holy Mother of God.

Giulia might be more naïve than Sidney, but she knew what the panting and grunting coming through the crack meant.

Fabian, you deserve to be kicked out of here. Giulia's conscience tried to make a case for humans giving way under loneliness or pressure or overwork. *Shut up. It's the same as cheating on your spouse. If you want to sleep around, get a divorce. Can you hear your own conscience, Fabian? You're cheating on Christ. Time to petition Rome.*

She realized she was still standing too near Fabian's room, the sounds rushing to their inevitable conclusion. A huge effort of will and sticking her fingers in her ears freed her to run upstairs.

Safe in her room, the enormity of what Fabian and Ray were doing slammed into her. She stood in the center of her cell, her head filled with the sounds of Fabian's and Ray's skin slapping together behind that betraying door. Her breakfast threatened to come back up before she managed to push the knowledge to the back of her head. Only when she could control herself did she check her phone and read the text from Sidney.

Mr D has info. Lunch tmw?

Good, Giulia typed. Noon?

A minute later: Mr D says ok. Whats it like???

Giulia laughed—quietly. That last question was definitely from Sidney, not Frank. She couldn't do justice to all of it in textspeak: the sheer number of Sisters, the minuscule rooms, the cavernous cellars, the personalities. And the forbidden sex. Mustn't forget that. Guess what i just overheard? No. She was definitely not texting those words. Instead, she texted, Lots of stories for you soon.

Giulia could almost hear Sidney's disappointed groan. Even a few sentences from her was an antidote for these cell walls.

"I need a dose of the real world. Why didn't I listen to my inner imp and bring that *Cosmo*? I could swear these narrow walls are trying to suffocate me."

She pulled at the veil around her head.

"Stop it. The walls aren't moving. The veil's not tightening around you like a vise. Quit thinking you're the heroine in an Asian horror movie. This isn't *Ringu*, it's Community Theater Convent, complete with stock characters and a mad-scientist organ soundtrack. " She shook her head hard, rattling the image of Ray and Fabian to a dark corner again.

She paced the short, narrow space.

"This black lace underwear isn't doing its job. Black was the wrong color—it's nun-wear. Should've put on the jade green set."

The window rattled as she opened it. "Brr. Not going for a walk in this. All right, Falcone, make yourself useful and see what you can do for the Novices while you're winning their confidence."

Her conscience murmured the word *hypocrite*.

"No. I like Sister Bartholomew. I want to ease her workload so she can get five minutes' rest. And if I learn something at the same time, the good deed cancels out the sin."

She yanked open the door to escape herself and collided with two Sisters.

"I'm so sorry! Are you all right?"

One of them seemed familiar—yes, the little old nun from the library last night. She only looked startled now, rather than angry.

"Snackar du svenska?"

Giulia looked at her, then at the dark-haired Sister behind her.

"Good morning, I'm Sister Theresa. Sister Arnulf is asking if you speak Swedish."

"I'm sorry, no." Giulia shook her head at the small Sister.

She nodded. "Du är ny här. Vi ses sen när barnflickan inte är här."

Sister Theresa gave Giulia an apologetic smile. "I'm sorry. I don't understand her either. The Novice who translated for her passed away last week, and I was recruited because I know some sign language."

Sister Arnulf patted Giulia's arm and smiled.

"Her friends arrive tomorrow, so she'll have someone to talk to in time for her birthday. She turns eighty on Friday." She touched Sister Arnulf on the shoulder and gestured toward the stairs. The little nun shrugged and followed.

Now that she knew the identity of Sister Bridget's other friend, Giulia was tempted to think Sister Fabian was purposefully thwarting her investigation. But she couldn't invent a friendship that didn't exist—it was too easy to disprove.

Giulia followed them to the stairs, but headed up to the fifth floor rather than down. It was Sister Bartholomew or failure, then, and Giulia was not going to fail. *I'm going to shove my conclusions in your condescending face, and if they're identical to what you're trying to force on me, I'll eat this veil.*

Halfway up the last flight, her head reached floor level. The two rows of wooden lockers still faced each other across the landing, and from what she could see through their screened fronts, still empty. She didn't smell a decomposing mouse, though. The walls had vibrated with all their shrieks the morning they found that surprise in one of them.

Smiling, Giulia climbed to the landing and turned left to the Novices' side.

"So this is where Fabian's old furniture ended up. When did it become a Community rule that the Postulants and Novices get everyone's leftovers?" Then again, these recycled pieces of furniture were in better shape than the sprung couch and tottery chairs from her time.

Voices sounded from down the hall and around the corner. *Sheesh, Falcone, rein in the talking to yourself before you miss a clue. You're a detective now, not a stressed-out nun.* She followed the sound and stopped at the wall outside the chapel door. The two months it took them to transform two unused bedrooms into this chapel were one of her happiest Novitiate memories. They had all been relieved to discover that the donated pale-blue paint actually complemented the donated ivory carpeting. She couldn't remember who'd given them the stark yet beautiful hand-carved crucifix from Assisi. The best part of it all was it belonged to them alone. No one was allowed in it except Novices and Postulants. Some days it had been the only sane real estate in the Motherhouse.

The noises became intelligible. Giulia peeked around the door frame.

Plump, pale Sister Vivian was blubbering into a tissue. A pile of wadded-up used ones covered the floor next to her. Sister Gretchen sat on her heels kitty-corner from the tissue mountain.

"Vivian, if you won't be specific about what's troubling you, how do you expect me to help?"

"I caaaan't. It's too, it's too …" She buried her face in a fresh tissue.

"Vivian." Sister Gretchen pinched the bridge of her nose.

Giulia backed down the hall and into the safety of the living room. *In my day, someone as up-and-down as that wouldn't have been allowed to enter.*

She stopped at the couch. *Did I just use the words "in my day"? Good Lord. I was a Canonical only eleven years ago. Next thing you know, I'll be yelling, "Get off my lawn" out my apartment window.* She knocked on her skull to rattle everything back into place. Her knuckles jarred an idea loose. What if Vivian's old Motherhouse had been so desperate for Postulants that they skirted the usual screening procedures? Perhaps Vivian was one of those hopeful, sincere girls whose *Sister Act* dreams got pulverized by the real thing.

Sister Bartholomew, coming upstairs, met Giulia on the landing between the last two flights.

Giulia put a finger to her lips. "This may not be the best time to go up there."

Sister Bartholomew tilted her head as sounds of sobbing mingled with Sister Gretchen's firm voice reached them.

"Sweet cartwheeling Jesus, is Vivian drowning our chapel again?"

Giulia choked. "Sister Bartholomew—"

She held up a hand. "Please call me Bart."

"Okay. Sister Bart, you may want to shelve that expression."

Her eyebrows met. "What expression … Oh, no. I'm going to kill my brother. He always says that."

Giulia grinned. "At least you said it to me and not Sister Gretchen."

"Sister Gretchen's great. She knows I'm still learning polite speech patterns."

"Did you learn the other ones at a job?"

"Yeah, my family owns a car repair shop. I grew up covered in grease and ignoring *Playboy* centerfolds on the pit walls."

"Pit?"

"The bay where cars get repaired. Sorry. The jargon is second nature. So are derogatory terms for male and female anatomy in three languages." She opened her hands. "Transforming this grease monkey into Sister Mary Bartholomew is a work in progress."

"Sister Bartholomew? Is that you?" Sister Gretchen appeared at the top landing. "I could use your help, please."

"Of course. Excuse me, Sister Regina Coelis."

Giulia continued downstairs, gnashing her teeth. Another opportunity lost as Saint Francis Day crept closer.

Through the landing window, she saw Sister Arnulf and her handler walking through the gardens bundled in plain black wool coats.

She reached her room after nodding and smiling to several Sisters in the hall.

"Never thought I'd encounter an endangered species: the rare Swedish Catholic nun. Only a handful left in captivity, folks. Tour starts in the Motherhouse and runs through the weekend. Take only pictures, leave only footprints." She yanked open the desk drawer. "If only Sister Arnulf was from Calabria, the language barrier between us wouldn't exist. God, a little help, please?"

Her Day-Timer lay open in the drawer, the still-sketchy outline she'd written based on her meditations during Mass accusing her like a criminal record.

"How is it my own conscience is worse than every relative of mine who says I'm going to Hell because I jumped the wall?" She yanked her black raincoat out of the wardrobe.

Three minutes later she was walking the long sidewalk outside the walls. She wanted a five-mile run but settled for three complete circuits of the wall, hampered by what Sisters attached to the Motherhouse would and wouldn't actually do.

"Was it autonomy I missed, those last miserable years? I was a model Sister, obeying the rules, fulfilling the needs, doing everything that was expected. Except for refusing to play up the nonexistent glamour of the religious life to naïve teenage girls."

Pre-lunch sidewalk and street traffic picked up, and she reminded herself not to mutter out loud.

That had been the cosmic clue-stick hitting her upside the head. If the life was so perfect, she should've been selling it like ice cream on a hot summer day. The girls should've heard a tinkly version of "Soul of My Savior" every time she walked into a classroom.

A mother with three small children nodded to her. She smiled back. After they'd passed her, the littlest girl said, "Mommy, why do nuns dress funny?" The mother shushed her. Giulia stifled a giggle. She used to think the same thing, till she wore the habit herself. Then it became a badge of honor. A symbol of Who she'd dedicated her life to. A reminder that she was the walking advertisement for the religious life.

She snagged her toe on a square of broken sidewalk and flailed, but caught herself. "Decorum, Falcone. Ugh. That word. It governed my old, Regina the model Sister, life."

She began the second circuit.

Model Sisters didn't wake up one morning with a big fat nothing where certainty used to be. That clue-stick had been whacking her in the head for quite a while. She'd chosen to ignore it until the emptiness consumed her.

The sidewalk by the west wall was blessedly free of civilians. She turned the corner, walking faster.

What if Sister Bridget woke up empty one morning? What if the shift from Maryland to Pittsburgh aggravated it? Canonical year might be cloistered, but knowing your family was at least in the same city as you mitigated the loneliness a bit.

Giulia itched to jog out this stress and feed her ideas with endorphins.

Since Sister Vivian was a hot mess, Giulia needed to find out if she was from Maryland or Indiana too. There was a chance Sister Bridget had been messed up as well, from distance or false abandonment or … but that would mean Fabian's analysis had been correct.

Sister Bartholomew wasn't a mess, but her family lived in Bethel Park. Ten miles from Pittsburgh. Her situation might be the opposite—never far enough away from the Motherhouse.

Giulia turned the last corner and began the long walk up the Motherhouse driveway. Lunch. Then … telling Sister Bartholomew the truth?

"How do I say it? 'Sister Bart. I'm really a private investigator hired by Sister Fabian to find out why Sister Bridget killed herself. Does it have anything to do with Vivian's crying jags and why you're afraid of the cellars?' Heh. That'd make her vanish down a rabbit hole. Maybe a partial truth. And a quick co-opt of the Driscoll charm."

ELEVEN

Except that every time Giulia saw Sister Bartholomew that afternoon, she was escorting another new arrival. Or fetching a clean towel. Or disappearing into a bedroom, sheets in hand, to make up a fresh bed. Sister Vivian and the two Postulants ran the same treadmill.

The weather shifted to cold, steady rain around two, and Giulia wandered the floors like the Ghost of Sisters Past. On her second circuit of the main floor she recognized one of her entrance group in the doorway and dodged into the back stairwell just in time.

She evaded all human contact on a roundabout path through the Community Room and three small parlors until she reached the refectory. Several Sisters manned the stoves and counters, none of whom Giulia knew. No one even glanced at her when she walked past them to the stairs to the cellars.

When the heavy door closed behind her, she breathed easier. "Better fighting spiders than being polite to Mary Stephen. I should forgive her—no, I did forgive her a bunch of years ago. I remember that Confession with its protracted discussion about what specific kind of sin that was." She squashed a daddy longlegs with the side of her fist. "Forgetting is something else. I'm not stupid enough to pretend her backstabbing and rumor-mongering never happened."

She stopped herself from indulging in foul language. Frank Driscoll she was not. She wouldn't cheat by using Italian, either.

gurgle

Giulia froze.

gurgle, clank

"Wait ..." She followed the noise into the seldom-used half-bath shoehorned between an empty fruit cellar and a bricked-up coal chute. "It's the hot water pipe." She crouched next to the chipped sink, worked her hand between the pipe and the wall, and snugged the joint a half-turn tighter.

hiss, clank ... gurgle ... Silence.

She stood and brushed her habit straight.

I am remembering way too many obscure details. Like the best way to tuck my hair into my veil and the trick to stop that gurgling pipe. Why did my brain cells bother to retain such obscure information? She backed out of the closet-sized room and paced the hall. *Falcone, you're going to forget what life is like outside these walls. That might make your cover tighter, but don't consider it for a minute.* The silence smothered her. "I think I prefer the clanks and gulps. Why doesn't Sister Bart? That everlasting annoyance should be nothing more than background noise to her by now. Something to add to the list of things to get her to talk about."

She paused in the doorway of the dim, empty laundry room. "And while I'm at it, I'll stop talking to myself."

Giving up on the chance that Sister Bartholomew's errand list would bring her down to the cellars—the laundry tables were free of towels and sheets—Giulia climbed back upstairs. Sister Mary Stephen's limp blonde bangs weren't visible in the parlors on the first floor.

Safe so far.

On the second floor, Sister Vivian passed her without acknowledgment as she accompanied two elderly nuns in walkers. One of the Postulants carried a mop and bucket into the bathroom.

Still safe.

When she reached the third floor, she could hear a violin repeating the third line of "O Sanctissima" drifting down from the fifth.

The bangs lurked in the doorway kitty-corner from Giulia's room.

Busted.

Laserlike eye contact forced Giulia to cloak herself in the mantle of her grandmother, always the lady. The hall stretched like Silly Putty as she walked across it.

"Hello."

"It's been a while, Regina."

"Six years, Stephen. Not since Final Vow retreat."

"I heard you left."

"Glomming onto rumors, like always. Done you any good yet?"

Their brittle smiles never wavered. The bell rang for lunch.

"I see you're still fighting those ridiculous curls."

"I see you're still afraid of your given name, Mildew—sorry, Mildred."

"What about—"

A dozen Sisters came out of their rooms. The door next to Sister Mary Stephen opened on a petite, perky redhead.

"Hey, Mary Stephen, chow time. Oh my Lord, it's Regina Coelis." She leapt at Giulia.

"How've you been, Josepha?" The tiny nun's welcome squeeze crushed Giulia's lungs. "Is your team still basketball champ of Alexandria Catholic Central?"

"Of course we are. The WNBA recruited three of my seniors. I rock." She bounded toward the stairs. "Come on, Mary Stephen, I'm starving. Got a table yet, Regina? I think there's room at ours."

Giulia smiled angelically at Mary Stephen. "I do, unfortunately. But I'm sure we'll have plenty of time to reminisce later."

Mary Stephen's mouth contorted. "We'll miss your charming presence."

Giulia won the "who'll move first" standoff, but blew it by tripping on the edge of the carpet. Mary Stephen's snort earned her a *tsk* from a Sister still in the traditional habit.

Sister Fabian intercepted Giulia as everyone waited for the Sisters using walkers to pass.

"If you have a moment, Sister Regina Coelis?"

"Certainly." Giulia caught Mary Stephen's too-interested glare as she turned away.

The Superior General led the way into the smallest of the little parlors on the first floor and closed the door.

"Report."

Giulia's mouth opened in automatic obedience.

Stop.

She suppressed a wicked grin. "I beg your pardon, Sister?"

Sister Fabian's mood-ring earlobes sprang into action. "I expect obedience, Sister. Have you confirmed my findings?"

Giulia braced her feet. "Perhaps you misunderstood me yesterday, Sister. As Driscoll Investigations' client, you will receive a complete report when we're satisfied that we've uncovered all the facts—"

"I've given you the Community's decision."

"No, Sister, you gave me your decision."

"I am the head of the Community."

Giulia waited, heart pounding from flouting years of ingrained obedience.

Color crept from Sister Fabian's earlobes to her throat. "I have just been informed that the apostolic visitation will be here next week."

"The what?"

"The Vatican. Pay attention. The Holy Father created a committee to inspect random Communities, and because of the merger, ours has been chosen for the honor."

"I see. So that's why you want this tied up in a neat little bow by Wednesday."

"We will present an obedient face to the deputation. You will give me your report, now."

"No."

The Superior General took a step forward. "The Community was well quit of you ... Sister."

Harpy. "I'm sure you don't want the Sisters to discuss this rather obvious meeting any longer." Giulia touched the doorknob.

Sister Fabian's nostrils pinched. "You were a disgrace to the habit for years. I see nothing has changed. This conversation is not finished." She stalked through the door Giulia opened for her.

Miserable, officious, obstructionist shrew. What would you have said if I told you I heard you and Ray "doing it" this morning? Her hand on the door trembled the least bit. *They say it takes more guts to jump the wall than to stay inside. Standing up to her might top them both.*

———

After lunch, Giulia sat with Sister Arnulf in the third-floor corner library and folded the corners of a square paper in and then halfway out. "You do this for the other side, too." She smiled at Sister Arnulf. "Why am I telling you this? You can't understand me." When they finished that step, she turned both their papers over and demonstrated the upward fold. "If only Eleanor knew Swedish along with origami."

She folded and turned and folded, Sister Arnulf mirroring her actions.

"Min Bridget älskade små hundar." Sister Arnulf met Giulia's gaze over the completed Scottie dog origami. "Jag ser dig med hennes vän."

"You have no idea how much I want to understand you, Sister." Giulia grabbed a pen and a clean sheet of paper from the box— and stopped. "What's the point? You can't read English, and I can't write Swedish."

Sister Theresa blew into the library smelling of rain and fast food. "Sister Regina, thank you so much for filling in for me this afternoon."

"Were the fries good?" Giulia put away the pen and paper.

"Always. McDonald's fries are my besetting sin. This annual ritual is an excuse and I know it, but we started it to celebrate Sister Lorraine's Investiture. She's the first young woman I shepherded into the Community."

She unbuttoned her coat and gestured to Sister Arnulf. "I'll take her back now." She made the sign for "bathroom," and her charge nodded.

As they left, Sister Arnulf gave a look to Giulia that she could have interpreted any number of ways: *I'll see you later. I'm tired of being led around like a child. You ought to speak my language.*

"I know it, Sister," Giulia said to the last possibility. "It's time to enlist Sidney and a Swedish dictionary."

TWELVE

FORTY SISTERS OF ALL ages crowded the first-floor Community room at seven-thirty that evening. The largest room on the first floor (after the refectory), it still resembled a subway car at rush hour with this many people in it.

The oldest Sisters were of course given the two sofas. Sister Fabian and the other former Superiors General occupied the privileged armchairs around the television. Everyone else brought chairs from the smaller parlors; a few who dared to wear jeans sat cross-legged on the floor.

Giulia, stiff, proper, and itchy in an armless wooden chair, cursed the inventor of pantyhose.

"I'm a Rangers fan," said Sister Susan from a rolling office chair, "but any excuse to watch hockey—even the Penguins versus the Devils."

"Thank you for not making the obvious joke, Susan." Sister Eleanor, in a similar armless chair, finished a row of a pale-blue baby sweater and turned her needles. "My sister's expecting her third," she said to Giulia. "Her last sonogram showed them a 3-D image of this." She held up a fist with her index finger pointing straight out.

Giulia chuckled. "No mistaking that."

The Postulants and Novices entered the room wheeling a cart loaded with two giant tubs of fresh popcorn; stacks of bowls, cups, and napkins; and a five-gallon sports jug.

"It's exactly the same routine from when I was a Novice," Giulia said in a low voice to Susan. "We're in a time loop. Someone call Doctor Who."

On the television, a high school chorus began the National Anthem. Sister Vivian handed Sister Fabian a bowl and cup first, then everyone formed two loose queues to serve themselves. Giulia waited until Sister Bartholomew and the other three had theirs before she took the last of it.

"Those girls need it more than I do," she whispered when she returned to her new friends. "They all look like they're about to drop. What is Sister Fabian thinking, to let so much work fall on them?"

"You know the answer to that," Elizabeth whispered back. "You've heard it from enough retired Sisters."

"We got up at five a.m. and washed everyone's clothes and sheets in a hand-washer, complete with crank wringer," Giulia muttered.

"The cook made us a single piece of fried bread. If she liked us, she'd make us two pieces," Susan continued.

"And that was all we got to eat all morning," Elizabeth added.

"So I don't know why these Novices think they work hard," Giulia finished.

The three of them grinned at each other.

"You're right, Sister Regina," Susan said. "The Novices and Postulants are overworked. I saw you buffing the chapel floor this morning."

Giulia waved it away. "I like to keep busy."

Susan chewed a mouthful of popcorn. "The stress is getting to you too, huh? Elizabeth here instantly adapts to any situation, but I'm a creature of routine—and small convents."

"Ssh." One of the retired nuns glared at them.

"Sister Fabian's nephew is on the team," Giulia whispered. "That's why we get an evening of ESPN."

"I wondered," Susan said. "She doesn't seem the type to let people indulge."

"We have more profitable uses for three hours of our time than watching television." Elizabeth sipped her lemonade.

Susan stared at her with hooded eyes. "Elizabeth, sometimes I want to shake you. What on earth is wrong with harmless pastimes?"

"We are to set an example for the world and you know it, Susan. How can we do that if we follow the path of their vices rather than leading them on the path of virtue?"

Giulia began, "But if we aren't familiar with current secular pursuits—at least superficially—how will we connect with the laity in ways they can relate to?"

Susan flopped back in her chair. "You two must've been separated at birth. It's like I'm listening to the Sanctimonious Hour. Elizabeth," she pointed at her fellow Sister, "look me in the eye and tell me you don't tune your clock radio to the Nets home games when you can."

Elizabeth blushed. "I know I should break myself of such a bad habit, but—"

Susan groaned. "Please discontinue the puns immediately."

"Ssh!" Two retired Sisters glared at them this time.

Giulia, Susan, and Elizabeth meekly settled in their seats and ate popcorn.

Midway through the first period, the Penguins scored. Sister Fabian cheered.

"That was her nephew," Giulia said.

"If only I could 'accidentally' change channels to a Fabian movie marathon," Susan said. In a voice pitched for Giulia's and Elizabeth's ears, she sang the chorus of "Turn Me Loose."

Elizabeth and Giulia elbowed her. Sister Bartholomew's head started to turn in their direction, but she stuffed popcorn in her mouth and faced the television again.

Giulia swallowed several times until she had her voice under control. "Sister Susan, you'd have a happier visit if you flew under Sister Fabian's radar."

Susan huffed. "You don't have to tell me. I've lived under three Superiors cut from her cloth already. But I'm fifty-one years old, I'll die in harness, and I'm sick of dancing to the tune of people like her."

"But your vocation—"

"My vocation has nothing to do with power-grabbers. Don't misunderstand me—I'd never throw away my vocation for the temporary satisfaction of getting the best of her." She jerked her head at the front of the room. "That's why you surprise me. You don't seem the type to suck up to her. I saw you coming out of one of the parlors with her at lunch."

"Sometimes I choose to compromise."

Elizabeth said, "Susan, one day someone's going to punch you. Sister Regina, she's not usually this abrasive. Put it down to travel and crowds. She's much better in one of our minuscule Florida convents."

"Yeah, the palmetto bugs don't lecture me." Susan finished her lemonade. "My apologies, Sister Regina. Why God chose me to serve His purpose, I'll never know. And people claim He has no sense of humor."

The first intermission began, and several Sisters headed for the bathrooms. Some explored the bookshelves. The Novices and Postulants gathered the cups and popcorn bowls and wheeled the cart through the doorway nearest the kitchen.

Giulia pretended to leaf through a back issue of *The Cord*.

Is that what I did? Throw away my vocation? I was so sure of it once—sure for eight years. Nine, if I count senior year in high school. Was my faith so weak that a few years of Fabian-clones and banishment to the hinterlands withered it?

A hand touched her shoulder. Susan said in her ear, "You left and returned, right? I remember you mentioned it last night at dinner. I did, too, before final vows. It's rough getting back into the rhythm, but it gets easier. Remember, God won't desert you."

She squeezed Giulia's shoulder and returned to her chair as the second period started.

————

A half-hour after the game ended (Penguins 2, Devils 0), Giulia paced her cell—*No!*—room. Two steps across, seven steps down, one step across (the desk crowded that end of the room), seven steps back.

"What's worse? The idea that I never had a vocation? That it was only family tradition and starry-eyed wishful thinking and Cradle Catholic indoctrination?"

Two steps across. Seven steps down.

"Or that I tossed it aside like an empty espresso cup? That I chose hate for the petty politics and Fabian's puppet strings over the will of God in my life?"

She stopped pacing and opened her wardrobe. Her reflection in the small oval mirror on the inside of the door showed a living flashback: herself in the last months before she jumped the wall. The same haggard face. The same caverns under her eyes. Those same two curls that always escaped her veil.

"I'm slipping back into it so easily. It hasn't even been two days yet. If I didn't have my phone in my pocket—" she patted its familiar rectangle— "I'd wonder if the Giulia Falcone who got makeup lessons from Mingmei and stopped bad guys with Frank was someone I'd only read about."

She turned her pocket inside out and studied her driver's license photo. "It'll take a little time to get back to normal when I get out. Normal. I need a shot of that."

She texted Frank.

Exciting evening. Popcorn and TV hockey.

The phone buzzed right away. Slacker. Why arent u detecting?

She made a face at the screen. I'm not on duty 24 hours a day.

Good. U kno I cant afford OT.

Giulia grinned as she typed, HEARD IT BEFORE. MAYBE YOU SHOULD FIND US MORE CLIENTS.

TASKMASTER. WOULD U LIKE TO KNO IM AT THE GARDEN SHARING PIE AND ICE CREAM WITH A WOMAN?

Giulia swallowed. YOU FOUND A GF IN THE 24 HOURS I'VE BEEN IN HERE?

There was a longer pause before the answering buzz. JEALOUS? HAHAHA. DONT WORRY. IM OUT WITH MOM 4 HER BIRTHDAY.

"Curse you, Frank. You know I just turned neon-green jealous."

A ghostlike tap came at the door.

HAVE TO GO.

THIRTEEN

SHE OPENED THE DOOR, a greeting to Sister Bart on her lips ... and was confronted with Sister Vivian. The Novice's lopsided smile and heavy-lidded eyes said bad things to Giulia.

"Hey, there, Sister Regina. You can't be headed for bed already. You've been in real convents where people keep human hours."

Giulia yanked her inside. "Quiet!" she whispered.

Still with that smile, Sister Vivian leaned against the closed door. "Aren't you tired of talking to Bart all the time? She's so naïve and bo-ring." She exhaled a fog of altar wine.

"Shouldn't you be on your own floor by now?"

"Don'chew worry about me, Sister. My family knows how to handle their liquor." She executed an elaborate wink. "I'd've brought some for you, but it's hard to sneak it out." She thumped onto Giulia's narrow bed and patted the covers. "Let's talk, woman to woman."

Giulia sat farther away than Sister Vivian indicated. *It's research. She knew Sister Bridget too. Ten minutes and I'll boot her up to the fifth floor.*

"Thass right. God, I miss college. We'd stay up all night gabbing, sharing secrets, trying each other's makeup ..." A slow headshake. "I like being a Sister, yanno. It's what I wanted to be ever since my great-aunt died. She was a pisser of a nun. Told the funniest jokes just this side of dirty. She made me think the convent wasn't juss a coop-full of ugly hens who couldn't get a man."

"I see."

Sister Vivian flopped crossways on Giulia's bed, resting her head on her hands. "I knew you'd understand. You've been around." She giggled. "I didn't mean that like it sounded. You and me, we're women of the world. Not like Bart and Bridget."

"Did they enter right out of high school?"

"Duh. Isn't it obvious? You didn't meet Bridget. She couldn't deal with it." Another slow headshake. "Bart's not doing too bad, except she sleepwalks."

Giulia leaned against the wall, doing her best to look worldly and at ease. "That's not too good. How does she keep away from the back stairs?"

"We put a lock on the door. S'str Gretchen caught her once and stopped her. So did I." She moved her gaze away from the bare dresser to Giulia's face. "It was frickin' creepy. Her eyes were mostly closed but not quite, and she wasn't walking normal. Just going thump, thump, thump down the hall." Her hands didn't move to cover a huge, wine-soaked belch. "Oops, sorry." She giggled again. "That's all you'll hear from me, too. Tol'ja I could deal with it. How d'you deal with the freaky bad stuff when you're a real, permanent nun, Sister Regina?"

Before Giulia could invent something neutral-sounding, the Novice scooted upright, leaned toward the wall, blinked several times, then swayed toward the opposite wall. Giulia put out a hand to stop her from falling off the bed.

"God, I wanna beer. My roommate had a fake ID our second year in college. We'd all pitch in and she'd get a twelve-pack and our suite would share it."

"I don't think beer's allowed in the Motherhouse."

"Oh, yeah, don't I know it. Nothin' fun's allowed here."

"There's hockey and popcorn nights."

"Puh-lease. Bart may think that's fun, but she acts like an old woman. Did she admit she's afraid to go into the cellars? Try to get her down there and then pretend you hear something moaning. She gets whiter than the old nuns' veils."

Giulia imitated Vivian's casual, confidential tone. "Was she always afraid of the cellars?"

"Nah. Only since Bridget killed herself." She leaned into Giulia's steadying arm, overbalanced, and bonked against her shoulder. "Did'ja hear she drank a whole bottle of bleach? Stupid kid. I would've showed her how to fix the altar wine so no one'd notice any difference. She didn't talk to me much, so I didn't know it got to her that bad."

"Did you know what was bothering Sister Bridget?"

Vivian looked sideways at Giulia. "Shh. Can't talk about it. Biiiig secret." The lopsided smile reappeared. "You'd'a been a great roomie. You're such a good listener. My college roomie was a good listener. She liked girls. D'you like girls? Everyone said nuns were wicked Lesbos, but they lied. I miss my roomie." A tear trickled down one plump cheek. "Your lips're kinda like hers, too."

She plunged forward, taking Giulia with her off the edge of the bed. Sister Vivian's sloppy kiss landed near Giulia's eye socket.

"That's quite enough, Sister." Giulia pushed her off and stood.

Vivian stayed face-down, weeping into the linoleum.

"Sister Vivian, this is not how a Sister of Saint Francis is expected to conduct herself."

"Not you too." The weeping volume increased. "You don't understaaaand."

"That's it." Giulia hauled her up. "Do you want every Sister on this floor to hear you? You know these walls are like papier-mâché."

Snot ran over Sister Vivian's upper lip. Her swollen eyes dripped tears. Giulia grabbed several tissues from the desk and shoved them in Vivian's face.

"Clean yourself up. We're going to try to get to your floor without turning you into tonight's surprise entertainment. Although that'll take a minor miracle. What's Saint Vivian the patron of?" Only a honk into the tissues answered her. "Never mind. Let's go."

Giulia poked her head into the hall; no one. None too gently, she dragged still-sniveling Sister Vivian into the hall. They skirted three doors with lights shining beneath them and took a wide path around the low-voiced conversation in the corner sitting room.

Sister Vivian tripped twice on the front stairs. Giulia hovered between frustration at not being able to take the lesser-used back stairs and gratitude that Vivian had mentioned the new lock on their floor.

Both sides of the fifth floor were dark. Of course—the girls worked too hard to keep secret late hours. Giulia pictured the layout of the living room, but a too-solid chair? couch? leapt out at their legs. She remembered to keep her reaction to a hiss.

Sister Vivian's naturally high voice jumped an octave. "Ow!"

Giulia clapped her hand over Vivian's mouth. "Do you want Sister Gretchen to find you like this?"

That'd put way too much spotlight on me. A visiting Sister helping the Novices with the cleaning is one thing. The same Sister with her arm around a drunk Novice late at night—well, can you say hideous scandal?

Snot and tears dripped down Giulia's hand, but she kept Vivian's mouth covered. A circle of light bobbed ahead of them, illuminated the wall, and flickered over their faces. Giulia blocked her eyes with her free hand.

"Sister Regina?" Sister Bartholomew whispered.

"Oh, thank God. Can you help us, Sister?"

"What?" Sister Bartholomew came closer, keeping the light on the floor in front of her. "Oh, no, is Vivian drunk? Never mind; I can smell it." She hefted Vivian's other shoulder. "Sister Gretchen's not up here yet, but I expect her any minute. Let's put this one to bed before she shows."

Sister Bart steered the shambling procession to the first bedroom after the chapel. Sister Vivian was all but out on her feet.

Sister Bartholomew yanked down the bedspread. "Idiot. What did she do, bust into your room bragging how she can hold her liquor?"

"More or less."

They heaved Vivian onto the blanket and took off her shoes.

"'S'at, you, Bart?" Vivian's voice faded out on the last word.

Giulia un-Velcroed the veil and laid it on the dresser. "So she's lost control like this before?"

"Not since the Feast of the Assumption. Wonder what set her off? Help me turn her over, would you?"

They rolled the now-unconscious Vivian onto her stomach. Sister Bartholomew unzipped the slightly-too-tight habit, muttering, "Gotta channel it better, dummy. Gotta deal with it." Between them, they tugged it off her in increments, finally working it out from under her legs. Giulia hung it on a hook behind the door and Sister Bartholomew flung the bedspread over Vivian just as she began to snore.

Blowing out a long breath, Giulia pulled two tissues from the box on the dresser and wiped her hands.

Sister Bart turned Vivian's head to the side. "At least if she pukes she won't choke to death."

She closed the door on the noise, and Giulia blinked to get used to the new darkness of the hall.

"Has she been that bad since she entered?"

"I don't think so, but I didn't meet her till after the merger. We were both Canonicals already."

Steady footsteps became audible on the landing.

Sister Bartholomew hustled Giulia down the hall and through the unlocked back door. "Thanks a ton for helping with Vivian, Sister. Sister Gretchen shouldn't find you up here this late. See you tomorrow morning."

Giulia clutched the banister to stop herself going headlong down the steps. Sister Bartholomew vanished behind the double doors.

She slid off her shoes and walked downstairs on the balls of her feet. *It has to be close to eleven-thirty. That alarm rings at six. And I'm sneaking around the Motherhouse covered in sticky snot and tears and drool that stinks of sour altar wine.* The third-floor bathroom door opened and she slipped into the corner parlor. *I should've smeared myself with honey and found that anthill before coming here. This place is like a* Jerry Springer *episode.*

"Där är du. Följ med mig."

Giulia's veil nearly flew off her head like hats did in comic strips. "Sister Arnulf."

The little nun took Giulia's hand and led her to one of the small tables. Giulia looked out at the dimly lit floor, but Sister Theresa the handler wasn't anywhere. She let Sister Arnulf sit her in one of the polished chairs.

"Sister, you know I can't understand you, but I'm working on the basics. Maybe tomorrow." She sighed at her own futility. "Why am I explaining this to you?"

Sister Arnulf drew a face on a piece of paper while Giulia muttered. Giulia couldn't tell if it was supposed to be male or female. It wore no veil, but had no hair either. When the face had rudimentary features, she added a dark circle on the right side of the forehead, pressing so hard the pencil lead snapped.

She pushed the paper in front of Giulia, pointed to the circle, pointed to her own forehead, and pointed to the paper again.

Sister Theresa entered, sporting a quilted flowery bathrobe and a typical case of veil-head.

"Sister Arnulf, I've been looking everywhere for you. Sister Regina Coelis, I know she doesn't mean to be a nuisance."

Sister Arnulf glanced at her babysitter and bent over Giulia. Her thin, wrinkled fingers patted Giulia's cheeks, then her own. She touched Giulia's forehead, then her own where she'd drawn the dark spot on the paper. Finally she circled her throat with one hand and pointed to the invisible mark with the other.

Giulia held up both hands in a helpless gesture.

Sister Arnulf made a frustrated noise. "Är du dum?"

Sister Theresa put a hand on Sister Arnulf's arm. "Säng—That means bed," she said to Giulia.

Sister Arnulf slapped the desk and the other two stared at her. The little nun's body was tensed like she was ready for a fight. Then a moment later she relaxed and nodded at Sister Theresa.

"Sorry. She's wandering even more this week." She cinched her robe. "You'd never think such a sweet old lady bombed Nazi arms depots in World War Two, would you?"

"Not in a hundred years. I didn't know there was a Swedish resistance in the war."

"Poor little Sister Bridget told me about it. They were sort of an adjunct to the Norwegian resistance. But if even half the stories she told Sister Bridget were true, our friend here was once a force to be reckoned with."

"Are you saying she flew bombers?"

"No, no. She was barely fifteen then. She and her school friends became pipe bomb experts."

Sister Arnulf looked at them with her head slightly tilted. Giulia was reminded of a cat trying to anticipate a bird's next move.

Giulia stuffed the pencil sketch in her empty pocket. "Good night, Sisters."

Sister Arnulf nodded when the paper disappeared. Giulia stared after them until the high crown of the older Sister's veil disappeared down the staircase.

"First thing tomorrow I'm texting Sidney with another set of basic Swedish phrases."

Her plans scattered when she opened her door. Someone had searched her room.

FOURTEEN

"FABIAN, YOU UNDERHANDED—" GIULIA stopped herself before the curse left her tongue. "It can't be anyone else but her. No one else knows why I'm here. No one else cares."

She closed the door. "Shut up, Falcone. One, you're talking to yourself. Two, these walls are laughably thin. Three, most of them are sleeping and without other sound to mask it, your voice will carry even easier."

She yanked and tugged the stuck top drawer of the desk until it straightened on its worn track. "Fabian's a Scooby-Doo level sleuth if she leaves clues this obvious. Everyone knows these drawers stick on their runners until you learn the trick to them. Everyone except Fabian with her fancy furniture. "

The folder about Sister Bridget was on the opposite side of the drawer now. Giulia opened it to a crinkled top page.

"Too bad for her I'd only written up one spreadsheet's worth of notes." She turned over each page. Two more were wrinkled. "Nothing's missing…" She catalogued her memories of each page.

"Right. It's all there. Thank the Lord I keep my cell in my pocket." She smirked. "And that I didn't bring the *Cosmo*."

She turned in place and opened her dresser drawer.

"Ick. She pawed my underwear." A giggle bubbled up. "If only I could ask her what she thinks of the lace and bright colors. So inappropriate for a Sister of Saint Francis, don't you know."

She crept to the door and inched it open. Every other room on the floor was dark, but that meant nothing. She closed herself back in and texted Frank.

ROOM SEARCHED. UPDATES WHEN I LEARN SOMETHING.

———

The line in the bathroom at 6:05 a.m. reminded Giulia of intermission at the Cottonwood Performing Arts Center.

Be sure to visit the wine bar before Act Two, folks! And when the show's over, Tracey's Chocolates are the perfect way to end the evening.

Giulia wanted a Tracey's turtle in the worst way—at this hour of the morning, too. Talk about stress eating.

The water pressure in the building had improved since her Novitiate years. Now it was possible to take a decent four-minute shower rather than waiting ten for the water to heat up. That was probably why Fabian spent the money: faster showers kept the puppets efficient.

Giulia towel-dried her hair. She should've showered last night, but the noise would've awakened too many people. Now her veil would be damp till noon.

Sister Josepha grimaced at Giulia as she stepped into the just-vacated shower cubicle. "The only good crowds are the ones cheering for my basketball teams."

Sister Mary Stephen took the sink next to Giulia.

"Morning," Giulia said after she spit.

Mary Stephen nodded, staring at Giulia's reflection in the mirror instead of her own.

Giulia, now self-conscious about her every movement, escaped as soon as she swallowed a multi-vitamin. Safe in her room (like that was safe anymore), she chose fuchsia underwear with silver-toned lace accents.

"Take that, Fabian. I hope you're gnashing your teeth as you pick out today's pair of granny underpants." The habit slipped over her "real woman's" underthings and she transformed into Sister Regina Coelis. She twisted her already curling hair into a knot and shoved it under the veil. The clock read 6:22.

Drawers closed, bed made, room neat and anonymous.

She turned on her phone and the message icon appeared in the top left corner, but it was from Sidney, not Frank.

OLIVIER PROPOSED! Cant wait 2 tell u!

Giulia's grin stretched her cheeks to their limit. "What a wedding that'll be. One set of food stations dedicated to carnivores and sugar-holics, the other for the all-natural cult. I wonder if they'll have a juice bar opposite the regular bar?"

6:32. She set the phone to *Silent* and walked—never run, no indeed—downstairs.

She tried to pay attention to morning prayers. Really she did. Why did the monotone-voiced Sisters always volunteer to lead?

Her mind wandered to Sidney and Olivier's wedding. It didn't stretch credulity a millimeter to picture Sidney eschewing a traditional white gown for one made from flax or bamboo. Both sustainable plants, of course. Or perhaps she'd choose a winter wedding and make her dress from her family's alpaca wool.

Like yesterday, Giulia joined in the responsories to all the Psalms while the rest of her was miles away in Cottonwood.

She'll be bubbly and sweet, and Olivier will be handsome and charming. She'll feed him gluten-free cake sweetened with honey, and he'll feed her something traditional with buttercream frosting—but no yellow dye number 5.

Office ended.

I didn't pay attention to a single word. I'm going to Hell.

Father Ray said another efficient Mass with a five-minute homily. As Giulia moved along the central-aisle Communion line, she got that prickly-neck sense of someone watching her.

When she turned away from the Communion rail, the Host doing its best to glom onto the roof of her mouth, she looked straight into Sister Mary Stephen's ice-blue eyes.

Giulia conceded the staring contest when she reached her pew. Her knees hit the kneeler, and meditation about Sister Mary Stephen trampled any thoughts of meditation on Communion.

Only twelve people remained in the Communion line when her tongue finally dislodged the Host from the Palate Gravity Field.

———

"I want chocolate." Sister Susan poked at her scrambled "eggs."

"I'd settle for non-institutional coffee," Sister Eleanor said.

"If only I'd brought a box from Tracey's Chocolates," Giulia said. "It's this one-woman shop where I li—I'm stationed. She makes raspberry truffles as big as a quarter, and she even grows her own raspberries."

Susan set down her fork. "Sister Regina Coelis, you just ruined breakfast—not that it took much."

Elizabeth said, "Susan, when you waste food it's tantamount to refusing a starving child a piece of bread."

"Elizabeth, you are the only person I know who could use 'tantamount' in everyday speech." Susan ate a forkful of reconstituted egg-like protein.

"Pay attention, Sisters," Eleanor said. "This is the next fold on the crane. Everyone expects an origami crane, so you might as well learn it."

Giulia folded her paper. What she really wanted to do was check her text messages.

Eleanor folded the top flaps into the center fold. "I keep trying to design a Saint Francis origami, but he always comes out looking like the Frankenstein monster."

"It'd be good for Halloween," Giulia said.

"Turn failure into success?" She turned the half-completed crane in her hands. "I'm sure I can create a pumpkin and a black cat. Hmm."

Susan leaned across the table. "Sister Regina, why is that blonde Sister with the bangs staring at you? Two tables to your left."

Giulia skewed her eyes over her shoulder. Sure enough, Mary Stephen's blue laser beams were trained on her. They cut off when she caught Giulia's gaze.

She smiled in apology to Susan. "We have a bit of a history. I'm afraid I needled her yesterday."

"Forgive me for using you as an object lesson, Sister, but Susan, you should—"

"Elizabeth, if you lecture me one more time about my feud with you-know-who, I will short-sheet your bed." Susan stabbed the last piece of sausage on her plate and stuffed it in her mouth.

Sister Elizabeth raised her eyebrows. "As you wish."

Sister Cynthia made a face at her wheat toast. "I hear that tomorrow's feast will live up to its name. Chicken parmesan and Texas sheet cake."

Elizabeth's eyes widened. "Seriously? Made the correct way, with pecans in the frosting?"

"I guess so. The chubby Novice—what's her name?"

"Vivian," Eleanor said.

"Yes, that's it. Sister Vivian said that her former Superior General learned how to make it when she was stationed in El Paso, and offered to help the cooks."

Cynthia finished her toast. "Real Texas sheet cake will make this trip worthwhile."

Giulia fostered a glimmer of hope. "Is chocolate involved?"

"The perfect way, Sister—in the cake and the frosting. The ratio is a lovely two to one."

"I approve."

"Elizabeth," Susan crossed her arms, "I don't want to hear one word about the spirit of poverty tomorrow."

"Susan, you know very well Saint Francis lived on only what he and the friars begged for."

"Elizabeth—"

"But like him, I graciously accept what I'm given—chocolate cake most of all."

The table broke up amidst laughter.

A familiar voice reached Giulia as she passed the front foyer. Sister Arnulf had buttonholed another new arrival. English and Swedish garbled together as Sister Theresa apologized and Sister Arnulf resisted her pulling arms.

Giulia headed for the stairs and her room, the only place she could safely check for texts.

"Sister Regina Coelis."

The Superior General sounded exactly like a cartoon snake's voice. Giulia choked down a smart remark. No need to aggravate her further.

"Yes, Sister Fabian?"

Every one of the dozen Sisters within earshot stopped whatever they were doing and found something to keep them in the main hall.

"I expect you in my office."

With an expressionless face, Giulia said, "I'm sorry, Sister, but I don't have time right now."

She felt the wave of astonishment ripple through the hall. Before her façade crumbled, she turned her back on Sister Fabian's outraged face and continued upstairs.

"Saint Francis Day is tomorrow," the cartoon snake hissed.

"I'm aware of that, Sister, thank you."

If they'd been anywhere else, a delighted and horrified murmur of conversation would've followed her upstairs. Instead, Sister Fabian's quick, deliberate steps headed toward the chapel hall and her private rooms. Giulia counted to twenty out of habit. So did everyone else, apparently, because at "twenty" the hurried patter of many sensible shoes scattered in every other direction.

Giulia's heart pounded as she climbed the four flights of stairs to the third floor with outward calm.

Only Sister Mary Stephen's gaze met hers as she crossed the carpet to her room. Behind her own closed door, Giulia stuck her head out the window into the shock of cold fall air.

You're a grown woman, Falcone. It's ridiculous for you to react like a ten-year-old disobeying her parents. You're past this. You're free. You owe her nothing.

She sneezed. *And you're cold. Get inside, dummy.*

She closed the window with one hand and groped for her phone with the other. No texts.

A moment later, she laughed at herself. What a desperate, trapped animal she'd become when no connection to the outside world killed her good mood.

That and Sidney's CAPSLOCK proposal text.

Sidney, six years younger than Giulia. With a happy, goofy family; an endless wonder at the everyday world; and a kind, intelligent fiancé.

Giulia, pushing thirty with both hands, had a laundry list of "issues," a family that hadn't spoken to her since a year ago June, and a short-circuited relationship with her boss.

He room attempted its Shrinky-Dink imitation again.

"No." She slapped the walls apart. "They move only in your own imagination. You keep this up and you'll be a human touch-me-not plant when you leave. Anytime someone comes near you, you'll curl into a trembling ball."

She looked down at the phone, open on the bed. The message icon had appeared.

Trans: What does the face mean? = Vad betyder ansikte? Was she unhappy? = Var hon olycklig? Cont nxt txt.

"Excellent." Giulia pulled out a page from her Day-Timer and wrote everything out.

The icon lit.

Was she afraid? = Var hon rädd? Mr D says dont forgt lnch.

A moment later she'd dialed the office and waited for Sidney to pick up on the second ring, like always.

"Driscoll Investigations, may I help you?"

"Congratulations."

"Giulia! We miss you. Did anyone recognize you? Is it just like you remember?"

"No and yes. Tell me about Olivier."

"He was so romantic. He took me to his parents' house for dinner and they made eggplant parm and fresh bread."

"So they cooked especially for you?" Giulia heard her own smile in her voice.

"Olivier said he told them how I eat. All his brothers and their wives and their kids were there. It was a huge meet-the-family night."

Giulia took a breath to speak at the same time Sidney did, and missed her chance.

"After dinner we got all bundled up and walked in the woods behind the house. The moon was shining through the trees and the leaves were all soft underfoot, and we stopped by this huge sugar maple and he really did get down on one knee and ask me to marry him."

"His family was in on it, then."

Sidney tee-hee'd. Giulia turned the phone up away from her face and took several deep breaths. She didn't want Sidney to think she was laughing at her. She hadn't realized how much of a delight Sidney was till this minute.

"Of course I said yes. His mom and dad and all his brothers were waiting in the hall when we came in." She paused. "Am I that obvious?"

"Well, with Olivier you are."

"Oh. That's okay then."

"Look, I have to go," Giulia said, "but I need you to do something for me."

"Sure. Go ahead. I've got paper and pen right here."

"I need a Swedish interpreter."

"Weren't my translations okay? I looked them up on Google."

"I'm sure they're fine; my idea isn't sufficient. I'm going to try them, but my pronunciation won't be correct and I'll have to write her answers phonetically. We don't have the time."

"What is this for?"

Giulia heard, *Tell me, tell me, I'm dying to know what's going on in there!* behind that polite question.

"There's a little old Swedish nun here who was friends with Sister Bridget, the one who killed herself. Sister Bridget was the only one who understood her, and she's trying to tell me something, but she doesn't speak English. So if you can find a translator, I can call him or her and put this Sister on the phone, and the translator can tell me what she's saying."

"Got it. No problem. I'll start on it right away. Oh, Mr. Driscoll, Giulia's on the phone. Did you want to talk to her?"

A moment of silence, and Frank's voice replaced Sidney's.

"Good morning. Anything to report?"

"The food's terrible."

"No one said detective work was easy."

"Thank you for your sympathy. Sidney's going to connect me with someone who can bridge a language gap. I'm working on the other Novices. What time are we meeting for lunch?"

"Noon, more or less."

"I'll be at the end of the driveway where you dropped me off. Tell Sidney congratulations again."

She folded the paper and pen and put them in the opposite pocket from her phone. At the same time, she squashed the jealous troll trying to take root in her heart.

A good two dozen Sisters milled around the hall now, although twice that number would still have room to stand at arms' length from each other. Ebenezer Scrooge's stairs, wide enough for a horse-drawn coach, had nothing on the Motherhouse halls. Ten months out of the year their temperature averaged sixty degrees.

Narrow, oblique rays of sunlight stretched half the length of the hall, touching a bareheaded Sister whom Giulia didn't recognize. Her open raincoat revealed a white blouse and black trousers. Her voice carried well beyond the circle of the four Sisters she addressed.

"Would you believe three of them took me aside between the foyer and first-floor landing? 'Sister, it was expected that everyone wear the habit for this celebration.' 'Sister, didn't you receive the email about wearing the habit?' 'Sister, a letter was sent to all attendees regarding appropriate dress.'" She shivered and belted her coat closed. "Of course I knew we had to wear the habit. Did any of them juggle three separate flights with two interminable layovers—one in Newark—and keep the habit in the exemplary condition everyone expects? Even polyester double-knit wrinkles after seven hours in coach."

"Mary Margaret, you're getting hives." A cheerful Sister with silver bangs steered the irate traveler toward the bathroom. "Come wash your face and take a Benadryl."

"And change out of your indecorous lay clothes before you scandalize the Superior General." A bony Sister with a monobrow hid her mouth against the back of her hand, but laughter honked through.

Giulia waited till the bathroom door swung closed behind them before she crossed the hall. No one passed her on the first two flights of stairs, but the second floor was even more crowded than the third. Giulia didn't recognize anyone or see Sister Arnulf.

"Sister Regina, I'm so glad I found you." Sister Theresa clutched Giulia's arm from behind. "Sister Arnulf's taken me all over the Motherhouse looking for you. That is, after I dragged her away from the foyer."

Giulia nodded. "I saw her there after breakfast. What is she so anxious to tell someone?"

"I can't figure it out. I sat her down at the computer in the first-floor library and found a translation site, but she must be speaking a dialect."

"Wouldn't she type it in for you?"

"She tried, but either the English keyboard stumped her, or she never learned to type. The technology of the computer itself seemed to frustrate her."

Giulia kept her mouth shut. She clearly remembered checking out the first floor Sunday night and seeing Sister Arnulf sending email from the communal PC. The way she pounded the keys. The anger.

Sister Theresa inched closer. "Don't think badly of me, but I grew up watching *The Muppet Show*. Every so often, I expect Sister Arnulf to open her mouth and say, 'Bork bork bork.'"

Giulia bit the inside of her cheek quick and hard. After a deep breath, she felt she could trust her voice. "I will work hard to forget you said that, or else I'll burst out laughing the next time she talks to me." She smiled to take away any hint of censure. "I wouldn't hurt her feelings for the world. "

The bathroom's swinging door opened. Sister Arnulf's face lit when she saw Giulia.

"Kom med mig. Jag ritar det igen."

Giulia and Theresa followed her the length of the hall to the sunny little library. As she took pencil and paper to possibly redraw the facial outline, Giulia took her own paper from her pocket and read, "Vad betyder ansikte?"

Sister Theresa's mouth fell open. Sister Arnulf's head jerked up and she started talking at light-speed.

Giulia held up one hand in a "slow down" gesture and tried to write with the other. When Sister Arnulf stopped, she handed her the pen and pointed to the paper. The little nun shook her head and started all over again.

"This isn't working." Giulia jabbed her finger on the paper several times. "If you won't write it down, I can't get it translated."

Sister Theresa raised her voice over the fast-flowing Swedish. "I thought you didn't know the language?"

Giulia said to her, "I have a friend who's familiar with a bit of it, and she gave me a few phrases to try. But it's not enough. I was afraid that'd be the case."

Sister Arnulf's voice slowed, then stopped as she looked between Giulia and her handler.

Sister Theresa said, "I've listened to her talking to as many new arrivals as she can. She repeats one word often enough that I took a stab at it on the Internet and got lucky. It's 'mole' or 'blemish' or something similar—I'm sure my phonetic spelling was at fault. Unfortunately, several Sisters have moles or facial blemishes. Even I do." She raised her bangs a fraction to reveal three small, flat moles. "You can usually see only the edges of the bottom two."

Giulia frowned. "Why would she be so concerned about a mole? Unless she thinks someone has cancer ..." She glanced at Sister Arnulf, who was staring out at the crowded hall.

Worry lines creased Sister Theresa's forehead. "Cancer never occurred to me. I'll mention it to Sister Fabian."

Sister Arnulf turned her head to glare at one or both of them, Giulia couldn't tell.

Sister Theresa gave them both a wry smile. "Sister Fabian asked me to chaperone her after Sister Bridget died. She's never taken to me. I'm not sure why."

Sister Arnulf smoothed her face when Sister Theresa gestured to her.

"Come on. Let's see if they need help decorating the refectory."

Giulia watched them navigate the hall, then looked down at her sheet of phrases. She crumpled it and tossed it in the wastebasket.

"Sidney, hurry up and find a translator."

FIFTEEN

THE NUMBER OF SISTERS in the hall increased so quickly Giulia was reminded of asexual reproduction.

She dropped her head onto her arms. "I'm going to Hell." A moment later she stopped laughing and checked the clock above the door.

"Still too early to sneak out to meet Frank. I may as well make myself useful to the Novices." She left the library and eased past the stressed traveler, now in a pristine habit.

"Don't I clean up nice?" The traveler pirouetted for her companions. "Behold the proper Sister of Saint Francis fit to represent the new and improved Community."

"You're going to get in trouble," the silver-haired one said.

"I'm already in trouble. Nineteen exemplary years besmirched with jet-engine exhaust. My review isn't till January, though. Perhaps my faux pas will be forgotten by then."

"Only if you hold your tongue." The same Sister steered Mary Margaret toward the stairs. "Come and talk to Edwen and Epiphania. They're like kids at Christmas with everyone back here."

Giulia circled around them and started down the front stairs. Crowded, but she wanted no chance of running into Sister Fabian. Her stack of "Keep Your Temper" cards was running low.

The bass notes from the organ vibrated through her feet as soon as she entered the long chapel entrance hall. The always-loose pane in the Saint Anthony stained-glass window vibrated in its casing.

By the time she entered the nave, the combined volume of the organ, singers, and other musical instruments was rattling her brain in her skull. She stopped across from the Third Station of the Cross and said to the prostrate Jesus, "Is anyone able to find contemplation space here?"

Perhaps Operation Sparkling Chapel was complete, because not a Novice or Postulant was in sight. The singers above and behind her began the last verse of "Make Me a Channel of Your Peace," an earworm if there ever was one. Giulia walked farther up the aisle toward the Virgin's alcove in a futile effort to get away from the din. The sun touched the replenished silver edging to the statue's veil, and it did indeed sparkle.

The trumpet hit a B-flat instead of a B and the choir director's tight voice snapped, "The last two lines again, please."

Giulia turned her back on the statue. She could brave early winter in the gardens for the sake of a little head space.

With a resounding three-octave B chord, the rehearsal ended. Giulia's footsteps crack-crack-cracked on the tiled vestibule floor in the new silence. Maybe she'd stay in here after all.

Many footsteps clattered down the narrow stairs from the choir loft. Giulia flattened herself against the wall for the singers to pass.

"Well, well, well. Good morning again."

Giulia counted to five. "Good morning, Sister Mary Stephen."

"Are you spying on the choir or merely taking up space this morning?" Mary Stephen's professionally trained voice made even snark sound melodious.

"I had business to take care of."

"I'm sure you did. That would be hanging on the fringes of the talented group, as usual, right?" Her wide smile took in her own business suit–tailored habit and Giulia's plain, used, unflattering one.

"If you spent less time watching what I did—"

"If you spent more time living up to your vocation—"

Giulia glared. "How would you know what living up to a vocation means? Unless you still think God's called you to be the Community's Rumor Mill."

Giulia's group-mate took one step nearer to her. "When the well-being of the group is involved—"

"Not that excuse again." Giulia pulled a deliberate smirk. "It was lame by the second time you tried it on our Novice Mistress."

"So you admit you were wrong the first time."

"Fat chance. The only thing wrong was your Hooverlike sucking up to her."

Sister Mary Stephen's nostrils flared. "You always were eaten up with jealousy. Just because Sister Fatima recognized my willingness to help—"

Giulia barked a laugh. "Is that what you call it?"

"As proved by the positions given to me."

"Hall monitor, snitch, and truant officer. Oh, and your most-deserved title: Number One Backstabber."

Sister Mary Stephen stepped even closer to Giulia. "You still claim the streamlined filing system was your idea?"

"I know it was. Remember, I caught you coming out of my room the night before you pitched the idea to Sister Fatima."

"We all worked on it!"

"Oh, and I was merely the recording secretary? Not a chance, Stephen. You snuck into everyone's room to appropriate whatever would make you look like the Indispensable Novice." Giulia stepped closer this time. "Ask Josepha if she remembers the day her sneakers got confiscated."

Mary Stephen's high color faded a degree. "What are you implying?"

Giulia plastered "wide-eyed innocence" on her face. "You don't remember one of your finest moments? That would be when you convinced Sister Fatima that any outside contact had to be detrimental to the intent of the cloistered Canonical year." Giulia's voice, as low as Mary Stephen's but not as trained, grew raspy. "So under the cloak of Formation you got yourself named 'Ethics Nazi' and snatched Josepha's high-tops out of her room when she wasn't there—because she kept letters from her girls' Pee-Wee basketball team in them."

"You—I—Sister Fatima said—"

"Whatever she said, you twisted it to suit your own purposes."

Mary Stephen choked, but recovered the next moment. "That's rich, coming from you. No one saw through your 'Model Novice' game except me."

"Don't blame me because you couldn't be Top Nun in everything. You're a great singer, you're smart, you're efficient, you have an eye for arranging flowers, and you can embroider fancy altar cloths without a pattern."

"Well—thank you—"

"But you can't force people to like you even though they kiss your sensible black shoes. Sister Fatima confided in me because we liked each other. Hildegard and Barbara hung out with me because we needed a change from you. They never kissed my shoes, because I didn't want it or need it. It's called friendship."

Mary Stephen's hands clenched. "Don't you pretend to be a saint on earth. You think I snuck around the fifth floor? Then you must've learned something from me, Miss Self-Righteous. I got a look in your desk drawer last night."

Giulia's ears sizzled. "You're still pawing through my life? Good God, you're certifiable. The best day of my Sisterhood was the day you and I got assigned to separate schools."

"Don't change the subject. I saw that folder. You didn't even bother to hide it."

"Because I didn't know Sister Snitch was still in business." Giulia got toe-to-toe with Mary Stephen, craning back her neck to look up into her face. "Did you get some kind of illicit pleasure feeling up my underwear?"

"Maybe it's a good thing I still don't trust you." She looked down her nose at Giulia. "I think Sister Fabian would be very interested to learn—"

"Sister Mary Stephen. Sister Regina Coelis."

Giulia and her adversary froze. Sister Fabian stood at the foot of the choir loft stairs. Behind her and on the opposite side of the vestibule, every member of the choir crowded the steps, horror and rapt attention on every face.

"I am appalled that two Sisters of Saint Francis would conduct themselves in this manner. In the presence of their fellow Sisters, no less. What kind of example are you setting for the Sisters in Formation?"

Giulia kept her eyes on the floor. Without doubt Sister Mary Stephen was doing the same. It was the only safe and humble-appearing action.

"Our Community is beginning a new era, joined in faith with our sister Communities on this solemn and joyful feast."

Giulia ground her teeth, dying to tell her where to get off, knowing she had to take it to maintain her cover.

"Retire to your rooms, please, and meditate on the sins of pride and anger. I strongly suggest you fast until dinner and offer it up in a spirit of humility. Both of you need to remember what that word means."

"Thank you, Sister." Giulia and Mary Stephen gave the expected reply almost in unison.

Giulia raised her head at last and met forty identical expressions of schadenfreude. *Of course. Any day Sister Fabian ripped into someone other than you was a good day.*

The choir filed past them, their faces shifting into neutral when they neared Sister Fabian. Mary Stephen caught up to the last of the line and followed them out.

Giulia slumped down against the wall until her butt hit the floor. "I have never wanted to let loose a string of curses worthy of Frank Driscoll more than at this moment."

Silence filled the chapel. Giulia gazed at the eternally burning candle flame above the tabernacle until her eyes unfocused.

"You two should just put on bikinis and mud wrestle."

Giulia started, gasped, and dissolved into laughter.

Sister Bartholomew squatted next to her. "That was better than a soap opera."

"They'll be—" more laughter—"talking about us for days." She groped in her pocket for a tissue and came up empty. The Novice handed her one, and she wiped her eyes. "So much for keeping a low profile."

"Maybe there's too much happening this week for them to gossip about it?"

Giulia honked into the tissue. "A houseful of women letting an epic catfight pass without comment? Please."

Sister Bart coughed. "You have a point."

Giulia stood. "I'm getting out of here. Thanks for the tissue."

"But you're supposed to be in your room, fasting." Her eyes became as big as a manga heroine's.

"There's only so much incarceration any human can take." Giulia remembered whom she was talking to. "Sorry. You're right."

The lunch bell rang.

"Go on. Get in there before you get in trouble too. I'll wait till everyone's in the refectory before I move. I wouldn't want to give further scandal."

SIXTEEN

GIULIA TOOK A HEAD count as she waited just inside the archway to the chapel entrance hall. One hundred forty-eight. No wonder the refectory resembled the wall-to-wall people and food stands of the Taste of Pittsburgh festival. When the Postulant Mistress passed through the refectory door last of all, Giulia walked through the chapel and the vestry and out into the supply hall. The garden door locked itself behind her.

"It doesn't matter; getting in is the easy part. Let them speculate on what I've been up to when I come back. Entertainment hostess, that's me."

The chill wind rustled the crimson maple leaves. Giulia breathed it in. "Freedom. What a beautiful scent."

She opened her phone and texted Frank. He replied ten seconds later.

Giulia jogged right, left, right, and around the narrow flagstone paths in the gardens. The wall ended at the driveway—much too close to the front door for her tastes, but some things couldn't be helped. She continued down the driveway, rubbing her arms—it felt like mid-November, not early October. Stupid to run out without her coat, but the escape window had opened and she knew better than to ignore it.

Frank's Camry idled halfway down the block. Giulia started to run toward it, but remembered what she was supposed to be. Slowing to a brisk walk only took an extra minute, but the sidewalk appeared to stretch with every step, keeping her from her goal: the Camry's open passenger door.

"Where's your coat?" Frank's annoyed voice snapped her hallucination.

"I grabbed escape when opportunity presented itself." She closed the car door and held out her hands to the vents. "My coat wasn't available."

"Geez, it's that bad?" He put the car in gear and drove away.

"Hello to you too."

"Hi. We're going to Scarpulla's Deli. They gave us the world's best sandwiches when we were on stakeouts." He beat a yellow light at a small intersection.

Giulia stretched her toes to catch the lovely heat from the floor vents. "Won't that be crowded and exposed?"

"Nope. They added booths last year when they reinvented as a '50s nostalgia place. We'll have just enough privacy to talk over the noise."

Giulia leaned back in the gray cloth seat. She hadn't realized how much the tension monkey on her shoulders weighed till she was—temporarily—back in the real world. Out where people didn't obsess over cobwebby ideas of behavior. Or paw through your underwear. *Frank did once, though, when Urnu the Snake and his sister tried to kill me.* A smile spread across her face. *I can overlook Frank's drawer-searching, since his goal was to keep the world from seeing me naked.* The smile vanished. *But I won't overlook Mary Stephen's snooping.*

"What are you thinking about? You look like you're ready to clock someone."

"Remember how I said you'd have to pay for counseling after this? If things keep heading in the same direction, you might have to post bail for me."

The upcoming light turned red and he braked too hard. "What kind of drama's going on in there?"

Giulia bounced a bit, pulling her veil off-kilter. "Stupid design." She adjusted it, tucking in her hair. "If I Velcro it tight enough not to slip, it gives me a headache. It's not just drama in there, it's melodrama. Complete with ghosts and clues no one understands and surprise villains poking their noses where they most certainly don't belong."

"How're you fitting in?"

"Hah. Where should I start?" She gave him a wicked grin. "If you were to drop me off within sight of a window and then kiss me goodbye … oh, the scandal. I think I'd enjoy the instant chaos."

Frank looked sideways at her. " Yeah, um, not while you're dressed the part."

"I know. I'm yanking your chain." She watched the lunch crowd hurrying along the sidewalks. "Are we there yet?"

He snorted. "What are you, four?"

"I want one of these amazing sandwiches. Wait a minute. What was a Cottonwood policeman doing on a stakeout in Pittsburgh?"

"I graduated from the police academy here. Bigger city, more opportunity, all of that." He signaled a left turn and waited for traffic. "Plus I got out from under my brothers' shadows."

"That's right, you're the baby."

He pulled into the deli's parking lot. "Spoken like the oldest. Maybe I should ask your brother what he thinks of you."

"He'll whine about how I threw shoes at him from the top of the stairs, neglecting to mention that he flung them back from the bottom of the same stairs. Then he'll announce that I'm a disgrace to the family and try to recruit you into the Latin Mass Society."

Frank turned toward her. "You threw shoes at your brother? But you're all about doing the correct thing. Your picture should be in the paper next to a manners advice column."

"Gosh, thanks. In other words, I'm still repressed and uptight."

He avoided her eyes. "No, that's not what I meant."

"Let's just get lunch and compare notes."

He opened her door. "I wish you weren't wearing that outfit. It sticks out."

She shrugged. "That's its purpose. If someone asks, you'd better tell them I'm your cousin. Nuns don't have intimate lunch dates with men."

Frank's Adam's apple bobbed. "Holy sh—crap. I didn't think of that. I keep thinking you're just Giulia."

"Good. That's exactly what I am: Giulia wearing a disguise." She looked up into his face. "Your eyes are bloodshot. What have you been doing?"

"You sound like Sidney. She's been pushing this disgusting herb tea on me every morning. I've been working late with Jimmy and the narc guys, pulling together the pieces of the MS Contin ring."

"The what?" Giulia shivered in the steady wind. "Can we go inside? This habit isn't all-weather."

He opened the restaurant door for her. A Babel of voices and a wave of odors crashed against them. Giulia picked out tomato soup, bacon, and pumpkin pie.

"They ain't been the same since the Steel Curtain."

"At least the Penguins scored—"

"...wants to be Paris Hilton for Halloween..."

Over all of it Elvis sang about love and loss. Laminated movie posters from 1950s classics muted the glowing white walls: *Love Me Tender, The Wild One, Harvey, The Girl Can't Help It.* Cherry-red swivel stools lined a long chrome and Formica counter, the shelf behind it loaded with milkshake machines, soda dispensers, and two old-fashioned coffee urns.

The hostess led them along the row of booths on the opposite wall. The black-and-white checked linoleum offset the red vinyl booths with their speckled tables. A few lunch patrons looked up when Giulia passed, and their conversations paused. She kept her face neutral. Most booths were occupied, and the busboy washed down one smack in the center just as the hostess neared it.

Frank unbuttoned his trench coat while Giulia studied the menu with a feeling akin to rapture. "Frank, I owe you. They have sopressata clubs."

He folded the coat and set it next to him on the seat. "Whatever that is, it can't beat a cheesesteak hoagie."

"O ye of limited palate. I'll give you a bite of mine and you'll understand."

Their waitress, wearing a pink-and-white striped poodle skirt, starched blouse, and cap, appeared with pencil and pad. She stared at Giulia, took their orders, and promised to bring their drinks.

"I haven't missed being on display like a department store Santa."

"Yeah, I caught the looks. Did you hear how the suits in front stopped discussing the cup sizes of their weekend dates?"

Giulia rolled her eyes. "No, thank God. So what is Sidney trying to make you drink?"

He groaned. "Eyebright and chickweed tea with a liquid B-vitamin complex added. I'd rather eat pickled beets than drink it, and pickled beets make me puke. Sorry." He leaned forward. "Don't tell Sidney, but the B-vitamin thing really works."

Giulia laughed. "If you admit her remedy works, she'll be worse than my uncle after he got born-again. He preached Pentecostalism at every family gathering. My cousin spilled beer on him once during a rant—accidentally, of course."

Their Cokes arrived. Giulia raised her classic-design glass. "To Sidney and Olivier."

Frank touched his glass to hers. "May they have a long life of compromise and Olivier sneaking out for red meat and sugar."

"And Sidney spinning alpaca wool for baby blankets."

"I'll be glad when you get back. She's bursting to talk about the proposal, the plans, all that girl stuff. We need you."

Giulia grinned at him. "Coward."

A plate filled with a tall sandwich and fries slid under Giulia's chin.

"And the cheesesteak for you, sir. Can I get you anything else?"

"No, thanks; we're good." Frank squeezed a Pollock painting of ketchup over his fries. "I haven't eaten anything today."

Giulia swallowed two fries at once. "I'm living on fake eggs and chicken-shaped cardboard. This is Heaven."

"Tell me what you've got." He reached into the folds of his coat and brought out a pen and a covered six-by-nine notepad from the inner pocket.

Between bites of spiced meat and fries—"All food should taste this wonderful"—she told him about Sister Fabian's useless folder of information, the Fabian-Ray affair, little Sister Arnulf, the Novices, and the groping of the underwear.

"She did what? What are you wearing underneath that thing?"

"Frank!" Giulia hissed. "Keep your voice down. You don't talk to nuns like that."

His head swiveled as he checked out the nearby tables. "Sorry. I think we just shocked a few Catholics."

"First you don't want to touch me because I'm in habit," she kept her voice to a whisper, "and now you forget it altogether. What's the matter with you? You're more professional than this."

"Hell, yes, I know. The extra hours over at the station are short-circuiting my internal censors." He drank the rest of his Coke. "I need about three days' worth of sleep."

"I want to know how you're faring with your old colleagues, but we don't have time right now. Do you have enough brainpower to focus on this case I'm working on?"

"Yes, of course. Sorry." He signaled the waitress with his empty glass. "Caffeine'll do it."

"At first I was sure that it could've only been Fabian in my room. You know, because I won't come to her office to give the daily progress reports she demands. I figured she figures I'm hiding reams of notes and coded secrets I've unearthed." She finished another quarter of the club sandwich and told him of this morning's Fabian snub.

The waitress brought two Cokes and took Frank's empty plate. He declined dessert. The women at the booth behind Frank left, sneaking glances at Giulia and whispering to each other.

"Maybe we should've gone somewhere private for lunch."

Frank's eyebrows gave the obvious answer.

"Yeah, all right. Where would an adult male and a nun go that wouldn't cause gossip? Nowhere. I hate this." She sucked down a third of her new Coke.

"Why would this nun search your room anyway? Do you two have unfinished business?"

"You could say that. She likes to use people as stepping stones to promotion. Yesterday was the first time we've seen each other in six years, and we kind of picked up where we'd left off."

Frank chewed an ice cube. "A catfight? You?"

She felt a blush begin. "She's an instant irritation. Plus, she doesn't like how I got out of her sphere and made something of a life for myself. When I was still in the convent, that is."

"She thinks you're still in-in?"

"Sure. So does everyone. Nobody's said a word about my cover story." She started the last quarter of the sandwich. "The place is chaos. For meals I'm at a table with Sisters from two different states. The merger's the best setting we could've hoped for."

"Back to the catfight. You think this nun went through your stuff because of an old grudge?"

"We've made it a new grudge now. We sort of had a huge fight in front of the whole choir this morning."

Laughter. "If only we'd planted a closed-circuit camera."

She scowled at him. "Thanks. Fabian actually came to my rescue. Not because of any love for me, but because Mary Stephen was about to reveal the contents of the folder Fabian gave me."

"In front of everyone? Good thing then."

"There's no lock on my door, so I won't be able to keep her out. I stashed the folder behind the bottom drawer of the dresser, so it'll take her more time to find it and she'll have to make noise. Those drawers like to stick." The last bite of sandwich disappeared. "She'll probably try again tonight if I'm up late. I'm putting all my notes in the phone now, so she won't find anything new."

"Good job. I had no idea the convent was such a soap opera. You'll notice I'm not commenting on the sex scene you overheard."

"Usually it's more covert than this. The soap opera-ness. I'm not commenting on what I overheard either. I'd prefer to retain this excellent lunch."

"Sidney will be thrilled, you know. You'll be retelling these stories for a month. Okay. Summary?"

Giulia sat straighter. "Fabian's hiding something. Sidney's looking for an interpreter so I can communicate with Sister Arnulf. Something's stressing the Novices besides the usual Canonical stuff, and I'm running out of time."

"Maybe I can help with one of those." He flipped several sheets in the notebook until he came to a page with multiple bullet points. "The phone call to Sister Bridget's parents would've broken me in the days of long-distance charges. They each got on an extension. The father cursed the Community, then apologized, then cursed Sister Fabian and apologized. The mother was still weepy, but she had some choice words for the way the merger was handled to coincide with this cloistered year they're in."

The waitress took Giulia's plate. "Coffee for either of you?"

Frank looked at Giulia. "I could use a cup. What about you … Sister?"

Giulia didn't crack the ghost of a smile at Frank's slight hesitation. "Coffee for me, too, please." When they had privacy again, she said to Frank, "Did they have anything definite?"

"No. Their suspicions are based on their daughter's drastic personality change after the merger. Seems she was on the quiet side but had a decent sense of humor until she moved here."

"So it was more than homesickness?" Giulia leaned back in the booth as the waitress brought coffee. "Thank you."

"They think so." Frank sipped his coffee, grimaced, and added sugar. "You never know what will send someone over the edge. One homesick college student will blubber and call mommy twice a day, and the one in the next room will join three different clubs and get over it in a month. A third may dive into the bottle."

Giulia's coffee cup hit the saucer with a *clink*. "Of course."

"What? Something with Sister Bridget?"

"No. The other Novice, not the one who was friends with Sister Bridget, came to my room buzzed last night. She's not from this Motherhouse originally either."

"One Novice kills herself, another's a drunk? What's wrong with that place?"

"It's not as bad as you make it sound. There's always an adjustment period after you enter. Moving far from home can compound that. That's why Formation—"

Frank's stare stopped her.

"Since when do you defend the convent?"

"Since always. I never said the convent as an institution was evil."

"Maybe not in those words, but you sure hinted at it. Only two days and you're brainwashed again."

"I beg your pardon."

"Listen to you. You sound like a repressed version of your old, repressed self."

"What gives you the right to denigrate my opinions about a previous lifestyle choice? Perhaps you object to how well I've gone undercover? Although that would be a strange objection for my employer to make."

He picked up his coat. "I think we're done here, Sister. If you don't mind waiting with me while I pay the bill, Sister."

Giulia got Frank's repeated use of "Sister" and slid out of the booth, following him to the cash register without a word. Patrons three and four booths down nodded at her, and she gave everyone a polite smile.

"Hope you enjoyed Scarpulla's, Sister. I think you're the first nun we've ever had in here." The cashier totaled the bill.

"Thank you, I did. Your sopressata is first-rate."

He grinned. "My uncle will be happy to hear it. We import it from the Old Country." He handed Frank his change. "Come again soon."

The contrast between the warm, crowded deli and the wind plus threatening clouds made Giulia hurry to the car. Frank opened her door first and she dived in, already shivering.

SEVENTEEN

Frank pulled out of the parking lot, silence between them. Traffic was even heavier. He navigated through two four-lane intersections, ran another yellow light, and turned into the entrance of the Heavenly Peace Cemetery. Compared to post–lunch hour crowds, the bare, narrow roads inside the cemetery were quite peaceful. Frank drove to the far side of the cemetery's older section and parked.

"Don't open your mouth." Giulia popped her seat belt and faced him. "You have no idea what it's like on the inside of those walls. I'm dealing with one woman just out of her teens and another one who's not legal yet."

"I get—"

"I said 'wait.' Barely two weeks ago their friend snuck into the huge, old cellars sometime in the middle of the night and drank a gallon of bleach. You think you'd be functioning normally after that?"

"I'm not talking about them, I'm talking about you. What happened to you in there? Suddenly you're throwing around buzzwords and acting all self-righteous and better than the poor unwashed laity." He popped his belt and stuck his face in hers. "Yeah, I know some buzzwords, too. You're my partner, remember? Half of Driscoll Investigations? Sister Mary Latin-Whatever doesn't exist anymore."

"Wrong. For the next few days she exists for Sisters Bridget and Bart and Vivian. I'm going to find out what's going on in the Motherhouse. The only way I can win their confidence is to be one of them again. That's not just a costume you wear for a play or makeup you apply to look a certain part. It's training yourself to think and act and talk and move a certain way. They're not going to trust an outsider. They barely trust themselves—I can see it. So if you don't like Giulia-as-Sister-Mary-Regina-Coelis, that's tough cookies. She's got a job to do." Giulia was so angry that the air from the vents was almost too warm.

Frank backed away. "Point taken. Sorry. Look, this is what I was going to show you in the deli." He took out a business-sized envelope from the opposite inner coat pocket. "Sister Bridget got a letter out to her old boyfriend a month before she killed herself."

"She wanted to leave?" Surprise cooled some of Giulia's anger. Leaving wasn't easy—anyone could ask her about that circus from Hell—but the logistics weren't difficult, especially for Novices. "Why would she kill herself when she could've just walked out the door?"

Frank paused in opening the envelope. "She could've?"

Giulia huffed. "Of course. It's not jail."

"Aren't there procedures to follow? Papers to fill out?"

"Of course, but if she was that desperate she could've gotten free and dealt with the mess from her parents' house." A thought hit her. "Had she been seeing her ex while she was still a Postulant? Was she pregnant?"

Frank leaned over the stick shift, holding the letter between them. "Nothing like that. She was fine with the nun thing. Here—read it."

Giulia squinted at the cramped handwriting.

It's different now that they moved us to Pittsburgh. This Motherhouse is huge and lots older than our remodeled one in Baltimore. More retired Sisters, too, and they watch us like wrinkled old hawks. I think they're trying to help the Novice and Postulant Mistresses, but, well... Retirement can be a difficult adjustment for people who've been busy all their lives.

Giulia touched the underside of the stationery. All the words were scored into the paper. "Her self-censoring isn't working."

I'm writing to you because I could really use your help. This is confidential, and I have to ask you to deceive some people. The Novice who got moved here from Indiana has a drinking problem, and she's stealing altar wine. I want to help her, but I have to do it so no one in authority will find out. She may be released from vows if that happens, and she wants to stay. When you write back, please pretend you're my aunt for the return address so no one will open the letter and censor it.

Frank said, "Do they really do that?"

"Yes. And no, I'm not going to get into it with you here and now. It always sent me over the edge, too."

"Damn. Sorry. Okay, the important part is next. See how she digs the pen into the paper on some words and how the dots on the *i*'s get more erratic?"

Tell me some steps to wean her gradually from the alcohol, please. And there's one more thing: another Novice here has some drug issues. I'm not sure what she's taking, but the pills are small and white and they seem to detach her from the world. Ny-Quil does that to me. I remember how good drugs like that feel when you're sick or stressed or have too much on your mind. In a way it makes you feel like you have a pile of big puffy quilts between you and the bad stuff.

'Would you research this for me and tell me how to gradually detoxify both of them? I don't want them to get caught. Vivian is somewhat self-impor-tant because she's finished 2 years of college, but Bart is so much fun. She's my only friend here, and she really helps me deal with it.

Giulia stabbed her finger at that last phrase. "Sister Bart and Sister Vivian said that, too—'deal with it.'"

"Meaning the gargoyles perched around the place, watching them?"

"Put a sock in it."

"Fine. Sure. You tell me what sent her over the edge, then. How's your self-possession holding up? Great, I see."

"You go through a miserable divorce and then move back into your ex's house with his new wife. I bet the Driscoll charm'll wither pretty fast."

"Oh, please. You're not gonna compare leaving the convent to a marriage breaking up."

"You bet I am. Don't pronounce judgment on subjects you know nothing about."

"God, you're just like my mother when you get high-and-mighty." He took a deep breath. "Sorry. How did we start arguing about my mother?" He took the letter and returned it to the envelope. "Back on topic. The ex-boyfriend overnighted this to me. He's a big, tough amateur hockey player—I called him after I spoke to the parents. He said it was like a whole different person wrote this letter. Apparently Bridget always used to write like one of those airhead girls, using *like* and *yanno* and *oh my gawd*. He mentioned brainwashing. He also said that Bridget never could tell a convincing lie and that no matter what the other Novice was doing, she was taking drugs, too. He's not still in love with her, but he's ready to tear off a few heads. If someone in your Motherhouse turned those girls into addicts, they'd better hope Rick never shows up at their door."

"It's not my Motherhouse," Giulia said automatically, but her mind was preoccupied. "Could whatever drug she was addicted to have depressed her to the point of suicide?"

"Without knowing exactly what it was, I can't hazard a guess. Think you can ferret that information out from your Novice friend?"

"In one day? Why not ask me to walk on water while you're at it?" She looked away from him, out the window, before she lost her temper again. Pine and silver birch mingled with orange and red maples back here, the colors reminding her of the faded carpet in the Motherhouse hallways. "I'll figure something out. Even though I think Sister Bart's got a key to this, I can't just walk into her room and say, 'I lied to you, I'm really an undercover detective and I want you to tell me everything that's wrong with you Novices, including the drugs.'" Her brow furrowed. "But maybe part of that will work. She already thinks I ask a lot of questions and I'm different from the other Sisters. I don't have to tell her everything..."

"Three months ago you never would've said that." Frank started to pat her leg, but stopped in mid-gesture. "Um... I mean... you're really taking to the job."

"And I think what you really mean is that you're a bad influence on me." She buckled herself in. "Let's go. It's already one-thirty. Someone's going to notice my absence."

He looked at the dashboard clock. "Already? I'm meeting Jimmy in half an hour." He began the long, winding drive back to the front gates of the cemetery.

Giulia watched the kaleidoscope of trees pass the car. "Are you earning a paycheck for Driscoll Investigations this week, or are you merely an adjunct to the Cottonwood police force?"

He laughed. "The latter, but hopefully not past tomorrow. Remember that new employee Blake's company wanted me to scope out? Turns out he funded his fancy clothes and car as a small part of the same wide-ranging dealer operation. Jimmy and the Pittsburgh Task Force are getting close to the top of the pyramid, but Blake's employee's no use anymore. Seems he's walking the path of righteousness now. His kid started school, and his wife wanted to join the PTO with a clean conscience."

"It's a first step on the right path."

"Giulia, if I ever wanted to change something about you, it would be the way you bring out your stock of moral aphorisms. You remind me of an eighteenth-century schoolbook when you do that." He smiled, perhaps to take away the sting. "And I know whereof I speak, because my grandfather had dozens. He was a collector."

Giulia wanted to kick herself. Sure, it was good that Frank kept her at arms' length while she wore the habit—it kept her in character, too. But her frustration mounted every time he made a remark like that or apologized for swearing in her presence. Their relationship—such as it was—seemed to have regressed to her barista days, when Cradle Catholic Frank was practically in awe that a former Sister would speak to him as an equal.

Giulia snapped her fingers. "I just thought of something. What if I don't clear this up by tomorrow? Will we forfeit the money?"

"Heck, no. Trust me to draw up a tighter client agreement than that. We get paid when we turn in our report in a timely manner. No date specified and whatever conclusion we reach."

"Good, because Fabian expects me to rubber-stamp hers."

"What a surprise."

He stopped talking to navigate. Traffic was just as dense as before. Giulia fingered her overlarge crucifix and eased back into

Giulia-as-Sister-Mary-Regina-Coelis. Ten minutes later, the car pulled up to the curb half a block from the Motherhouse driveway.

"Text me." Frank shifted into Park.

"As soon as I know something."

He unbuckled his seat belt. "Finish soon, okay? I want you back in the office."

She smiled. "As a buffer between you and Sidney?"

He grinned back. "There's that. You have more patience with her than I do. But it's not just that, it's more like, well, I'm used to you around there now, and ..."

"Is this where you sing two verses of 'I've Grown Accustomed to Her Face'?"

He frowned. "That's not what I mean."

She started to make a smart remark before she realized his face was closing in on hers. Both her hands came up between them. "What are you doing?"

He stopped with his chest just touching her hands. She watched the progression of thoughts on his face until the conclusion clicked and he jerked back.

"Sorry. Sorry, Giu—Sister." The frown returned. "Forgot the boundaries. Won't happen again."

Giulia suppressed a sigh. "It's just the wrong place and wrong time." Her eyes looked over his shoulder at the mother with three young children crossing the street in front of the car. The mother glanced into the windshield as they waited for a space in the traffic.

Without another word, Frank exited his side and came around to open her door. "Have a pleasant afternoon, Sister." He spoke to her, but his voice was pitched to be heard by the people around them on the sidewalk.

"Thank you." She didn't offer to shake his hand or initiate any other physical contact. When she turned away, an older couple inclined their heads to her and she nodded back. *Nuns are like cable TV: always on. What on earth was Frank thinking to get in "kiss" mode with me dressed like this? Talk about burning hot and cold.*

The wind knifed through her habit. She walked quickly—but decorously—up to the driveway. One hand held down her skirt in case it tried to imitate Marilyn Monroe's in *The Seven Year Itch.* She scanned the Motherhouse windows as she came around the end of the wall. No one looking out of the fifth floor or the fourth; movement on the third near the bathroom; two faces in the corner parlor on the second.

"Blow me into Fabian if it'll make your narrow little lives happy, ladies," she muttered. "She'd love another reason to chastise me in public. She would've flipped her veil if she'd known I was parked one hundred feet away in imminent danger of a kiss."

A car and a taxi passed her, the breeze fluttering her veil. *Cold,* she thought, and right on its heels, *Camouflage.*

Abandoning decorum at the edge of the wall, Giulia ran. As the new arrivals piled out of the car and taxi with suitcases, she ducked between them with welcomes and hellos. The first one out rang the doorbell and as the same delighted nun checked names against her clipboard list, Giulia slipped out of the foyer—and bumped into Sister Arnulf.

The little nun nodded at Giulia and blocked the path of the first Sister to make it through the arrival gauntlet. When Giulia saw Sister Arnulf's "game face," she ditched any idea of trying to communicate with her in this chaos and tried to disappear into the main hall.

"Sister Regina Coelis, thank Heaven." Sister Gretchen ran toward her. "Sister Fabian shanghaied my Novices, and all the flowers for tomorrow will arrive in fifteen minutes. Can I borrow you again?"

"Sister Regina Coelis?" The fluting voice of the "welcoming committee"—in reality, just Sister Alphonsus—cut through the gabble in the foyer. "May I beg your help for these two retired Sisters?"

"Argh," Sister Gretchen said at Giulia's ear.

"Of course, Sister," Giulia said. Over her shoulder, she whispered, "I'll meet you in the back chapel hallway as soon as I can."

"Sister Emma is in 435 and Sister Joan is right below her in 335. You're an angel." She flipped two pages back over her clipboard and turned to the waiting group. "Now, Sisters, you're down on the second floor at the far end. We're rather short on guides right now, so if you don't mind..."

Giulia lifted both Sisters' suitcases. "The elevator is right around this corner."

EIGHTEEN

HALF AN HOUR LATER, Giulia pushed open the doors to the back stairs. The empty silence in the stairwell was a relief.

"Breathe. They're just old. You'll be old someday, shuffling your creaky legs forward six inches at a time, shouting because you're going deaf."

Her shoes made small taps on the plastic runners, the echoes dying when she reached the thin carpet on the treads to the first floor. Blasts of fall air puffed under the door. She clenched her teeth and pushed against the force of the wind.

A delivery man came through the propped-open garden doors carrying a box of mixed carnations. Sister Gretchen stood in the hall before three other boxes, talking to an invoice.

"Two dozen white mums, eighteen areca palm leaves, six bunches stargazer lilies, three dozen carnations—oh, good, pink and red, perfect for the stargazers."

"Everything okay, Sister?" The delivery man stood by the doors, hands in the pockets of his "Sunday Flowers" jacket.

"Yes, thank you—oh, did you bring the blocks of floral foam?"

"Yes, Sister, there's five of them in the box with the lilies."

"Oh, okay, I see them. Thank you very much."

"Sure thing, Sister. Want me to close these doors for you?"

She nodded, already ripping through the masking tape criss-crossed over the protective cellophane. Giulia walked up and tapped her on the shoulder.

"What would you like me to do first?"

"Vases, thank you, on the shelves in the first cupboard. The biggest one, and four of the medium-sized ones. Into the vestry by the sink."

Giulia lugged the smaller ones two at a time, the big one last. Sister Gretchen followed with the palm leaves and lilies.

"You've put together flower arrangements before, haven't you?"

"I have, but only for regular Sunday Mass." Giulia loosened the carnations from their bunches. "I would've thought Sisters Edwen and Epiphania did the arranging."

Sister Gretchen shook her head. "They can't do the lifting anymore. Sister Epiphania's got Parkinson's now, too. Her hands shake too much for this delicate work." She brought out florist's scissors and made fresh cuts on the lily stems. "Sister Charlotte and I are familiar with the look Sister Fabian expects for the chapel tomorrow. Charlotte's helping her Postulants finish the table centerpieces for tomorrow, so I said I'd take care of the flowers."

Giulia set the green foam bricks in the vases and secured them with florist's tape. "A backdrop of palm leaves in all of them?"

"Yes, three each in the four smaller ones. Use the bigger ones for them and save the five narrowest for the central piece."

"Right. Got them. Is there another pair of scissors?"

"In the drawer next to the sink."

Snipping sounds filled the vestry for a few minutes.

"Sister Regina, I hope you don't mind if I ask you a question."

"Of course not."

"What made you leave and return?" Sister Gretchen crinkled the cellophane from the mums into a noisy ball and pushed it to the side.

"It's a little complicated."

"We have time." She turned toward Giulia, scissors in one hand and a puffy mum the color of new snow in the other. "I'm not just asking out of idle curiosity. Well, maybe a little curiosity," she smiled, "but also because so many of the Sisters are giving up the life. I worry about my Novices."

"This won't be complimentary. Are you okay with that?"

Sister Gretchen glanced over her shoulder at the open doorway to the sanctuary. "I am, but we should keep our voices down. You probably remember all the eager ears in this place."

Giulia snorted. "Yeah. Anyway. Did you reach the point when you were so busy that you realized you hadn't prayed a prayer or contemplated in silence for years?"

The scissors in the Novice Mistress' hands snipped a mum stem so hard the end bounced off Giulia's veil.

"Sorry." She picked it up. "Yes, two years ago. I was shepherding an intelligent loner through the discernment process. You know."

"I do. I was that intelligent loner once."

A pause. "I'm sorry you're still bitter about it."

"I'm not bitter about myself. One of the reasons I was assigned to schools at the farthest places we staff was my refusal to 'shepherd.'" She ripped a long piece of floral tape and secured a block of foam inside a smaller vase.

"Ah. Well, my mother passed away just after that young lady started her Postulancy. When I cleaned out my mother's apartment after the funeral, I discovered a scrapbook she'd kept of my life." She stuck palm leaves in one of Giulia's prepared vases. "Like this, at the back—start with one in the center and overlap the other two. The scrapbook was full of embarrassing childhood pictures and sweet memories."

Giulia adjusted palms.

"Twenty pages at the end of the book were dedicated to my years in the Community. Pictures of my Investiture, my temporary vows, my final vows. I looked so happy."

"We all did. It was a rush. We belonged to a very exclusive club." She placed more palms.

"Those look good. Now alternate carnations and mums in a ratio of three to one." She demonstrated with the vase in front of herself. "This florist always gives us the best. I haven't seen a limp flower from them, ever. You may think those photos of me all young and giddy were the trigger, but they weren't. It was the rest of the scrapbook. There were newspaper clippings of me with my students at science fairs, at graduations. The kids looked young and giddy, but every year I looked older and bitterer. Is that a word?"

Giulia smiled. "Not technically. How's this?" She stepped back from the flowers.

"All right …" Sister Gretchen reversed the position of the mums and the carnations on the left-hand side. "Use one bunch of three stargazers, and make the display symmetrical. Sister Fabian is a stickler for symmetry."

"We aim to please." Giulia eyeballed the first stem's placement.

"Back to the scrapbook. I stared at myself on page after page and saw an old, angry woman—and I was only forty-three. This wasn't what I'd signed up for. I talked to my spiritual advisor and ended up taking a sabbatical." She nodded at Giulia's finished display. "That's good. Can you do two more just like it?"

"Sure." Giulia ripped a length of green tape. "My advisor suggested a sabbatical, but it wasn't what I needed."

"The opposite was true for me. I spent that summer in my mother's apartment, attending Mass, working in a soup kitchen, reading in an independent bookstore that just happened to make wonderful smoothies." She finished one of the smaller displays and prepared the foam for the large central one. "By the middle of August, I'd gained six pounds and realized that my life without the Community was incomplete. Darn, this mum has a bent stem. Low in the front with you."

"I'm glad you found your place."

"It wasn't easy, but you must have had a much more difficult time."

Giulia placed the lilies in her second vase. "The paperwork would make even a government official weep."

"You still seem—if you'll pardon me—a little uncomfortable with Community life."

"I was gone for just over a year. It's a big readjustment."

"And I'm sure this controlled chaos isn't helping. Hmm. Two pink carnations on the right and three on the left. This won't fly."

"I have an extra pink. Trade you for a red."

"Deal. Sister Bartholomew tells me that Sister Fabian is paying extra attention to you." She bent sideways and whispered, "My sympathy."

Giulia laughed. "If patience cancels out venial sins, my 'Get into Heaven' account is in the black."

Sister Gretchen chuckled. "I witnessed the smackdown this morning. She has a long memory, you know."

"It is what it is. I freely admit to having trouble with obedience, then and now." A lily flopped forward. "Do we have any wire?"

"In the hall cupboard above the vase shelf."

Giulia fingertip-clawed down a small bundle on a shelf two inches too high for her. Cold air whistled through the garden doors at her back. She kicked aside the edge of the rubber-backed runner and dragged the door closed against the wind. When she knelt to straighten the runner, a small orange pill rolled out from beneath its corner.

Looks like one of those orange-coated low-dose aspirins. Edwen or Epiphania dropped it, I bet.

She brought it in with her and showed it to Sister Gretchen. "Do you know if this is someone's prescription? I thought it was a low-dose aspirin, but now that I see it closer, I'm not sure." She turned it over in her hand.

"I've seen one before down here." She took it from Giulia. "On second thought, I've seen one like it but a different color. This might be one of Edwen's heart pills."

"I'll give it to her later." Giulia pocketed the little pill and unrolled a length of wire.

Sister Gretchen said, "Have I thanked you for all the help you've been for my Novices?"

"You have. It's selfishness on my part: I like to be useful."

"I'm sure you've heard about poor Sister Bridget. Putting everything else aside, Sisters Bartholomew and Vivian are doing thirty-three percent more work this week." She leaned stiff-armed on the counter. "That sounded callous. Truth be told, I've put Sister Bridget's suicide in a locked room in my head for now. Sister Vivian's working through some issues, and she doesn't trust me enough to talk freely about them. The merger's been difficult on the Novices and Postulants." She shook herself and added another mum. "Are you putting your there-and-back-again in a locked room and using work as camouflage?"

"For now."

"Sometimes it's the only choice, as long as it's temporary. That's what I'm telling myself." She plucked a bent leaf. "Your turn. What made you hang up the habit last year?"

Giulia added the last mum to her third vase. "I woke up one day and I was empty. Like one of those hollow chocolate rabbits at Easter."

"Try moving that mum a little to the right, behind the striped carnations. All of a sudden?"

"No, of course not. When I traced it back, I realized it had been building for about two years." She reached for the lilies. "Part of it was the same as yours: constantly busy and never taking proper time to pray. It's so easy to keep busy."

"Trade me the lily in your hand for this one, would you? Yours is taller." She made a face at the arrangement and adjusted a carnation. "I'm training the Novices not to fall into that trap. If you chose the world over the emptiness, why did you come back?"

Giulia finished placing the lilies and looked over all three vases. "This is where I can do the most good. I realized it's not all about me."

"I may use you as an object lesson soon. I hope you don't mind."

"Heh. No, I don't mind. Do the four small ones look similar enough to pass the Fabian test?"

"Ssh." She glanced backwards. "Walls. Ears."

"I didn't miss that part of it at all."

Sister Gretchen stepped backward and surveyed the arrangements. "Ditto. If I believed in karma, I'd say being appointed Novice Mistress was punishment for my sins in a past life. Not training the girls; living here. Can you fan that palm leaf on the far left out so it overlaps the one next to it?" She did the same for the vase on the far right. "I remind myself daily to be charitable because I'm setting an example for the girls. Some days it's harder than others."

"I used to say that I'd rather get run over by a semi than end up here in my old age, sniping and spying and complaining about the food."

"Especially the coffee. I think these will pass inspection. The watering can is underneath the sink, but we'll avoid hernias if we carry them out dry."

Giulia brought one vase to the Blessed Mother statue. It nestled into a pre-cut groove in the marble platform at her feet. She did the same for the statue of Saint Joseph while Sister Gretchen placed the other two on low tables on either side of the top step. Together they hefted the large central vase and set it on a matching table before the altar.

Giulia filled the watering can seven times to soak the dense blocks of floral foam in all five vases. Together she and Sister Gretchen walked down to the tenth pew to get the full effect.

"Should we turn the flowers by Mary and Joseph inward so everyone can see them better?"

"God forbid." Sister Gretchen whispered. "We'll have Sister Fabian on one side and Sisters Edwen and Epiphania on the other lecturing us about symmetry and the proper respect to the Saints."

In the vestry again as Giulia swept leaves and stem ends into the trash, Sister Gretchen flattened the boxes and slid them onto the shelves below the counter.

"How long are you staying?"

"I've been assigned to a school in South Dakota, so just till Friday. Assuming I don't clock Mary Stephen over the head with one of these vases and get kicked out."

Sister Gretchen choked so violently that Giulia thumped her on the back several times before the fit subsided.

"I'm sorry, but that fight in the vestibule was worthy of a daytime tell-all show. All it lacked was the both of you throwing chairs at each other." She ran water into her hands and slurped it. "I gather you two have a history?"

"Long, intense, and quite detailed. I've been trying to avoid her as much as possible. My goal was to fly under the radar for the duration." She shrugged. "On to Plan B."

"If Plan B involves Greco-Roman wrestling, please wait till I can see the show."

"I was thinking more like making sure the coast is clear before I venture into a room."

"How adult of you. I'll have to resort to watching *Jerry Springer* reruns on the Community PC." She winked.

Giulia laughed. "We all have our guilty pleasures."

NINETEEN

SISTER FABIAN'S VOICE STOPPED Giulia before she rounded the curve in the back hall. Her shoes squeaked once on the imitation wood flooring, but that small sound couldn't penetrate the Superior General's closed door.

If the "grateful" recipient of the chastising answered, her voice was too low for Giulia to hear. More garbled Fabian noises followed, and the door opened. Sister Bartholomew walked out on unsteady feet. Giulia recognized the look on her face: drained, humiliated, furious.

Father Ray appeared at the doorway. "Smile, Barty. It's all part of your vow of obedience."

Bart stopped, but kept her back to him. "Yes, Father."

Ray chuckled. "Run along now. I'll see you Friday morning for Confession."

"Yes, Father." Bart walked much too quickly toward Giulia.

Before Giulia could scramble into some kind of hiding place, Bart grabbed the railing and swung herself onto the stairs. The wide stairwell swallowed her light footsteps a minute later.

Giulia stayed put until Ray returned to Fabian's rooms and closed the door. *Fabian, he's got no business tag-teaming the Novices' Formation with you. You're all about appearances, so why are you risking a scandal?*

The door to the gardens opened and Vivian scurried in. Giulia caught a glimpse of her reddened cheeks and swollen eyes before the Novice bee-lined for Sister Fabian's rooms.

I can't confront either of you while Vivian's in there. May Job's plague of boils be visited on you, Fabian. You're going to drive them both away, vocation or not.

Giulia walked upstairs against the flow of traffic moving toward the chapel. Sister Mary Stephen glared at her from the opposite side of the landing, but was carried away by the crowd.

The empty third floor greeted her with a tangible sense of peace. So, so tempting to crash on her narrow bed for half an hour.

Don't give in to temptation, Falcone. You're a Sister of Saint Francis again. The thought of skipping prayers would never cross your mind.

But the thought to check messages would cross Giulia Falcone's mind. She closed herself in her room and pressed the power button. Nothing.

"I'm starting to feel like Yukon Cornelius every time he tosses that pickaxe in *Rudolph the Red-Nosed Reindeer*. I get a big, fat nothing every time."

She pocketed the phone and returned to the hall. One of the Sisters she'd escorted earlier that afternoon stood at the top of the stairs.

"Oh, Sister Regina Coelis, I'm so glad someone's still on this floor. I thought I had it in me to walk instead of taking the elevator like an old woman." Sister Joan smiled, tripling the wrinkles on her aged face. "But I'm a little daunted. Could you lend me a steadying arm?"

"Of course." Giulia held out her right arm. Sister Joan looped her left hand through it and clutched the railing with her right. One step, balance, one step, balance; they made slow progress down the first flight.

"I'm making both of us miss the Rosary, dear. Please forgive me."

Giulia smiled. "Don't worry about it. I can always say it before bed."

"But will you keep awake?" A cackle came from the shriveled lips. "I'm usually asleep by the third Mystery."

"Bare feet on a cold floor is my secret," Giulia said. "Changing position every five Hail Marys works, too."

They began the next flight.

"Brrr. Bare feet in this weather?"

"When you absolutely, positively, have to stay awake..."

"Don't tell anyone, but I've cheated a little and finished a Rosary the next morning in the shower." She wiggled her fingers on Giulia's arm. "That's why God gave us ten of these, you know."

Giulia tried to make her polite laugh sound sincere. Such a narrow life, to take childlike pleasure in bending one of the countless rules that defined the day. Yet was it really narrow and joyless?

Giulia sure didn't know that kind of innocent happiness in such a small thing.

"You're one of the happiest Sisters I've met this week," Giulia said as they started down the penultimate flight of stairs.

"Some of them do look like they suck lemons in secret, don't they?" Sister Joan took her hand from the banister and crooked a finger at Giulia. When their veils touched, she whispered, "People like that aren't happy no matter what life they choose. The door's open; walk out, I've told some of them. But no, they go all holy and talk about their Vocation with a capital *V*. Well, Sister, it's no one's vocation to be a boil on the butt of the Church." She gave Giulia a sly smile. "If you'll excuse my rough language, of course."

Giulia writhed her lips so her laughter wouldn't echo through the stairwell. "I never heard a word."

They resumed their descent.

"I may try your barefoot Rosary trick tomorrow night. They'll hold prayers at the usual times, I'm sure, but I plan to eat and be entertained all day."

"Such an example to set for the younger Sisters."

Sister Joan glanced at Giulia, then returned her wink. "We're all adults. I'll answer to my own conscience, and they can answer to theirs."

They reached the deserted first floor. Even at this distance, the noise of one hundred-plus voices reached them.

Sister Joan paused. "I apologize for my legs. They need a moment's respite. From the sound of it, they're still on the Rosary. Perhaps we'll be spared the righteous indignation of the lemon-suckers."

"Stop it, please," Giulia said, "or you'll make me laugh during the Office."

"It'd wake some of them up." She patted Giulia's arm. "Now that was uncharitable of me, and I ask your forgiveness. Besides, you've gained favor in Heaven this afternoon: you just helped the helpless. That makes me an instrument of charity and wipes out my nasty remark's venial sin. See the glow of sanctity on my face?" She lowered her voice as they neared the hallway that led to the chapel. "If you can't, the wrinkles might be hiding it."

Giulia coughed, swallowed, and coughed again.

"I'd better stop talking or you'll have hiccups. I'd be entertained, but that'd be wrong of me, let alone distracting to the Community." As they reached the vestibule, she whispered, "Would you mind walking me into the refectory for supper? You're the perfect height, and I'm feeling a little creaky today."

Argh. "Of course I will. Let's find a pew toward the back."

Giulia clenched her teeth till her jaw popped. Even though chances of catching Sister Bart before supper had been slim, now they were nonexistent. She'd have to try another post-dishes hunt.

TWENTY

AT LEAST THIS NIGHT after supper her fellow Sisters did her an unwitting favor. A good third of the crowd headed for the chapel to see a presentation on the Superior Generals'—former and current—vision for the new, combined Community. A rumor that Sister Gretchen and three more Sisters from her group would be acting out scenes from old movies lured another thirty or so into the Community Room. "Abbott and Costello routines are my favorite," Sister Joan said as Giulia walked her there. As soon as she helped her settle in a sturdy high-backed chair, Giulia excused herself and escaped through the opposite doorway. Several small groups claimed space in the first-floor parlors. The parlors upstairs followed the same pattern.

From the fourth floor, a stealthy climb to the darkened fifth. Living room on both Novice and Postulant sides: empty. Chapel: empty. Just as she'd expected. Next, all the way back down to the refectory, where she located the Postulants. Both of them sweeping the floor and Sister Charlotte setting handmade centerpieces on each table: a papier-mâché Saint Francis holding a bright yellow mum.

"Beautiful work, Sister," Giulia said.

"Thank you, but my Postulants did the lion's share of the work. I merely came up with the design."

Giulia walked around the minuscule piles of dust and a few withered peas and into the working areas. Dishwasher empty; kitchen empty except for two enormous chocolate sheet cakes on the long center island.

She borrowed a sweater hanging in the front foyer to check the gardens, but no one besides herself was out in the cold and dark.

The cellars it was, then. The refectory was empty now; good. Lord knows she'd had it with being scrutinized and stared at, even by the Postulants. The chocolate cakes called to her like sirens when she passed them. The steel-core fireproof doorway that led downstairs from the kitchen squeaked before she could catch it. She held herself still, but no noise came from below. A gut feeling told Giulia that Bart was going to try and run away from this... discussion.

Giulia smelled the smoke three stairs from the bottom.

Fire! No ... no. Wrong kind of smoke.

She stayed at that height and sniffed. *Not cigarettes, not clove cigarettes either ... more like ... pot.*

"Oh, for crying out loud. This isn't high school." She hit the floor and peered into the first storage room. Too dark to see anything, but that meant no one else was in there either. The room on the other side of the hall was its twin: empty and dark. Next, the small, outdated bathroom opposite the laundry: a cloud of smoke poured out as soon as she opened the door.

Coughing into her sleeve, she flipped the light switch. Gray haze obscured the toilet, sink, and mirror.

This isn't the kind of pot my students used to smoke. It's like it's been cut with some kind of herb. She closed her eyes, which had started to water, and concentrated on her sense of smell.

It reminds me of … cooking. Thanksgiving. Stuffing. Sage. She inhaled again. *Yes. Sage.*

She backed into the hall and closed the bathroom door. A bobbing light to her left caught her eye. She tiptoed that way, into the main laundry room. The smoke was everywhere. She squinted and saw a veiled shape walking around the edges of the room, flashlight in one hand and smoke pouring from the other.

This looks like something out of a bad horror movie. What on earth are you doing, Bart? Because it had to be Sister Bart spreading all that smoke. The shape was too narrow to be Sister Vivian, and the Postulants didn't have veils. Plus, these actions were extraordinary enough to fit in with the "something's off" vibe she'd been getting from the Novices ever since she'd arrived.

Brushing away the scented fog with one hand, Giulia followed a few paces behind Sister Bart. The light stayed pointed toward the floor, outlining the baseboards and corners. The other hand waved itself toward the ceiling, letting the smoke drift into the corner. After a moment, Sister Bart coughed into her hand—the hand that held the smoking bundle.

She dropped the bundle and the flashlight and leaned on the nearest table, coughing like a two-pack-a-day addict.

Giulia hesitated. The deep, wet coughs persisted.

I have to get her into the fresh air.

She touched Sister Bart's arms. The Novice jumped at least six inches—straight up.

"It's me, G—Sister Regina. You need air. Come on."

Sister Bart shook her head, dragged in a deep breath, coughed some more, and squatted. Her hands groped for the bundle and the flashlight.

Giulia swooped down and grabbed both items. "I've got them. Let's go."

She took the Novice by her sleeve and led the way up the stairs. Sister Bart shoved her face into her other sleeve and kept coughing. Giulia took a quick glance at the kitchen—still empty—and closed the door behind them. She tossed the smoking bundle into the sink and turned on the water.

"Stems of sage leaves tied with twine. Okay, sure."

The cupboard next to the sink held measuring cups and bowls. She held a one-cup glass measure under the water and shoved it into Sister Bart's free hand. When the tied stems were a soggy mess, she wrapped them in foil and threw them in the trash.

Sister Bart refilled the cup and drained it. Only then did she sit against the metal counter, taking deep, long breaths.

Giulia washed the cup and put it away. Sister Bart turned off her hand-sized flashlight and put it in her pocket.

Before the Novice could make a break for it, Giulia put a hand on her shoulder that was both friendly and restraining. "We can't talk here; it's too open. Not to mention loud."

"There's no private place here." Sister Bart's voice was low and hoarse.

"There's the cellars … Is the air freshener still in the broom closet?" She started walking toward the dishwasher as soon as Sister Bart nodded. "Come on. We'll need at least two."

She pulled the chain hanging from the twisty fluorescent bulb. "Ugh, I don't miss that industrial-strength dishwasher cleaner at all. Does it still look like toxic waste? Here we are—oh, yes, excellent." She took two full spray cans of unscented Febreze off the second shelf from the top. "Here. Come on. We'll neutralize the cellars while we discuss this."

"Sister—"

"Don't talk yet." Giulia glared at her. "Follow me."

She opened the door and hit the spray button. *Unscented, my eye. Gack.* Down four steps and a 180-degree turn-and-spray. Behind her she heard the door close. The sagey marijuana smell dissipated enough for her to descend to floor level and turn on the lights. The smoke hung from the ceiling like mist on an upside-down river.

"Good Heavens. What were you doing with all this smoke?"

"Smudging the rooms." Sister Bart's voice wasn't as hoarse, but it was far from normal.

"What-ing the rooms? You take the rest of the hall; I'll take the little bathroom."

"But—"

Giulia turned on her. "In ten hours, people will be in that kitchen to make breakfast. By that time, the smell from all this smoke will have penetrated that door and might still be strong enough to set off the smoke alarms. Speaking of which—" She climbed back up three steps and squinted at the ceiling-mounted alarm. The cover hung open and the nine-volt battery dangled from only one set of connecting wires. "At least you thought this through. All right, let's get spraying."

Sister Bart stood her ground. "We can't. I don't know how long the smoke is supposed to stay."

Giulia stood on the second step so she was eye level with the Novice. "What exactly were you trying to do down here?"

Sister Bart squared her shoulders. "I told you. Smudging. I called my sister-in-law and she told me how to do it."

"Do what, exactly?" One minute more of this and Giulia was afraid she'd shake her.

"It cleanses the house. It clears out old energy and … and spirits. She does it once a year. She says she's never encountered a spirit that won't leave with a gentle nudge."

Giulia tried to think of something to say, and failed.

Sister Bart stepped closer, her jaw squaring like her shoulders had. "I took some of the dried sage from the garden and bundled it like she told me, and disabled the smoke alarms down here. I lit the sage and then let the smoke drift into the corners and around the doorways, just like she said." She rubbed her eyes. "I didn't think it would smell so much, though."

Giulia closed her eyes, counted to five, and opened them again. "Are you telling me you covered the cellars with sage smoke— which smells like pot, by the way—because you think the cellars are haunted?"

"You don't live here! You don't know what it's like early in the morning when the pipes gurgle just like, just like," her voice dropped to a whisper, "someone swallowing a lot of liquid."

"Those pipes were making that noise back when I was a Novice. The Motherhouse is more than one hundred years old."

"They fixed it. They had plumbers down here in July. They ripped out parts of the laundry and bathroom walls and replaced pipes and connections, and it stopped. Right after Bridget killed herself it started up again."

Giulia rubbed her face. "They'd probably have to replace half the pipes in the entire building to stop all the noises I've heard."

"That's what Vivian said, but she was in 'I'm so superior' mode. Like she's had experience with anything other than desk jobs and booze. I'm the one who can take an engine apart and put it back together. I know what liquid flowing through pipes is supposed to sound like." She pointed behind her with the spray can. "I'm telling you that Sister Bridget's letting us know that she's angry. She wants justice and we're like Hamlet. We know we're supposed to do something about it, but we're too scared."

First things first. "Before we discuss this in detail, we are eliminating this smoke. Whatever your sister-in-law does in her house, you can't disable the smoke alarms here and turn the cellars into a theater special effect gone haywire." She stood. "If the bathroom bothers you, start with the big laundry room. Go."

Giulia walked down the hallway spraying odor-neutralizer in waves over her head. When she reached the bathroom, she sucked in a huge breath, opened the door, and emptied a quarter of the can into the three-by-six-foot space. After ten seconds she exhaled with a huge *whoosh* and took a tentative sniff. Now it smelled more like mulched leaves and chemicals.

"Not enough." Another inhale, and she sprayed the room again.

When she joined Sister Bart in the laundry room, the entire left half of the space already had the same chemical mulch odor. Giulia started with the right-hand corner near the doorway and met Sister Bart in the middle, both their cans rattling on near-empty.

"At least now it smells like we just decided to freshen the air down here." Giulia set her can on the nearest table. "Let's fix the smoke alarms."

She carried a metal folding chair to the stairs and steadied it while Sister Bart—taller than Giulia by four inches—reconnected the battery and wrestled the plastic cover back in place. Giulia held her breath again through the alarm's self-test, but the little green light blinked on and stayed steady. "Our guardian angel's watching over us tonight. I gather you stood on the table to unhook the alarm by the washers?"

"I was careful."

"Then let's carefully go reconnect it."

Sister Bart reconnected the wires and ran another successful self-test. Giulia waited for the Novice to reach the floor before she spoke. "So how'd you get that interesting letter to your sister-in-law out of here uncensored? The same way Sister Bridget got one to her former boyfriend asking about ways to break drug addiction?"

Sister Bart jumped back and crashed into the table behind her. "She sent what? When?"

"Was Sister Bridget addicted to prescription drugs?"

"No, no, of course not. Who started a malicious rumor like that?"

"Why are you and Sister Vivian going to such extremes? Her with the drinking and you with this?" Giulia spread her hands in a gesture encompassing the de-smoked rooms.

A beat of silence.

Sister Bartholomew stood upright and picked up her can of air cleaner. "Thank you for your help with this, Sister. I'm afraid I didn't consider all the ramifications of my actions before I began. It's been a busy week." She took a step toward the doorway. "We should return these aerosol cans to the supply cupboard."

Giulia stood. "We should. I hope no one used these today who'd remember that they should still be full."

"It won't matter this week. Everyone's done so much cleaning and spiffing up of the old furniture and unused rooms, we've had to get new supplies in twice."

They walked upstairs and into the still-empty kitchen. As Giulia set her spray can on the closet shelf, she caught a whiff of the imitation-pot smell from her sleeve. She stuck her nose in her other sleeve. She pulled the end of her veil around and sniffed that, too.

"We forgot to Febreze ourselves." She pushed Sister Bart's arm up and the Novice sniffed.

"Oh my God, I'm dead."

Giulia snorted, quietly. "Shush. Come back into the cellars real quick. I'll spray you and you spray me."

They finished off both cans, waited a minute, and smelled their sleeves.

"Mulch and chemicals. Not too bad. Throw yours in the wash tonight and start fresh tomorrow. Just in case." Giulia got a way-too-vivid image of Sister Mary Stephen bumping into her newly scented habit. "That'd fulfill Sister Gretchen's wish for a TV-style cage match."

"What?"

"Nothing. A comment on my earlier catfight with Mary Stephen." She started up the stairs. "I'm caught between the need to avoid people and—" She stopped.

Sister Bart bumped into her.

Giulia turned around and made a shooing motion. "We could meet any number of people if we go through the first floor. Half the population is in the chapel and the rest are in the Community Room for the movie-skit show. Let's go out the other end of the hall … Oh, crap. We won't be able to get back inside."

Sister Bart smirked. "Language?"

"I never said I was a role model."

"Sorry. That was out of line. I have a key to the other back door, the one from the gardens by that narrow flagged path from the driveway."

"Excellent. Let's go, then."

Giulia followed her down the hall and up the narrow flight of stairs to the opposite door. The hinges screeched when Sister Bart opened it, but the wind covered the noise. Giulia turned off the light, and the door locked behind them.

"I am completely fed up with December taking over October this year." Giulia's teeth already wanted to chatter.

"It's my element. My family's originally from International Falls, Minnesota. We either learned to love the cold or got out of town."

They pushed into the wind, navigating the path by the oblique illumination from the streetlights.

"So it wasn't you who wanted to get out of town?"

"Nope. It was my dad. Twenty-three years of pumping gas in forty-below weather finally got to him." She inserted a dulled key into the lock. "Guess he and Mom shouldn't have gone to that family resort at Raccoon Lake for New Year's. Twenty degrees above zero in January was just warm enough for Dad to decide Pennsylvania was the Promised Land. Shh." She opened the door a crack and listened. "All quiet. The presentation must be over."

Giulia followed her inside, ready to lock Bart in the tiny vestry bathroom and pepper her with questions until she caved.

The distinctive sound of someone puking cut off her thoughts.

TWENTY-ONE

"What the—" Giulia followed the retching, splashing noises into the vestry, Sister Bart a step behind.

Sister Vivian balanced on hands and knees on the vestry floor. A line of vomit trailed behind her from an open closet. While they watched, she splattered another load of chunky liquid on the linoleum, her face, and her clothes.

Sister Bart ran to her and held her veil away from her face. "Vivian, you are dumber than a bag of hammers."

Sister Vivian groaned, clutched her stomach, and puked on Sister Bart's lap. Giulia grabbed the trash can from beneath the sink and caught the next pungent load.

"Is repeated puking your new weight-loss plan?" Sister Bart kept the other Novice's veil away from the worst of the mess with one hand and held her semi-upright with the other.

"You don't un—understand," Sister Vivian said.

"You're wrong, Vivian. I completely understand."

166

The trembling body in her arms moaned again. Giulia shoved the pail under her mouth. Vivian's body clenched and heaved, but only a spoonful of bile came up this time.

"That looks promising," Giulia said.

"About time. How much did you drink?"

"Dunno." A shuddering breath. "I had some after I ran her errand and the rest now. They got in some good stuff for Saint Francis Day. Ohhhh ..." She bent over herself in a series of dry heaves.

"Great. Did you water it down so no one notices?"

"'Course. I'm not stupid. Ohhh, my head hurts. Wish I had a bottle of Jack. Works faster than this stuff."

Giulia set the pail aside. "That's exactly what you don't need. Whisky on top of wine? You'll puke your stomach inside out." She yanked several paper towels from the roll over the sink.

"Ew ... Oh, no—" More dry heaves.

"Thanks for that image." Sister Bart took the towels and wiped vomit from Sister Vivian's face and hands. "Looks like you're done. Let's head upstairs."

"All that way? Just gonna sleep here." Her head clunked onto Sister Bart's collarbone.

"Oh, no, you're not," Giulia and Sister Bart said as Sister Vivian slumped unconscious in Sister Bart's arms.

"I didn't sign up for this." Sister Bart patted Sister Vivian's head. "You're like my daily Station of the Cross." She looked up at Giulia. "I'll take her arms if you'll take her feet."

Giulia grimaced. "I'm tempted to leave her here." She squatted in front of their Pietà from Hell and worked the unconscious Novice's legs around in front of her. "Ready? One—two—three."

167

They hefted the limp, smelly nun into a dangling V position between them.

"Ow. My lower back will hate me in the morning." Sister Bart wormed her hands into a firmer grip of Sister Vivian's armpits. "If only we could use the elevator."

"We'll be lucky if everyone stays on the front stairs." Giulia, last through the vestry door, kicked it closed. "In addition, if only there were a door between the vestry and the sanctuary."

"We wouldn't have these 'if onlys' if our self-appointed taste-tester for altar wine understood that there's a time and a place for everything." She backed onto the first step.

"Even for illicit drunkenness?" Giulia whispered now.

"Oof. You know what I mean. I have to turn around. I can't walk backwards all the way to the fifth floor."

They set Sister Vivian's dead weight on the landing between the first and second floors. Sister Bart knelt with her back to Vivian's head, and Giulia hefted the damp armpits into Bart's hands.

"You owe me, Vivian," Bart whispered.

Giulia returned to her half of the burden. "Ready?"

"Let me get my legs under me." She grunted, swayed, and stood.

On the landing between the second and third floors they set her down to uncramp their muscles.

"You're a liar," Sister Bart whispered to the still-unconscious Sister Vivian. "If your weight is down to one hundred fifty, I'm a candidate for the priesthood."

"Want to switch positions?" Giulia flexed her fingers.

"Yeah. Thanks."

Just as Giulia took hold of Sister Vivian's armpits, she heard voices coming near the door one flight below. Sister Bart's face lost all color. Giulia jerked their burden toward the landing corner, and Sister Bart flung Sister Vivian's legs against the wall. The voices reached the door and stopped, fading away to the left a moment later.

"They went to the small parlor instead?" Giulia whispered.

"Must have, thank God. We'd better get a move on."

They lugged their swaying burden up three more flights of stairs, only bumping her rear on the steps a few times.

"She's going to have a black and blue butt," Giulia whispered.

"Maybe it'll make her think before hitting the bottle next time." Sister Bart scowled at the ankles in her hands. "And don't give me the 'alcoholism is a disease' lecture. It's an addiction, and she doesn't want help."

Giulia bumped open the door to the fifth floor with her hip. "Second door to the right, right?"

"Yes."

The dark hall was empty and the bedroom door open. They swung the Novice onto her bed.

"I have a strong sense of déjà vu," Giulia said as she removed Sister Vivian's miraculously clean shoes.

"If we're reliving the movie *Groundhog Day*, I vote for ritual seppuku now." Sister Bart rolled up the veil so the vomit-stained part didn't touch the floor when she set it down.

Giulia lifted Sister Vivian's shoulder to get to her zipper. Together they removed the sodden habit. Giulia got something indefinable on her hands and wiped them clean on another part of the black dress. "It soaked through to her slip. I'll get this shoulder."

"Whatever sins I've committed, Vivian is the punishment." Bart pulled off the other strap and eased the slippery material over the Novice's bra and down to her hips.

Giulia tugged it off. "Where should we put these clothes?"

"Shower stall. After I clean the vestry I'll rinse them off when I clean mine." She looked down at her smeared dress and wrinkled her nose.

"What do you mean, after 'you' clean the vestry? I'm not leaving you to deal with that mess by yourself."

Bart gave her something like a smile. "Thanks."

Giulia rolled the veil and slip and ran with them to the bathroom. *I have to trust that Sister Gretchen is too busy to look into the showers tonight.* She placed the clothes in the corner of the farthest shower stall. When she returned to Vivian's room, Bart was about to turn off the light. Giulia saw a towel under Vivian's head and half the bedspread folded over her.

"You're a good friend," Giulia said.

Bart snorted. "I feel sorry for her, when I don't want to slap her silly. You'd think someone so 'experienced and sophisticated' would give up the booze after the first half-dozen binges."

"Did she throw up while I was in the bathroom? I still smell it."

"I think that's us."

Giulia looked at her sleeves. "These habits never thought their lives would be so exciting."

"That's not the word I'd use." She pushed open the back stairs door. "We'd better haul it."

The stairs remained blessedly bland, dusty, and empty. Giulia heard conversation on the third floor, but since she and Bart weren't carrying an unconscious woman like a sack of potatoes between them, she walked past the door without glancing at it. The back hall was also empty. Giulia couldn't tell if the stench had seeped around the closed vestry door or if she was still smelling her own clothes.

Bart opened the door. "Whoa."

Giulia suppressed a gag reflex. "I'll run hot water if you'll get more trash bags."

"Extra rolls of paper towels are underneath the sink. We shouldn't use the mop on this."

"Agreed." Giulia cranked open the small window over the sink. For the first time that week, she welcomed the cold, clean air. A minute later she carried several soaked towels and the reeking trash can over to the end of the vomit trail. When Sister Bart joined her on the floor, she said, "I don't plan on eating beef stroganoff until next year. Especially mixed with red wine."

"They serve it every couple of weeks here. I'm doomed." Sister Bart scooped a reddish-yellow puddle into a pile of towels and then into the pail. "It's freezing in here, but thank you for opening the window."

"Desperation drives us to extremes. About the food: can you stick with salad and rolls? Ugh. Why are we even discussing food?"

"You started it."

"My deepest apologies." Giulia scooted farther down the meandering line of vomit. "Now we have an excuse to wash these habits."

"I'm not feeling particularly thankful." She lifted one knee. "Watch out for hidden splatters."

"Sister Gretchen's going to have to be told about this." Giulia gagged again. "Excuse me."

"Please. The only thing keeping my supper down is not wanting to add to the mess."

"For which we are truly thankful. Amen." Giulia tied up the current trash bag and inserted a fresh one.

Sister Bart laughed. "You and my sister-in-law could've been separated at birth. She has this irreverent streak just like you, toward her gods and ours. I love discussing faith with her."

Giulia started to say, *Try working for an irreverent boss who sometimes thinks you're too holy to kiss and sometimes kisses you till your toes melt.* Fortunately she remembered who she was supposed to be. Instead, she soaked more towels at the sink and handed half of them to Sister Bart. By this time, they'd reached the unlocked closet that held the altar wine and the gold-plated special-occasion vessels. Two cases of Mont La Salle Abbey red altar wine nestled under the bottom shelf. Sister Bart tugged the left-hand one out far enough to open one of the top flaps.

"Three bottles used. She's getting better at shoving the corks back in. Idiot."

"How has she gone this long without getting caught?"

"Father Ray likes us." Sister Bart's voice had a shade of irony in it. "He asked if Vivian could set up the vessels for Mass each morning and if I could put them away afterwards."

Giulia sat on her heels. "Sister Mary Thomas agreed to that?" Giulia remembered the stern nun from her own Novitiate. "Back in my day, only death would've separated her from altar duties. Maybe not even that."

Sister Bart concentrated on a series of projectile stains on the baseboard. "She got transferred in June." Her voice got even softer. "Big blowup with Sister Beatrice about budget overruns."

"For what? New altar cloths?" Giulia wished her phone had an "instant record" button. Her mnemonics trick for memorizing details needed no distractions to work best. Repeating the essential details in her head, she dumped another set of paper towels into the trash can.

Sister Bart shrugged one shoulder. "We never did learn the whole story. But Sister Thomas got stationed out in the Midwest and Sister Mary Magdalene started baking all the Hosts herself. And we switched to cheaper altar wine. Tastes like it's just this side of vinegar. This stuff—" she gestured with her head— "is what we used to buy, according to Sister Gretchen."

"They didn't work out the merger on a whim. All four Communities needed to consolidate or go bankrupt."

"I would've suggested selling this drafty relic and splitting everyone up into small houses." Sister Bart pushed the wine carton back into place and locked the closet doors. "And selling the useless gold in here."

"Don't let Sister Fabian hear you say that."

"She already did. Well, she overheard me talking to Bridget in August." She tied up the trash bag. "It's the only time I stood up to her."

"What did you say?"

"Told her that God would be more honored by inexpensive electroplate that lets us pay our bills and practice charity." She shook out a new plastic bag with a gunshot-like *snap*. "Oops. I put a hole in it." With a crooked smile, she pulled another one off the roll. "That was not a good day. Days. More like a week. Did you know that your knees don't develop calluses till the very end of a lengthy penance?"

Giulia gave her a similar smile. "I do. And that pantyhose sticks to raw skin like superglue if you forget to put on bandages."

"Comrade." She bumped fists with Giulia. "Poor Bridget got caught in that unfriendly fire."

"That didn't send her over the edge, did it?"

"No. Sister Fabian called her in for several heart-to-hearts during the rest of August. She always came upstairs looking like she'd gone twelve rounds in a mixed martial arts cage." She stood next to Giulia and surveyed the floor. "I think we got it all."

Giulia stretched. "Now we mop. I'll fill the sink." When Sister Bart put a hand on the bucket under the sink, Giulia said, "One less piece of equipment to clean."

"Gotcha. One sponge mop coming up." She peeked into the hallway before opening the door all the way.

Giulia poured half the bottle of vinegar into the standing hot water. Adding that to the smells already in her nose made her eyes water. "C'mon, wind. You've been blowing all day. Now's not the time to take a nap."

Sister Bart lifted the mop over Giulia's shoulder and plunged it into the mixture. "There's more Febreze in the hall closet. Could you give the sanctuary a once-over?"

"Good idea." Giulia sprayed the altar, the gigantic crucifix, even the carpet. The conglomeration of odors trapped in her nose foiled her efforts to make sure the chapel smelled only of air freshener and hothouse flowers.

When she reentered the vestry, the dirty water was sklorping down the drain. Sister Bart held the sponge under running water and squeezed it repeatedly by hand. The wind had remembered its business and blew in through the open window. Steam from the hot water pouring out of the faucet blew against Sister Bart's fluttering veil.

"Enough. You're going to catch pneumonia." Giulia reached around her and cranked the window closed.

"This place needed the fresh air. All I smell now is vinegar and Febreze."

"Good. I couldn't tell. My nose surrendered half an hour ago."

They returned the mop and air freshener to the hall closet.

"Sister Bart, I would like to talk to you."

Bart stiffened, one hand clutching the closet door.

Laughter from the back stairs reached them, then three voices singing "Moses Supposes," from *Singin' in the Rain*. One voice stumbled over the tongue-twister lyrics, and Sister Fabian's voice corrected her.

Giulia and Bart ran for the vestry and peered into the chapel. A small group of Sisters wandered the perimeter, discussing the Stations of the Cross. Giulia pointed to the flowers. She and Bart walked sedately to the floor displays and pretended to make small adjustments. Bart "finished" first and walked down the populated side aisle.

One of the Sisters stopped her. "Sister Bart, you're just the person we wanted to see." She pointed to the second station. "Who painted these?"

Bart switched into full tour-guide mode. Giulia wanted to curse. The Sisters asked more questions, complimenting the immaculate chapel. No one made an odd face when Bart stood next to them. The habit-spraying must have worked.

At that point, Giulia conceded temporary defeat.

Up in her room, she shoved the desk chair under her doorknob and removed her veil. Stain-free, but when she put her nose into it, she smelled several incompatible liquids. When she tried to strip off the habit, the bottom stuck to her half-slip for a moment. She peeled both garments away from each other and they rewarded her with an eye-watering mix of odors.

"Thank God double-knit likes to be scrubbed. What color is that splotch? No. Maybe I don't want to look that closely."

She took the spare habit from the wardrobe. "What I didn't bring is a spare slip. Silly me: why didn't I plan for such contingencies as a vomit-speckled habit?"

She rolled up the veil, slip, and habit and stuck them on the window ledge. "This will stink up the room. All right, Falcone, be brave." She cracked the window an inch, and the cold punched her naked midriff.

"Whoa. Clothes, now." She scrambled into the clean habit and veil. The wind rattled the casement, and the loose end of the bundled habit fluttered. Giulia smashed that end flat and jammed it in the narrow opening. When she turned around, the room played its contracting-walls trick again. She rubbed her face and smelled the ghost of vomit.

"That's it. I'm sick of this hamster wheel. Cell, prayers, food, freaky happenings, cell. I need four different walls. And clean hands."

She stepped into her shoes, worked the chair out from beneath the doorknob, and strode—quietly—to the bathroom. Three hand-washings later, the most thorough nose inspection only picked up the smell of generic soap.

The noises of conversation penetrated the closed bathroom door once she turned off the water. The next moment the door opened, and Sister Joan shuffled in.

Giulia smiled at her. "You look happy enough to convert every lemon-sucker in the Motherhouse."

"Sister Regina! You really should have stayed for the movie skits. That Sister Gretchen does the best Moe Howard impression I've ever seen." She entered the first stall.

"I've heard she's very good. Would you like me to wait and help you back to your room?"

"You are an angel from Heaven. Yes, please, and thank you." The sounds of Sister Joan's skirt rustling and her rump hitting the wooden toilet seat followed her voice. "I gave in and took the elevator, if you're wondering. I looked for you or one of the Novices, and both the Postulants were taken." A grunt, more clothing noises, and a flush. "I should complain to the management." The stall door opened and Sister Joan managed the few steps to the sink.

As she dried her hands, she said in a low voice, "But I'm much too old to pretend to be grateful for the lecture our revered leader would favor me with."

Giulia put her head on the wall between the small mirrors over the sinks. *Breathe slowly. In. Out. In. Out.*

Sister Joan tapped Giulia on the shoulder. "Are you all right?"

Giulia held out her arm. "Sound echoes more than you'd think in here. We should go."

Sister Joan took it. "Then please help me to my room. I promise to be a model of decorum until my door closes behind us."

"Us?"

The wrinkled fingers patted Giulia's arm. Giulia led them with slow, even steps out of the bathroom, through the Sisters heading to their rooms, and three-quarters of the way down the hall. Sister Joan closed Giulia in with her.

"You're a very good listener, my dear. My voice is too low to carry far, but I should know better than to flap my lips in such a public space." She eased herself into the wooden desk chair. "I was Novice Mistress to that little snip. Even at age eighteen she had that hungry look."

Giulia sat on the edge of the bed.

"I wasn't out for power. I didn't want to be Novice Mistress, but I never refused an assignment. Those were the last days of the old Investiture ceremony: the girls wore real wedding gowns, and we cut off their hair in the vestry right before they received the veil." She smiled to herself. "They looked so lovely and so happy. Even Sister Mary Fabian—right up until she received that name."

"I wouldn't have been too thrilled either."

"I always harbored the suspicion that the naming committee had watched one of the actor Fabian's movies on TV the night before."

"I thought it was appropriate because she had such a beautiful voice."

"Oh my dear, when did any of us back then get an appropriate name? I mean, 'Epiphania'? Do you know what I answered to for forty-three years before they let us take back our given names? Ischyrion."

"Oh."

"Yes, exactly. I tell you, when I was an idealistic little girl dreaming of the mysteries of the convent, I never pictured myself saddled for life with an unpronounceable obscure saint's name." She stretched her back. "But those days are over, thank the Lord. What I wanted to say to you concerns the Novices and my former pupil in Formation."

Giulia gave her an inquiring look.

"I see that you're helping them—they certainly need it. Why some of these other young ones don't pitch in is beyond me." She shook her head. "Anyway, there's something 'off' about them. Do you see it?"

"Yes, I do."

"I heard about that poor little thing killing herself the other week. Whatever her situation was, they should never have let it get that far."

"I've seen Sister Gretchen counseling the plump one, Vivian."

"Counseling. Don't try to whitewash the troubles with buzzwords. Those girls are overworked in mind and body. I saw it within two hours of my arrival." The pale brown eyes sharpened on Giulia like lasers. "Why are you helping?"

Giulia blinked. "I like to keep busy."

"And you're trying to fit back in. Don't look surprised. I'm a nosy old biddy. I mentioned how graciously you became my walking stick—if you'll pardon the expression—and I got an earful."

"Oh."

"Don't look so worried. They don't realize what guts it takes to leave and return. I never did, but I saw several go through it." She leaned closer to Giulia. "Someone who doesn't like you saw you escape before lunch. Now that woman doesn't know the meaning of quiet Community Room conversation."

"Mary Stephen." The thought of combating more of her spite doubled Giulia's exhaustion.

Sister Joan patted Giulia's knee. "If you're worried about your reputation—and you might be after that scene in front of the choir—"

Giulia groaned.

Sister Joan laughed. "I'm sorry I missed it. Two Sisters sitting near me had it practically word for word. Anyway, your reputation is intact. It's obvious your nemesis has a grudge against you the size of Texas. Besides, you returned from your excursion just in time to help me up to my highly inconvenient room, for which I am quite grateful."

"Thank you. I hope others see it that way, too."

"Some of the older Sisters listen to me. I have a bit of a reputation for seeing what's what. Did you know I once stopped a burglary with a chalice?"

Giulia snorted. "Excuse me. I didn't mean that in a rude way."

Sister Joan flexed one sticklike arm. "The image is funny. I know. People have that reaction all the time. Foolish man, breaking into a minor church in a rundown part of Wilkes-Barre. Drugs drive people to extremes. Well, there I was, late Saturday night, setting everything up for early Sunday Mass. My head was in the cupboard where the altar vessels were stored, and I heard a noise in the sanctuary. There was this skinny kid prying open the box where people put in the money to light a votive candle."

"You didn't try to stop him yourself?"

"Of course I did. I was no fragile flower. My family trains guard dogs. I cut around to the door by the baptismal font, snuck up behind him, and conked him on the head with the pewter chalice. When he dropped like a rock, I thought I'd killed him. I only meant to knock him unconscious, which, thank God, is what I did. It's a good thing my arm isn't what it used to be, a decade or so away from wrangling German shepherds."

"What happened then?"

"I called the police, of course. They took the young man away. He'd been stealing from all the churches on our side of town. I went to his trial, and put in a word for a treatment facility, but I never heard anything about him again." She planted her feet in line with the chair legs. "I'm not merely a doddering old woman rehashing past glories out of nostalgia. My point to all this is: the plump Novice is into drugs or alcohol. I know that look. How she's getting them during her Canonical year eludes me, but she is. You seem to have Sister Gretchen's ear. She mentioned after the performance what a help you'd been."

"You think I should say something to her." Giulia gave her a tired smile. "I do, too. It's all about timing, though, and these past few days haven't exactly been long and leisurely."

"I thought you'd noticed it. What about the other one?"

"Not that I can tell. I'm still trying to pin down what they're all on edge about."

"The suicide, of course."

Giulia frowned. "But what drove her to suicide? When I find that out, I'll be halfway to learning what the current problem is."

Sister Joan yawned like a sinkhole. "I've reached my limit. Getting old is annoying. Time was I could stay up till midnight and be ready to lead prayers at six a.m."

She stood, and Giulia stood with her.

"You've got a head on your shoulders. I have faith in you. You're going to turn over the rocks in this whitewashed sepulcher and make it a good place for those girls again."

"It's not that bad here."

Sister Joan shook a finger at Giulia exactly like Giulia's grandmother used to. "Don't lie to me, Sister. There's no Confession till Saturday and you want to be able to take Communion tomorrow. I've watched you today and tonight. You're forcing yourself to look calm and productive, but you really want to jump out of your skin."

Giulia's cheeks heated up.

"Never underestimate a former Novice Mistress." She cackled. "I haven't lost my eye for a skittish Sister. Now you get to bed and have a good time tomorrow, like I'm going to. The day after is time enough to expose addictions."

"I'll do my best." Giulia smiled down at her. "Will you need help tomorrow morning to get downstairs?"

"No, I'll be fine. I'm ten years younger in the morning. It's afternoons and evenings my age creeps up on me. Good night now." She lowered her voice as Giulia opened her door. "I'm glad we caught most of the Rosary tonight. I'm in no shape to count Hail Marys on a cold floor."

TWENTY-TWO

THE HALLWAY WAS EMPTY again, the only sounds muffled laughter coming from the small parlor. Giulia walked quietly on the edge of the rug.

She detoured into her room and took the Day-Timer from its place in the zipper pocket of her suitcase. Her clock read 9:40, but her body kept insisting it had to be at least midnight.

As she headed downstairs to the chapel, she passed three Sisters huddled beneath a reading lamp in a corner of the first-floor hall. A thick photo album rested on the center Sister's lap

"How young we were. Elaine, look at your hair. It's a Brillo pad."

"I told you there was a reason I loved the veil."

Elaine looked up briefly when Giulia passed, but returned to the photographs after the briefest of polite smiles.

The chapel hallway was dark and empty now, the moon showing through breaks in the clouds only as blue or red or green gleams of light through the stained-glass windows.

The red-glass sanctuary lamp illuminated nothing beyond the top of the tabernacle. Giulia felt her way along the tops of the pews up the center aisle.

The toe of her right shoe hit the carpeted step that marked the sanctuary. She genuflected in the center opening of the Communion rail and stepped inside the sanctuary proper. Her eyes eked a bit of illumination from the red lamplight, but she still ran her left hand along the marble railing until her right touched the concave wall of the statue's niche. She felt down to the baseboard and touched the combined outlet and light switches. With a silent flick the recessed lights in the ceiling illuminated the blue and silver veil, and the low-wattage floodlight mounted on the floor shone on the Virgin's upturned face.

Giulia looked over her shoulder. Yes, the light reached the first pew. She returned the way she came, genuflected again, and sat in the leftmost corner of the center pew.

What I wouldn't give for a free wall and several colors of magic marker to create a clue collage.

She set the Day-Timer on her knees and uncapped the cheap ballpoint pen. The clean whiteness of the sheet of paper stared at her like a challenge.

Sister Bart.

Giulia covered the page front and back with bullet points about the sage-smoke incident, the fear of the cellars, the *Hamlet* hints about Sister Bridget haunting the Motherhouse. A second page about Sister Vivian filled just as quickly with alcohol-related information. A third for Sister Arnulf remained mostly clean—Giulia still wanted to weep with frustration at her inability to communicate with the little old nun. Hopefully Sidney would come through with a translator tomorrow.

A fourth for Sister Fabian. Giulia wrote:

What are you hiding, Fabian? That is, besides your illicit relationship with Father Ray. Why did you wait so long to call us in? Why didn't you just wait till after Saint Francis Day for this investigation?

But Giulia knew the reason: she, Giulia, was easier to hide amidst one hundred and fifty nuns from all over the country. During a regular week at the Motherhouse everyone knew everyone else.

Fabian's strategy should've worked. Giulia slides in under everyone's radar, plays the obedient nun, tells Fabian exactly what she expects to hear, and slides out again.

I fought against Fabian for years. What made her think I changed?

She looked down at the next blank sheet of paper and wrote:

Sister Gretchen.

Overworked

A touch dense

Concerned for the Novices (good)

Brief sabbatical and returned

Sabbatical…flowers…

She flipped back to her earlier notes on Sister Bridget, adding a summary of the letter she'd sent her ex-boyfriend.

She added *Deal with it?* to the bottom of that page, scratched it out, and started a new page.

Novices "dealing with" the following:

Move from Maryland and New Jersey

Lose (one of them) a friendly, easygoing Superior General

Same for Novice Mistress? Perhaps, but Gretchen is a good one.

Lose proximity to family (despite cloistered year). Big psychological effect?

Community Day overload of work: how do they each deal with stress? What sends them over the edge?

Her hair tickled her forehead.

Forehead. Blemishes.

She wrote on Sister Arnulf's page:

The face with the zit/mole/scar. Who has one?

Theresa

Ray

Sister Edwen—nasty chicken pox scarring on her temples

Beatrice—hairy growth on chin

Gretchen—beauty mark on her upper lip...

Gretchen? No way.

Yet...

Blemishes and drugs and alcohol. Arnulf and Bridget. Arnulf and her blemish drawing. Fabian plaguing the Novices.

What made Fabian change? She's turned into Fabian's Evil Twin—and Frank doesn't have enough Irish expletives to describe Regular Fabian, let alone this enhanced version. Cosmo says that regular sex makes people calmer, more easygoing. Wrong. If she'd ridden me the way she's riding the Novices I would've volunteered to clean Porta-Potties to get away, and been happy to do it. Or, depending on my vice of choice, I might dive into a bottle. Or take drugs.

Her pen couldn't write fast enough to keep up with her thoughts.

But what drugs? How did Bridget get them? Even if they've re-laxed the mail inspection rules, Sister Gretchen would ask to see the contents of a package.

Giulia dug into her pocket, but the orange pill wasn't there.

Right. It's in the rolled-up habit on my windowsill. If that's not an aspirin…

Her pen hovered over the paper.

Fabian supplies them? No. She's tied to the Motherhouse. Not as much as a regular Sister, but still.

Ray.

Her pen point dug into the paper.

Ray comes & goes with complete freedom through the garden door, like the priests have always done. His relationship with Fabian is intimate (gag) enough that he'll help her make the Novices compliant with drugs. (For what reason? Why the drugs?) And he has a facial blemish.

"Holy…"

She reread it all. If her logic was sound, Fabian was getting Ray to supply her with some kind of narcotic to chain the Novices to her.

Drugs. The employee Frank was investigating. She flipped back to the top of the first page and wrote:

TELL FRANK: CAPT. TEDDY BEAR'S CASE: POSSIBLE DRUG CONNECTION?

She turned back to the Father Ray page. Vivian was dealing with the pressure by adding altar wine to the mix. Bart was… Giulia didn't yet know how Bart was relieving the pressure. And Bridget, trapped and ashamed of her addiction, cleansed herself with bleach.

"Dear God."

She stared at the statue till her tired eyes unfocused and the Virgin dissolved into a silvery-blue watercolor.

"Mary, I could use a little help." Giulia's whisper sounded way too loud in the empty chapel.

"You and me both."

Giulia jumped. Sister Bart leaned her arms on the back of Giulia's pew.

"Sorry. I didn't mean to startle you. I thought you heard me walking up the aisle."

"I was zoning." Giulia closed the Day-Timer.

"Mary looks good. Bridget did the gilding last month. Or should I call it 'silvering'?"

"I know what you mean."

Silence.

"Sister Regina Coelis, I'm glad you're down here. I owe you an apology."

Giulia turned in her seat. "What on earth for?"

"For how flippant I was this evening in the vestry. You've been a Sister for years, and I'm only a Novice. I forgot my place."

Giulia dropped her head on the back of the pew. "Are you serious? No, don't answer that. Of course you are."

"Sister Gretchen passed me in the hall when I was taking my stained habit to the bathroom. As soon as she came close enough, she got a whiff of the mess. So we had a long talk. I like Sister Gretchen, but I really didn't want to rehash all that tonight."

"Some conversations you can't avoid."

"Yeah." She slumped back in her pew. "She reminded me that Novices aren't quite equal with post-vow Sisters, and that as nice as you are, I can't forget that."

"Look, I understand how it's supposed to work, but—"

"Please. I bend enough rules as it is."

Giulia raised her hands. "Then I accept your apology."

"You came down here for peace and quiet and space, right? I had the same idea you did: everyone'd be gabbing or heading for bed because of the big day tomorrow, and nobody'd be down here praying. I had to get away from those four walls. Even our beautiful little chapel wasn't room enough."

"I know what you mean about the walls. Lately they look like they're closing in on me."

"You too?" Bart stared at the softly lit statue of Mary. "I kinda hoped that would go away once you took vows. I have this recurring nightmare that all the dead Sisters from this Community are pushing on them, so they trap me in that five-by-nine cage forever."

Giulia looked at Bart out of the corners of her eyes and saw a reflection of herself: haggard, exhausted, sad. And addicted to … what?

"Come help me turn off the lights."

Bart followed Giulia inside the Communion rail and over to the Virgin Mary's niche. If she wondered why Giulia needed help to flip two light switches, she didn't say so. When Giulia turned left toward the vestry instead of right toward the nave, Bart still followed.

"We got it all," she whispered down Giulia's neck. "If we'd missed a spot, you or I would've smelled it when we crossed to the inside of the Communion rail."

Giulia waited till they were in the vestry and out of sight of the nave, just in case. "We're done cleaning. I'm buying you a cup of coffee."

"Thank you ... you're what?"

"Coffee. Escape. Are you willing to freeze for two blocks?"

Sister Bart's mouth opened but nothing came out for a few seconds. "It's after ten," she said at last.

"So it is. Do you have your keys?"

"Of course, but—"

"Then we can get back in." Giulia pushed open the door from the vestry to the back hall. "Quiet. Just in case she's in her rooms."

Bart sent a frightened glance down the hall toward Sister Fabian's section. Giulia didn't give her a chance to protest further. She turned the doorknob in one smooth, slow movement until it made only a faint *click*. The door opened without sound, Giulia pulled Bart through, and eased it closed with another muffled *click*.

"Whoever ordered this early cold snap needs to be fired," Giulia said. "At least the wind decided to take a break. Let's haul it."

"But—"

Giulia strode down the flagged path to the driveway. She was sure Bart would follow—Giulia had railroaded her into the quick escape to keep her off-balance. That, combined with the training in unquestioning obedience all Sisters received, left no doubt in Giulia's mind that Sister Bart would trail behind her like a duckling.

"Wait—"

Giulia didn't speak until they were on the sidewalk outside the wall.

"You don't like good coffee?"

"No, of course not. I mean, of course I like good coffee, the stuff in the Motherhouse is dishwater." Bart caught up to Giulia.

"I'm a Canonical. Remember? Cloistered? We're not supposed to be out at all, except for emergency errands and filming the Mass for shut-ins at the cable access station."

An SUV throbbing with rap music passed them. Giulia didn't reply to Sister Bart's questions. When the light changed, she crossed the street without looking for her duckling. Sister Bart touched the sidewalk right after her, right on cue. Giulia pulled out her cell and called Frank, walking faster the colder she got.

"You have a cell phone?" Bart's astonishment capacity appeared full.

Giulia counted the rings. *Pick up, Frank. It's Tuesday night. Don't be out on a date.*

"Hello? Giulia?"

"Mr. Driscoll, this is Sister Regina Coelis."

Frank's voice changed to match Giulia's formal tone. "Yes, Sister. How can I help you?"

"I realize it's late, but I would like you to meet me at the Double Shot on North Tupper. Do you remember where it is?"

"It's the coffee shop … uh … two blocks west of the convent, right?"

Giulia heard him yawn. "That's correct."

"Okay. I was just leaving my last conference. I could use some caffeine. Twenty minutes."

"Thank you. You'll be able to find us, I'm sure."

"Us? Got it. Be there by ten-thirty."

"Thank you." She closed the phone. "Why didn't they establish the Motherhouse in San Diego? Or Hawai'i. I could handle traveling to Hawai'i right now. Come on; it's just past the bar."

"Sister, who did you just call? Why are we meeting this guy at the Shot?" She matched her longer stride to Giulia's. "I mean, we couldn't really meet him at the Motherhouse, but what's going on? How are we going to get back in without anyone seeing us? My white veil sticks out like Day-Glo paint. And what am I going to tell Sister Gretchen?"

They passed the consignment shop (closed), the tattoo parlor (closed), Lou's Grocery and Lotto (open and smelling tantalizingly of chocolate chip cookies). They reached the alley between the grocery and Sam-n-Al's On Tap.

A dark, hooded shadow banged into Giulia.

"Git outta the way."

"Excuse me?" Giulia's icy teacher voice came out automatically.

"I said—oh, yer nuns. Comin' into Sam's fer a snort of Blue Nun?" The shadow laughed.

The streetlights revealed him to be taller and heavier than either of them. Giulia hoped that the habit would work its magic and he'd make another bad joke and leave them alone.

"If you'll excuse us—" Giulia took Sister Bart's arm and edged around him.

"Hey, little White Veil. Haven't seen you on the outside fer a while."

TWENTY-THREE

GIULIA STARED AT SISTER Bart. The Novice's face was as white as her veil in the oblique glow of the bar's neon beer signs.

"Saw the fat one today. How come she's makin' all the deliveries now? Yer better lookin'." He grinned at Giulia. "Too many babes hidin' under them veils. You ain't bad neither. I like 'em younger, tho'. Like her." He reached out as if to chuck Sister Bart's chin.

Before Sister Bart passed out right there on the sidewalk—Giulia had never seen anyone that colorless and still vertical—she stepped between them.

"We have to go now. Please excuse us." She gripped Sister Bart's arm, deliberately digging in her fingernails to shock her out of her fear. With firm, fast steps, she walked her past the bar and into the Double Shot coffee and bakery.

The door hissed closed. Sister Bart moved away from it, even though its coffee-cup shaped window had already fogged over.

"Sit down before you fall down." Giulia pushed her into the nearest chair. "Do you need a glass of water?"

"No. I'm all right." She looked past Giulia at the door.

"I doubt he's coming in here. Can you stand?"

The Novice stood. "I'm fine. See?"

"All right, then, come up to the counter with me."

The café had few patrons at this hour on a weeknight. An older man typed into a laptop in the corner table farthest from the door. Two college-age women shared a piece of three-layer chocolate cake at one of the center tables. Square hanging lamps illuminated five other empty tables lining the walls and two on the triangular floor space. In the back room, a gray-haired woman kneaded dough. Dizzy Gillespie played from an iPod dock on a shelf behind the counter.

Giulia scanned the menu on the Dry Erase board propped next to the iPod. "Look at that flavored syrup assortment. I died and went to Heaven."

"I, um, haven't had a good mocha in months." Sister Bart stared at the double line of plump scones.

"I'm holding out for the chocolate in that cake tomorrow." Giulia smiled at the multi-pierced male barista behind the counter. "A large cappuccino with pumpkin spice syrup, a large mocha, and two scones." She glanced at Sister Bart. "Blueberry? Almond?"

"I'm allergic to nuts. Blueberry, please."

"Two blueberry scones, please."

He poked the interactive computer screen. "Eight seventy-five. Would you like butter or lemon curd for the scones?"

Sister Bart said, "Butter."

Giulia said, "Butter for both, please," and handed him her debit card.

Sister Bart carried the tray to the table kitty-corner from the door. Giulia balanced napkins and two plastic knives on the Day-Timer.

"These people know how to make scones." Giulia split hers and buttered both halves.

Sister Bart had already started hers. "This is wonderful. Thank you."

"No problem. We both needed to get out of there." She savored her first bite. "Mmm. Perfect. Now let me tell you what's going on. Do you know that Sister Bridget's parents don't agree with Sister Fabian's explanation for their daughter's suicide?"

"Yeah. When they came up for her funeral they just glared at everybody. Vivian and I found lots of stuff to clean in Sister Fabian's part of the hall when she talked to them in her rooms."

Giulia blocked her expression with her scone. "Was it loud?"

"Like a roller coaster."

"Huh?"

"You know—they start off slow and even, then they ramp up and up until they get to the top. Then there's that pause while you think about it, and wham! You're screaming down a six-story drop."

The barista brought their coffee, and they took their first sips at the same time.

"Oh, yes."

"Oh, man."

They laughed.

"So this is what I meant by a roller coaster," Sister Bart said. "We heard calm-sounding voices at first, then they got louder and angry, and finally we heard Bridget's dad call Sister Fabian—"

she lowered her voice— "A lying 'b.' You know. Then the door slammed open and we got out of Dodge."

"I wish I could've been there. Okay then, the next thing they did was threaten the Community with a wrongful-death lawsuit."

Sister Bart gulped a mouthful of coffee. "They did?"

"They did. That's where I come in." Giulia sipped her own coffee to draw out the moment like a good storyteller. "You know I left for a year and then came back. Sister Fabian found out I worked for a private investigator during that time."

"She never forgets anything."

"Yeah. She called me in, told me to contact him, and informed him in her most Fabian-like manner that the Community wished to hire him."

"Were you there?" Bart finished the first half of her scone.

"Yes. She told me I would be the liaison for the Community."

"And you obeyed."

"It served my purposes as well as hers. I wanted to find out what really happened to Sister Bridget, too."

The smile left Sister Bart's face. "I can tell you."

Giulia shook her head. "I know what she did. I want to know why."

Sister Bart jumped away from the table and came back with a spoon. Rather than answer Giulia's implied question, she scooped whipped cream from the top of the cup.

After a minute, Giulia said, "Are you willing to help me?"

Sister Bart set down the spoon. "You know what it's like there, sort of. The way things are right now make it hard for anyone to speak up."

"There's no justice unless people speak up." She leaned forward. "How did you know that creep in the alley?"

"I—"

The door opened and Frank Driscoll entered. Sister Bart got a "saved by the bell" look on her face. Giulia watched Frank put on "Charlie Chan" with each step—genial, fatherly, and knowledgeable.

"Sister Regina Coelis. Good to see you." He shook Giulia's hand.

"Thank you for coming out here so late. Frank Driscoll, Sister Mary Bartholomew. Sister Bartholomew, Frank Driscoll, head of Driscoll Investigations."

Sister Bart shook Frank's hand.

"I'll just get some coffee and join you."

While Frank paid the barista, Giulia said to Sister Bart, "He's an honorable man. You can trust that he'll find answers for Sister Bridget's parents."

Sister Bart spooned the last of the unmelted whipped cream from her coffee cup and said nothing.

Frank returned and sat with his back to the door, Giulia on his right, Sister Bart on his left. He took his first swallow of coffee. "I needed that. Been a long couple of days." He looked at Giulia. "Okay, Sister. What do you have for me?"

"It isn't pretty. We have one Novice with a drinking problem. I don't know about the Postulants. They've been too busy for me to exchange three words with either of them. The merger may be a very good thing in the long run, but right now it's creating enough resentment to fuel three soap operas. Homesickness and personality clashes are a definite factor. However, it's my opinion that Sister Fabian's official conclusion is a travesty."

"Sister Regina—" Sister Bart looked back and forth between Frank and Giulia. "I didn't realize you were going to tell a stranger Motherhouse business."

Giulia chose her words to keep Bart on their side. "That's what I meant when I said I was helping Driscoll Investigations. Who on the inside would contradict Sister Fabian's conclusions? But you know, and her parents know, that Sister Bridget's suicide wasn't the natural outcome of a depressed, unhappy girl who shouldn't have been allowed to enter in the first place."

"That's what Sister Fabian's report said?" Sister Bart bristled like a cat confronting a Great Dane. "Of course she wasn't. No wonder her parents hit the roof. Bridget was the sweetest, nicest person in the city of Pittsburgh. She was wicked homesick, sure, but she always had a funny story to tell us. And just ask Sister Arnulf whether Bridget wasn't meant to be a Sister."

"I've been trying," Giulia said.

Sister Bart *tsk*'d. "Sorry. I forgot it was Bridget who would sit with her up in our parlor and translate stories of her Nazi-fighting days. The two of them would get all animated and excited, and Sister Arnulf would add sound effects—bombs whistling, humming the Swedish national anthem, German soldiers cursing. I think it was cursing—we don't speak German." She drank more coffee. "Sorry. I didn't mean to get sidetracked. But Sister Gretchen—that's our Novice Mistress, Mr. Driscoll—would definitely have spent more time with Bridget if her psych scores were below par." She licked her finger and picked up stray crumbs from her finished scone.

Frank opened his mouth and Giulia kicked him. He winced and shut it again just as Bart swallowed a whole blueberry.

"Sister Arnulf said all the time that Bridget was a model Sister. We know, because the first time she said it Bridget wouldn't translate, and Sister Arnulf poked her until she did. Anyway, the whole idea that Bridget was unstable is ridiculous."

"We need proof of that," Frank said. "Suicide points to the opposite. I apologize, but that's the case."

"I know."

Giulia set down her empty cup. "Sister Bartholomew, how does that creep in the alley know who you and Sister Vivian are? Why does he know who you are?"

Sister Bart jumped. A snort escaped Giulia before she could squelch it.

"If you're going to keep bouncing like that every time I mention something you're trying to avoid, I'll start thinking you have springs for muscles."

Sister Bart stared at Giulia, then at Frank, then at Giulia. "What are you doing?" she hissed.

Giulia rested her hands on the table, aiming for calm and steady. Sister Bart's hands, tapping the table in something like 3/16 time, gradually slowed to a standard 4/4. Giulia's foot was prepared to kick Frank's shin again if he even looked like he was about to say something.

"If we have any hope of clearing Sister Bridget's name, we need to know what only you can tell us." Giulia turned to Frank. "Mr. Driscoll, as we were walking here tonight, a strange man accosted us and quite obviously knew Sister Bartholomew." She spoke to Sister Bart again. "What is going on? What are you and Sister Vivian doing outside—in your cloistered year, as you yourself pointed out—and what's the nature of your contact with people like him?"

Sister Bart pinched her lips together.

"He mentioned 'deliveries.' Does he have anything to do with the addiction help Sister Bridget asked her former boyfriend to provide?"

Sister Bart clenched her fists on the tabletop.

Giulia reached across the small, square table and squeezed Sister Bart's fists. "Who coerced you?"

Sister Bart started to pull away, but at the word *coerced*, she froze. "How did you know?"

Giulia breathed a quick prayer of thanks—and kept her foot poised over Frank's, just in case.

"You've been reminding me for half an hour how you shouldn't be outside without permission because it's your Canonical year. There's no way you'd be sneaking into a garbage-filled alley between a bar and a grocery store to meet such a charming specimen of the opposite sex."

A strangled laugh came out of Sister Bart. "Yeah, he's not my type." She pulled her hands away from Giulia's and wrapped them around her nearly empty cup. "It was in the coffee."

"What was?"

"I don't know, but it made Bridget and Vivian all floaty."

"Not you?"

"I couldn't tell over my nut-allergy reaction." She looked up from her coffee. "You've got that 'I'm listening to Sister Arnulf and I don't understand a word of what she's saying' look."

"It would help if you started at the beginning. Mr. Driscoll, could you take notes?"

"You're better at—um, of course."

He took a pen and the six-by-nine covered notepad from his inner jacket pocket. Giulia liked his prompt response to her shoe squashing his toes.

She transferred her attention to Sister Bart, who was staring at the innocuous brown notebook like it was a hungry wolf spider.

"You know we have to write it down."

"I know. Might as well be killed for a sheep as for a lamb, right?" Bart downed the last of her coffee. "I quit cigarettes cold turkey on my seventeenth birthday. But right now I'd throw my mother under a bus for a Marlboro."

Giulia's smile conveyed encouragement.

Sister Bart focused on Giulia's chest. It took Giulia a moment to realize she was talking to the San Damiano crucifix hanging in her cleavage.

"The others got moved up here in April. I'm from Bethel Park, so I was here all along. The merger caused a lot of upper-level shuffling. My first Novice Mistress was sort of encouraged to retire. Sister Gretchen used to be a kind of traveling visitor to retired and invalid Sisters. She'd listen to them reminisce, bring them books, and give them Communion. Sister Fabian was in Sister Gretchen's entrance group, so it was kind of a slam-dunk."

"I thought you liked Sister Gretchen."

"Oh, I do. She's a great teacher and she can be a lot of fun when we're not on duty. I just think she's a little overwhelmed with the new responsibilities. The whole merger thing is still settling in. This is the first time everyone's gotten together from all the Communities."

"All right." Giulia glanced at Frank, but his bizarre homemade shorthand was keeping up with the conversation. "You were the only Novice before the merger?"

"Not at first. There were two of us, but Nancy's mother died and she went home to take care of the family." She moved her gaze to her coffee cup again. "Our priest situation changed soon after the merger, too. We used to have this really ancient guy. He was like everyone's great-grandfather, but he mumbled."

"Father Eugene."

She met Giulia's eyes this time. "Did you have him too? Was he any better then?"

Giulia smiled. "No. What happened to him?"

Sister Bart shrugged. "We heard he got diagnosed with Alzheimer's. I felt guilty after that because he irritated the heck out of me. Oops. Sorry. Language."

Frank's brow furrowed, but he kept writing.

Giulia stifled a smile. "Father Ray replaced him?"

"He used to be his substitute. Father Ray is good friends with Sister Fabian. I'm sure she pulled strings to get him assigned to us full-time." Emotion crept into a voice Bart had kept even and colorless thus far. "That was in June."

Frank drained his coffee. "Can I get anyone a refill?"

Giulia said, "Espresso, please, and thank you."

Bart goggled. "You can drink that before bed? Man, I'd be buzzing around my room till dawn."

"How about decaf, then, Sister? Or tea?"

"If you're sure you don't mind, decaf would be great."

"Sugar or cream?"

"Two sugars, please." When Frank went to the counter, Sister Bart leaned across the table and whispered to Giulia, "He's not what I expected."

"Were you having visions of Hercule Poirot?"

"More like Sherlock Holmes—so smart he makes you feel sub-human. But Mr. Driscoll has this confident air. It makes me feel like he can take almost anything I say and not be shocked."

Giulia smiled even as her mind leapt to several conclusions.

As though he heard her thoughts, right then Frank set a fresh cup before Sister Bart and sat down with his own. "Your espresso is coming in a minute, Sister."

"Thank you."

"Thank you, Mr. Driscoll," Bart said. "This is very generous of you."

Frank turned on his most charming grin. "It's no trouble at all."

Bart sipped, swallowed, and began worrying at her thumbnails.

Giulia said, "So Sister Fabian got her friend Father Ray assigned to the Motherhouse. I'm not really surprised that she wields power over more than the Community."

Bart spoke to Frank. "You're going to think I'm a terrible representative of the Sisterhood, but our Superior General is all about control and power."

"I've met her, Sister. Please don't worry about what I may think."

The barista brought Giulia's demitasse. She inhaled, sipped, and sighed. "That is wonderful."

Bart shuddered. "Not at this hour."

Giulia laughed. "Coffee is my friend."

"Coffee and I have an armed truce." Bart sipped hers again. "Let's get this over with. When Father Ray became full-time adjunct, he and Sister Fabian started hosting these 'get to know you' lunches in her suite. They started with the oldest Sisters, a few at a time, then took us next." She gulped and tried to cover it by drinking coffee.

"He seems pleasant enough." Giulia said to Frank, "He's a glad-hander, always smiling, hugs you hello, that kind of thing."

Frank made notes.

"We thought, Vivian and Bridget and me, that they'd take us in a group. But they invited Vivian first by herself. She put on her 'I'm so sophisticated' attitude like they picked her because she's older and wiser." Her smile twisted. "That sounds like sour grapes. But I sure didn't want to be alone with Sister Fabian for an hour. Neither did Bridget."

"What happened?" Giulia sipped more espresso, using the movement as cover herself.

"She came back upstairs all loopy, breathing wine fumes on us. I don't know what those two were thinking. Her psych tests must've shown she had a drinking problem. Sister Fabian reads all the results."

"She does?" Frank shook out his wrist.

"Power is everything to her," Giulia said. "Any leverage she can acquire, no matter how insignificant it may seem, she'll get her hands on."

Bart talked faster now. "Bridget and I knew that Vivian'd been sneaking altar wine. Right before Father Ray became our priest, Sister Mary Thomas got shipped off and the three of us got her sacristy jobs."

"Fabian did it on purpose."

Bart blinked. "I never thought of it like that. I bet you're right. That explains a lot. Christ on a crutch."

Frank coughed.

"They called Bridget down two days later. I didn't see her afterward, but that night I heard her puking in the bathroom. Two days later it was my turn." More coffee.

Giulia saw her hands tremble the least bit.

"They served the same food everyone else had, and they were all smiles and encouragement about how well my nursing grades were before Canonical year. When she wants to be, Sister Fabian can be witty, and Father Ray knows some great one-liners."

Silence, broken only by the Dave Brubeck Trio from the counter.

"They had a special dessert. Strawberry shortcake with real whipped cream. They handed me a cup of coffee with milk in it. That's not how I like my coffee, but I was in major politeness mode. I was thirsty, the milk had cooled it, so I took a big swallow."

Giulia, watching her, thought, *She rehearsed this.* Out loud, she said only, "And?"

"It was almond-flavored creamer. Real almond extract, not imitation. In half a minute my eyes were puffy and tearing, and hives broke out on my face and neck."

Frank said, still writing, "Anaphylactic shock?"

She shook her head. "I don't have it that bad. It scared the two of them, though. She actually ran to get Sister Gretchen, because she used to be a nurse. But Sister G knew all about my usual reaction, so she got them calmed down."

Giulia forced herself not to nudge Frank under the table.

"I got to crash on my bed the rest of the afternoon, and the hives didn't bug me as much as usual. Nothing really bugged me for about six hours."

"Why?" Giulia tried to sound merely concerned.

Frank turned a page and wrote so Giulia could see: I GET ABUSE SIGNALS.

Giulia said to Bart, "Did you take too much of your allergy meds?"

"No. I can control it with over-the-counter pills. Their coffee had tasted funny, under the creamer. A little bitter."

"They drugged the coffee?" Giulia heard the disbelief in her own voice. "I'm not doubting you. I'm appalled."

"Why did they drug it?" Frank stopped writing. "We are talking about the head nun of the convent—Community—and its priest, right?

Bart flushed. "If you follow the scandals in the news, it's not so out of the ordinary."

"I believe you, Sister. I've heard much worse. I was trying to come up with a reason."

Bart turned Bambi eyes on Giulia. "Promise you'll believe me."

TWENTY-FOUR

GIULIA DIDN'T LEAN FORWARD or change her expression, even though she wanted to tread on Frank's toes to make sure he was ready for this.

"Of course we'll believe you," she said to Bart.

Bart kept the Bambi eyes on Giulia. "Sister Fabian came up to check on me. At least that's what she said to Sister Gretchen in the hall outside my room. She was so sweet and soothing, telling me how she'd noticed that I was the responsible one of us Novices, and how she could see that I was helping Bridget cope and keeping Vivian in check." Her mouth trembled a moment, but she breathed in a huge lungful of air and it stopped. "The next day she called me into her office and gave me an ultimatum. Father Ray was there, too. They told me that Vivian and Bridget and I were going to work an extra job for the Community. They showed me a bottle of little pills."

Frank raised his head. "What were they? What did they look like?"

"I don't know what they're called. They were mixed colors, gray and white and pale blue and pale orange."

Giulia said, "I found a small orange pill in the back chapel hallway today."

"I didn't get any orange ones today," Bart said. "It must've been from Vivian's packet. Sister Fabian said I'd be delivering the pills on a rotating schedule to people who'd be expecting me. She'd give me permission to walk outside the grounds and down two blocks."

Giulia said, "Why did you agree to this?"

"They threatened Bridget and Vivian. Said they'd claim Bridget was an addict and Vivian was a drunk and kick them out of the Community. Bridget wanted to be a Sister since she was something like five years old. Vivian wants it too, as messed up as she is. It would've ruined them."

"But—" Frank said.

Bart shook her head till her veil flapped. "But nothing. Sister Regina, tell him."

"Mr. Driscoll, the vocation is difficult to explain to an outsider. You can believe that was effective leverage." After a moment, she said to Bart, "They didn't threaten you personally?"

Bart ran a finger around the rim of her coffee cup.

"We can't help you if you aren't honest with us."

"I know." Her lips formed words that looked suspiciously like *Christ on a crutch*. "I got into some hard stuff in high school." Her voice dropped lower than the Brubeck piano solo. "I kicked it before I entered, but they knew about it. They said if I went to anyone inside the Community or outside of it, they'd put in a word to the right places that I was still an addict and had been getting my fix from the alley guys. What hospital would hire me after that?

What car repair shop would, besides my dad's? People believe clergy implicitly, even these days after the pedophile scandals."

"*Go mbeire an diabhal leis iad.*"

Giulia cleared her throat. "Mr. Driscoll?"

Frank's gaze appeared to turn inward, replaying what he'd just said. "My apologies, Sisters. I have a bad habit of slipping into Irish whether or not who I'm with understands it. That expression means 'May the devil take them with him.'"

A pale imitation of a smile appeared on Sister Bart's face.

"How did you carry the pills? A purse would be obvious, especially if your contact was a man," Frank said.

The smile faded. "Four or five dozen wrapped longways in a tissue." She flipped the headband of her veil inside out. "They're tiny pills. Sister Fabian showed me how to make it the right size and flatness to fit in here." She shrugged, a sullen teenager gesture. "In case the cops happened to do a sweep for small-time dealers when I had to meet one."

"Despite all that, you're telling us now." Giulia caught and held Bart's gaze. "Did they do anything else to you? To any of you?"

"No." Short and sharp.

"Bart—"

"I said no. Isn't turning us into criminals enough?"

Giulia let it go for the moment.

Frank set down his pen. "Sister, if you'll forgive me, I'd like to ask you a blunt question." He waited for Bart's nod. "Why didn't you—all three of you—just leave?"

"It's not that simple."

"Why not? You're not a minor. You're perfectly free to tell both of them where to get off and walk out the door whenever you choose."

"Mr. Driscoll." Giulia pitched her voice to be heard only by the three of them. "Please remember we're in a public place."

"I know that. What I don't understand is the mindset of remaining in the situation she—you—describe when there's no reason to."

"There is," Bart said in a stronger voice. "There's the vocation."

"Exactly," Giulia said. "A vocation sets us apart. You don't walk away from God's choice for you lightly."

"I was raised Catholic. I know all about vocations and calling and serving. One of my brothers is a priest."

"He is?" Surprise made Giulia drop her character of "Sister Regina Coelis."

"Yeah, Evan. Second oldest. Sidney wants him to do the wedding."

"She's not Catholic."

"Olivier is, and Sidney's willing to accommodate him. You're going to have to help with her RCIA instruction, you know."

"That's going to be interesting." Giulia caught an odd look from Bart. "Mr. Driscoll, we've veered from the topic at hand. If your brother is a priest, why is it difficult for you to understand the concept of a vocation?"

Frank picked up the pen again. "I understand the concept, Sister." He placed a slight emphasis on the title. "What I wish someone would explain to me is why three grown women with, presumably, working brains, let a nun and a priest force them to be drug couriers."

"Every decision must be made in light of the vocation." Giulia met Bart's gaze, and she nodded.

"Brilliant. Just brilliant." Frank grabbed his coffee, swallowed, and grimaced. "Cold." He clunked the cup onto its saucer. "That word *vocation* does my head in. My brother trots it out every time we argue dogma. You—" he jabbed the pen toward Giulia. "I expected more of you. You should know better than to let these girls get caught in this kind of trap. What are you there for if not to protect—"

"I'm there to find out what drove one of them to messy suicide, remember?"

"And what's taken you so long? You waste time texting Sidney about Swedish translations. You waste time walking on egg—"

"I'm wasting time? Yesterday you were all about how well I'm doing in this situation and that the initial timeline was flexible." She snatched the pen from his hand. "I've told you from the beginning that this was a bad idea, and you insisted I was the only one who could do it. Every part of this is your own fault."

"My fault? You're the one who's supposed to be the professional here. If you can't handle the work—"

"What? Get out of the convent? You don't have the first clue what goes on in there. You talk about evidence gathering and witness massaging, but you're talking out of your—" She stopped.

Silence filled the coffee shop; music no longer played from the iPod. Bart gaped like Giulia had sprouted horns and a tail. From the corner of her eye, Giulia saw the barista texting at warp speed.

Frank's gaze followed hers. His lips moved, but no sound came out.

Which Irish curse fits this soap-opera situation? Giulia pulled herself into ramrod-straight teacher posture. "I beg your pardon, Mr. Driscoll. A Sister of Saint Francis is expected to behave with decorum at all times."

Frank held up both hands. "Please, Sister, the fault is mine." He turned to Bart, frozen in place like the Medusa had come by to offer refills. "Sister, I could tell you of the weeklong double shifts I've worked, but that's no excuse for my behavior just now." He put on his most charming smile. "Sister Regina and I used to work together in a somewhat informal setting. Now that she's returned to her life in the convent, I ought to remember the proper manners."

"I, um, please, don't worry about it."

Giulia handed Frank his pen. "We should get back."

"Let me drive you," Frank stood. "It's freezing. Where are your coats?"

"We didn't bring them."

"What?" Frank started to say something else, then visibly shifted gears. "Then I'll definitely drive you. I'm parked right out front."

Giulia picked up her Day-Timer and followed him as the barista came out from behind the counter, still texting. Bart trailed behind her like a duckling again.

The wind had finally given up, but the cold felt even worse after the warm, lighted coffee shop. Frank unlocked the passenger doors for Giulia and Bart, walked around to the driver's side, and started the engine.

"If we sit here for just a minute, the heat will kick in. Please excuse the cold air from the defroster."

The Camry's heating system began to warm the front seats right away. Frank put the car in gear and pulled into the empty street without another word.

Sister Bart said nothing during the two-block ride, not even a "thank you" when Giulia aimed the heater toward the back seat. Frank made a U-turn just past the Motherhouse driveway and pulled up to the curb.

"Sisters, it's not a good idea to drive you to the door. I apologize."

"You're right," Giulia said. "We understand."

"Thank you for the coffee and the ride, Mr. Driscoll. It was, um, nice meeting you." Bart got out and stood on the sidewalk, rubbing her arms.

Giulia said rapidly, "Sorry. There's more going on than she said in there. I'll text you."

"I'm sorry too. I trust you to clean up my mess."

Giulia exited before he could say anything else, and ran up the driveway with Bart.

A tiny Kia Soul followed them.

TWENTY-FIVE

The car—or Giulia and Bart—tripped the porch's motion sensors. The next moment, glaring white light flooded the front steps out to the end of the driveway.

"Who can be showing up at this hour?" Giulia continued onto the steps.

"People have been arriving at weird times all week. Lots of them took red-eye flights to save money." Bart's voice sounded both wary and tired. "They're going to want help."

"Good thing you have a key."

"The doorbell rings in Sister Alphonsus's room." Sister Bart led the way this time, back down the steps.

"All the time?"

"Ugh, no. Just these two weeks. I don't think she'd be all bubbly all the time if she was on permanent overnight doorbell watch."

All four car doors opened, and the driver plus three Sisters squeezed out of the artsy rectangular vehicle.

It's like a Catholic clown car. Smiling, Giulia walked up to one of the nuns. "Good evening, Sister. May I help you with your suitcases?"

The ancient Sister grasped the sleeve of the younger one next to her. "Syster Winifred, var snäll och hjälp mig med mina resväskor."

Sister Winifred gave Giulia a tired smile. "Good evening. Sister Peregrin doesn't speak any English, I'm afraid. She and Sister Georgia are here to visit Sister Arnulf."

The driver, a slicked-back businesslike young man, had already opened the hatchback and was setting a handful of black suitcases on the ground. Next to him, Sister Bart paused in picking one up. "Is she expecting them?"

"Yes, but we're about two hours later than we said we'd arrive." Sister Winifred clapped gloved hands over her ears. "Is it always this cold here in October?"

"No. We were supposed to give everyone a warm, sunny Indian summer welcome to Pittsburgh." Sister Bart slung a messenger bag over her shoulder and picked up a medium-sized suitcase. "I have a key, so we can go right inside."

Giulia walked around to the hatchback as the driver set the last suitcase on the ground. "I'll get these." She squatted, picked up two suitcases by their padded handles, and grabbed a small Pittsburgh Penguins duffel bag with her other hand.

"Stopp! Jag tar den."

Sister Peregrin moved faster than Giulia expected and snatched the duffel bag out of her hand. It clanked and crinkled. The elderly Sister hugged it to herself and the noises stopped.

"Tack."

"She said 'thank you,' " Sister Winifred called over to Giulia.

In the combination of shadows and floodlights, Sister Peregrin's smile looked more like a warning than anything else.

Sister Georgia said something to Sister Winifred, who reached into the back seat and brought out a fringed, knitted shawl. Giulia froze in place. *A translator. Dropped into our laps.* She would've high-fived Bart if both their hands hadn't been filled with suitcases.

The driver closed the hatchback. "Thanks for taking care of these. I have to head back to the airport for my next load, assuming the plane lands on time. Never tell your grandmother that you'll do her a favor anytime she needs one. Mine took 'anytime' literally."

"Not a problem. Cute car. I thought it was a little small for a regular taxi."

"It's bigger inside than it looks, like Time Lord technology." He looked down at Giulia. "I mean, if you get the reference."

"Geronimo!" Giulia said. "Although my favorite is still Tom Baker."

"I'll grant you that. I'm a Pertwee man myself. 'Night."

Bart unlocked the front door. Sister Winifred thanked the driver. Giulia climbed the steps in line with Sister Peregrin and Sister Georgia. When everyone was in the foyer, Bart flipped the deadbolt and set down the two bags she'd carried in.

"I'll run upstairs and get Sister Arnulf and Sister Theresa. I'm sure they're asleep, so I may be a few minutes."

Giulia helped the visitors with their coats. Sister Peregrin set the Penguins bag between her feet and stood guard over it exactly like a father penguin. Giulia turned her face away from the group until she could control her expression.

The Swedish Sisters looked around at the foyer's portraits of the Pope and the Community's founder, the muted blue walls, the wood-patterned linoleum. Giulia listened to their comments, but understood nothing.

Sister Winifred sank into one of the armless chairs. "What a day. Thirty hours in airports or on planes, and being examined like we're a new brand of terrorist."

Giulia sat in the opposite chair. "The airports in Sweden have similar screening procedures as the ones here?"

"Not nearly as invasive, but international travelers get the joy of scrutiny by Customs. I remember when the habit commanded deference and respect." She rubbed her hands over her face. "It was long and annoying at home. It wasn't too bad at London because we didn't leave the plane. But when we got to New York City, everyone had to go through the new scanners."

At the word *scanner*, Sister Peregrin turned to them and said, "Svin."

Giulia smiled. "You don't need to translate that one."

"I've been with the Göteborg convent for seven years, and I've never heard these two Sisters use any language stronger than 'Jesus, Maria, och Josef.'"

"What happened?"

She touched the top of her veil. "The screeners at the airport didn't know what to make of the high crowns on these. We were all taken aside for extra searches. I had a difficult time convincing the Sisters that we needed to remove our veils to prove we weren't hiding anything under them."

Giulia stared at her. "They made you remove your veils?"

"It gets worse. I removed mine first, to show the Sisters that it wasn't a big deal. They weren't happy, but they complied." She looked Giulia up and down. "Your habits are so much simpler. Look at mine—this gathered skirt could make two of yours. Our long sleeves are fitted enough that they passed inspection, but our skirts and undergarments are too bulky. Apparently they looked suspicious." She gave Giulia a wry smile. "Our first female screener brought in a second one and told us we had to be 'patted down.'"

"These little old Sisters? What terrorist profile could they possibly fit?"

"Now, Sister. You know profiling is illegal in the United States." She winked. "I must've conveyed my unhappiness with the procedure when I explained it to them. I thought *svin* was an extreme for them, but they gave me an education in obscure Swedish curses."

"It's a good thing the screeners didn't understand them, then."

"Lord, yes. The screeners were as polite as possible in such a bizarre situation, but we still had a total stranger's hands feeling every part of our clothing. And bodies, through the clothing." She sighed. "I feel violated. I was afraid my companions would go through the roof. Well, as far as their arthritis and hip replacements would let them."

"I'm amazed they put you three through that kind of search."

A shrug. "We weren't the only ones taken aside. I'm just grateful they both stayed silent through most of the search. Unfortunately, when the pat-down reached our, well, our panties, they indulged in invective from their youth. Including the word *Nazi*."

"No." Giulia covered her mouth with her hand.

"Yes. But, thank God, the habit still has some cachet. The screeners pretended they didn't hear the 'N-word' and finished rather quickly." She put her hands behind the small of her back and stretched. "I wonder what that closed-circuit tape will look like."

The two Sisters stopped their tour of the foyer in front of Giulia and Sister Winifred. Like a well-rehearsed vaudeville routine, they spoke in turns in rapid Swedish. Within four sentences, their voices began to ratchet up and they stepped on each other's lines. Sister Winifred tried to translate at first, but gave up.

"Winifred! Peregrin! Georgia!" Sister Arnulf walked toward them as fast as Giulia had ever seen her.

The two Sisters abandoned their tirade and met their friend halfway, all three laughing and talking at the same time. Behind them, Sister Theresa yawned like a cave.

Giulia stood. "Sister Theresa, this is Sister Winifred."

They shook hands. "We expected you hours ago," Sister Theresa said.

"I was just telling Sister Regina about our unfriendly-skies experience." Sister Winifred yawned this time. "Is there any possibility of hot tea or cocoa? We haven't eaten since we crossed the Atlantic Ocean."

"Let's get your bags up to your rooms first and we'll raid the kitchen." She stopped. "I have no idea where they put you."

"Wait a second." Giulia squatted by the end table that held the telephone and came up with Sister Alphonsus's clipboard. "I assume they've put all of you together..." she flipped one page and ran her finger down the next. "Here's Sister Georgia... yes, and

Sister Peregrin next to her. Sister Winifred, you're two doors down from them. Third floor: 310, 312, and 314."

Sister Winifred translated for the two new arrivals. With a glance at Giulia, Sister Peregrin picked up her Penguins duffel. Giulia tucked the Day-Timer under her arm as she and the younger Sisters shared the rest of the luggage between them.

"Sister Bart, can you get—" Giulia looked around. "She never came back?"

Sister Theresa shouldered the messenger bag. "I thought she did, but I was preoccupied with getting Sister Arnulf down here in one piece."

The three Swedish friends continued to talk nonstop.

Sister Winifred said, "I probably look like I've been flying for thirty hours."

Giulia smiled. "You do have that 'lead me to a bed and lock the door behind you' look."

"Oh, a bed. That sounds wonderful."

"Not before tea and sandwiches," Sister Theresa said. "I've traveled to Africa several times. Air pressure changes plus layovers plus living on those tiny foil packs of peanuts will give you a spectacular headache if you don't eat some real food."

"I believe you. I haven't been out of Sweden in ages. I'd forgotten what a rigmarole the trip to the Motherhouse is."

The elevator reached the dim, quiet third floor. Everyone stopped talking and proceeded to their rooms, moving as only nuns trying to be silent could move. Giulia detoured to her own room, yanked out the bottom dresser drawer, and set the Day-Timer on the floor under it.

When she re-entered the hall, the three younger Sisters were sorting suitcases and bags. Sister Arnulf and Sister Peregrin began a low-voiced conversation. Sister Georgia said something to Sister Winifred, who said something to Sister Theresa, who pointed to the door next to the elevator.

"Let's head to the kitchen," Sister Theresa said. "We have ham and turkey and bologna, and I think we have Kaiser rolls."

Sister Winifred's stomach rumbled. "Excuse me. Lead us to it, please." She spoke to Sister Peregrin, who set her bags in the wardrobe and followed Sister Arnulf into the hall.

"I'll wait for Sister Georgia," Giulia said. "What's the word for *kitchen*?"

"Say *I köket*. That means 'in the kitchen.' She won't try to ask you anything, so don't worry about the language barrier. She's a docile old dear. She'll follow you without an argument."

"Sister—" Giulia said, but the rest of the group had already piled into the elevator and vanished downward. Inside the bathroom, the toilet flushed. When the bathroom door opened, Sister Georgia glanced past Giulia at the empty hall.

"*I köket.*" Giulia pointed down and hit the elevator button.

Sister Georgia nodded and preceded Giulia into the elevator. They made the short trip in silence, Sister Georgia fingering the oversized rosary attached to the traditional Franciscan cord at her waist. Giulia still remembered how to tie the special three-strand knot at the end of it.

The light in the kitchen reached a little ways into the refectory, and Giulia guided Sister Georgia between the tables.

"Vilka vackra dekorationer."

Giulia started to say that she didn't understand, but they reached the dishwasher hallway and a minute later the kitchen. Sister Georgia repeated her remark.

"She says the decorations are beautiful," Sister Winifred said from her position at the counter next to one of the refrigerators.

"The Postulants created them," Sister Theresa said, spreading mayonnaise on a slice of wheat bread. "Sister Arnulf's been helping them with the papier-mâché and the painting all month."

"Syster Georgia, vill du ha skinka eller kalkon?" Sister Winifred indicated the tray of cold cuts.

Sister Georgia held out one half of a roll over the ham side of the tray. "Skinka, tack," she said and took the already-used knife out of the mustard jar.

"I feel positively rebellious, violating the sanctity of the kitchen at this hour," Sister Winifred said.

Giulia beelined—decorously—for Sister Winifred. "I wonder if I can ask you a favor. I don't know a word of Swedish, and I'd really like to talk to Sister Arnulf about something."

Sister Winifred swallowed a bite of her turkey on wheat. "Of course, but it can wait till tomorrow morning, I'm sure."

"I'd really—"

"Because, to be honest, I can barely put together a coherent English sentence right now." She smiled.

"Could you at least ask her—"

"Tomorrow morning, after prayers."

Giulia forced a polite smile. "Of course. Thank you. If you're all right here, I'm going to head upstairs."

"Oh, yes, we're fine. Thank you for all your help. We'll be sure to thank Sister Bartholomew when we see her tomorrow—that is, today."

Giulia looked at the clock on the stove. "Happy Saint Francis Day."

"That's right, it is." She translated Giulia's sentence for the three Sisters, who chorused it back to her.

"If you need something else, I'm in room 323."

"Oh, no. I'm sure we'll be fine. Thank you."

Giulia headed back through the gloomy refectory, moving cautiously between the tables so she wouldn't bump any and topple the centerpieces. The front hall was lit only by two dimmed wall sconces now. Chairs and lamps assumed strange shapes in the half-light. The newel post at the foot of the stairs reared its wooden pineapple top like a snake.

Speaking of snakes, Fabian's rooms are a short walk through the doors to the back hall. I think waking Fabian up to give her a piece of my mind is an excellent way to end this day.

She got all the way to the double doors before knowledge gleaned from years of watching murder mysteries kicked in.

Never tell the Bad Guys that you're onto them unless several armed cops are standing next to you at the time. I can't barge into Fabian's tastefully redecorated bedroom and announce that I Know All. If she and Father Ray have a well-planned scheme for supplying these dealers, they must have a well-planned cover-up, just in case.

TWENTY-SIX

"Do you ever obey even the simplest rule, Regina?" Sister Mary Stephen's words hissed at Giulia.

Giulia jerked to a stop just outside her room. Her nemesis leaned against her own doorway, an open book of devotions in her hands.

"What rule do you think I'm breaking?"

"Wandering around at all hours. Gabbing with new arrivals long after proper Sisters are in bed. And shall I mention how much time you're spending with Sister Bartholomew? We were taught about the subtle danger of the Particular Friend." Her smile conveyed anything but concern.

Giulia covered the distance between them in measured steps. *Would everyone on the floor wake up if I slapped that smarmy expression off her scrawny face?*

"Stephen, you must be exhausted. How do you watch over every move I make and keep up with your own responsibilities as well?"

"I care about the reputation of our group. You obviously don't." The volume of the hiss decreased.

"Oh, please. The only reputation you ever cared about was Sister Mary Stephen's and how it could be parlayed into more power." Giulia kept her own whisper low.

"Don't give me that 'I'm so superior' look. It may intimidate your students, but they didn't suffer through Formation with you."

Giulia laughed once and bit her lip before another laugh burst out. "Was I the cross you had to bear?"

"God, you're arrogant. Is that why you flout the rules?"

"Spare me. For all you know I could've been in the chapel saying a late Compline."

Mary Stephen snorted.

"What's your real problem with me?" Giulia fought to keep her voice low. "It can't be your manufactured rivalry from the Novitiate. We haven't seen each other in six years. Nobody holds a grudge that long."

The tall blonde slapped the devotional shut. The sharp noise echoed off the walls. "Why doesn't the world mete out favors to the deserving?"

Giulia raised her eyebrows. "This isn't the world. It's the religious life. Different paradigms."

"Obviously." She turned her back on Giulia and stopped just short of slamming her door. Or the piece of her quilted plaid bathrobe stopped her when it snagged on the strike plate.

Giulia heard a frustrated growl from the other side of the door as a hand freed the material. The door closed all the way this time.

Their conversation apparently hadn't disturbed anyone on the floor, since all the other doors remained closed. Giulia opened her own. *I know it's bad when I almost think of this shoebox as a sanctuary.*

The rolled-up habit had moved.

Giulia closed the door.

The tiny wastepaper basket was out of place. She pulled out the bottom dresser drawer and removed the Day-Timer. Only her fingerprints marred the dust bunnies.

"I wonder what Stephen will say to Fabian about the puke-smeared habit? Perhaps a tirade that dovetails with my inappropriate lingerie … oh, no."

She opened the top dresser drawer. "Damn you, Stephen. Crap. Sorry, Lord. Didn't mean to swear. Can I beg indulgence because it's the second time this week she's pawed my underwear?"

Giulia shook out one set of lace-trimmed silky undergarments. "I hate you, Mary Stephen," she repeated with each snap of the fabric. "I hate Fabian, too, but you bring hate-ability to a new and personal level."

The violet tap pants had holes in the seams and the smooth material was riddled with pulls in a pattern resembling the five fingers on a human hand. Ripped lace dangled from the matching bra's cups. Both underwires had been wrenched into angles and curlicues.

"Oh, no. I've only worn it twice." She tried to work the kinks out of one wire and it snapped in half. As she untangled her fingers, two long blonde hairs came away with them. She scrunched the set into a misshapen ball and flung it into the back of the drawer. "You thieving, covetous rat. Screw decorum and charity and everything else that's trying to turn me into a doormat."

226

She yanked open the door and stalked across the hall to Mary Stephen's room. When she was two steps short of her goal, the elevator gave a muted *ding*. All of the midnight snackers exited, whispering things Giulia didn't understand. The new ones smiled at her. Sisters Theresa and Winifred whispered, "Good night." Sister Arnulf stopped a moment, patted Giulia's arm, and nodded.

When they were all closed in their rooms, Giulia looked at Mary Stephen's door, at her watch, at the door again.

What good is confronting her at this hour going to do? We'll just stage another scene like we did in the vestibule. If I were as sneaky as she is, I'd go into her room tomorrow and manhandle her stuff. Her shoulders slumped. *But I'm not. I'm one of the good guys, blast it all.*

Adrenaline still pumped through her. She needed to do something, anything to defuse it. She returned to her room, and the first thing her eyes focused on was the habit on the window ledge. She grabbed the bundle, left the narrow window cracked to defuse any lingering odors, and headed to the Novices' floor. Bart had said she stashed the other two habits in their bathroom. Scrubbing all the habits clean was exactly the therapy she needed.

The thin curtains let in enough moonlight to see the shapes of the living room furniture. She tiptoed through the room, giving the couch a wide berth this time. No one appeared, awake or sleepwalking, as she passed the closed bedroom doors. With the lightest of touches, she pushed open the swinging bathroom door a few inches.

The shaded nightlight illuminated very little. She pushed the door farther and heard a small noise. She waited. Nothing—then the same muffled noise.

She slid sideways through the opening and held the door as it closed. The light she'd seen wasn't the nightlight, because that was lying on its side in the middle sink. She followed the feeble, slanting glow to the farthest shower stall. Another sound reached her—short, sharp breaths, then a tiny *mew* like a kitten.

Giulia pushed aside the shower curtain. Sister Bart sat on the tiled floor with her miniature flashlight next to her, its light bouncing off the shining wall tiles. She'd bunched up her red-and-white striped nightgown way above her knees. Rows of narrow scabs and scars covered her left thigh, like the pattern a woodpecker's beak makes on a tree. She looked up at Giulia, a razor blade in her left hand, a thin trail of blood dripping from it onto five new slices in her leg. The cuts dribbled narrow stripes of blood, making Bart look like a splatterpunk candy cane.

TWENTY-SEVEN

"WHAT IN GOD'S NAME are you doing?" Even in her shock, Giulia kept her voice to a whisper.

"Sister Regina, I, I ..."

Giulia shifted into teacher gear. She'd handled students who cut. First step: deal with the blood. She dropped the rolled-up habit, dashed into the nearest stall, and yanked a yard of toilet paper off the roll. A moment later she was on her knees next to Sister Bart, pressing the wadded tissue to the stack of five cuts. She eyeballed the rows of scabs next to the tissue and the rows of scars next to them.

"I don't see any redness or swelling on these scabs." Giulia's voice echoed a trifle and she lowered it further. "What are you cleaning them with?"

Sister Bart kept her eyes on the floor opposite Giulia. "Peroxide, then water, then Neosporin and bandages."

"I'm glad you're not as stupid as you look." Giulia checked the bleeding. "Almost stopped. Nice, shallow cuts. What did you do, find a website called 'Self-Mutilation for Dummies'?" She pushed the tissues hard against Sister Bart's leg. "Where are your supplies?"

"They're behind the dirty habits."

Giulia felt the heat from Bart's blush even if the light was too dim to see it for certain. She shoved the ball of habits aside. An extra-large Costco-brand box of tampons nestled in the corner. She almost approved of the good camouflage, but rescinded it when she realized it just meant Bart planned her cutting episodes well.

The box held a bottle of peroxide, a smaller box of bandages, two tubes of Neosporin, and a two-thirds-full package of double-edged safety razor blades. It frightened her.

Giulia whispered over her shoulder, "What do you do, use a new razor every time?"

"Well, yes. I don't want to get the new cuts infected."

"At least you have some sense." She went and yanked off more toilet paper before swabbing the cuts with peroxide.

"Ouch—not so hard," Bart hissed.

"Not the right kind of pain? Too bad." Giulia made another trip, this time to the sinks. She returned with wet toilet paper. She wiped the slits clean and dabbed Neosporin on them. "Oh, look. Two bandages exactly cover them. Of course that means you measured this out all nice and precise. Don't expect me to admire your planning." She repacked the tampon box. "Can you walk?"

"Yes."

"Then put Pandora's box away and meet me back here in ten seconds."

Giulia washed all traces of peroxide off her hands. As she gathered up all three stinking bundles, the door opened and Sister Bart poked her head in.

Giulia shoved a habit lump at her. "Let's go. I don't care how late it is, you and I are washing these tonight."

"But, Sister—"

Giulia stood nose-to-chin with her—Giulia's nose, Bart's chin. "Sister, you will obey me without question, or I will wake Sister Gretchen and rip the bottom of your nightgown off right in front of her."

Bart gulped and muttered, "Yes, Sister."

Giulia glanced at the back doors: locked. Rather than risk rattling a chain against metal fire doors at this hour, she headed back to the living room and the front stairs. Bart followed.

Giulia's shoes made only faint taps on the carpet. Bart's bare feet, nothing. The silent, dark Motherhouse seemed even bigger and darker than usual to Giulia this time through it. The hum of the refrigerators in the kitchen sounded almost welcoming. She slowly turned the doorknob to the entrance of the cellars, remembering how the door squeaked earlier that day.

She pushed in the switch, and the bare bulbs lit the stairs and enough of the hallway to get them to the laundry room.

Sister Bart, still behind her, turned the switch to the hanging fluorescents in that room. "Man, those are bright."

Giulia ignored that. "Is there something other than the industrial-strength powder detergent?"

"Sorry, no."

She wrinkled her nose. "If we're stuck, we're stuck." She went straight to the hopper sink in the corner and turned on the cold water. The ever-present bar of Fels-Naptha soap sat on the ledge.

"Does any place besides prisons and convents use this stuff anymore?" Giulia unrolled the first habit—hers—and winced at the stench. "Even when my younger brother spent a summer worshipping the porcelain and I helped him hide it from Mom and Dad, it didn't reek like this."

"It's the stroganoff. She told me that sour cream upsets her stomach." Sister Bart hovered at Giulia's side, her hands twitching on the counter.

Giulia attacked the crusted vomit with the block of soap. "Despite what I said in the Double Shot earlier, I don't understand you three."

The hands froze. "About what?"

She banged the soap on the habit against the bottom of the sink. "What do you think? Bridget let it kill her. Vivian's going to fall down a flight of stairs or choke to death. You're going to slip one night and sever an artery." A small sound—of protest?—reached Giulia's ears over the splashing water. "Don't squeak at me." She wrung out the habit and snatched the slip. "Why in the name of all the saints is Sister Gretchen allowing this?"

"Um, well, she doesn't know."

Giulia lifted the slip up to the light, then scrubbed the hem again.

Bart fidgeted.

Giulia wrung out the slip the way her grandmother had twisted the heads off chickens on the farm. Sister Bart handed her the veil.

Giulia tossed the slip aside and ran the stiffened black cloth under the water.

"Why. Not?" Her teeth hurt when she closed her mouth again. She forcibly stopped herself from clenching them this time.

Bart whispered, "Sister Fabian said—"

"Sister Fabian can rot in Hell for all I care!" Giulia stopped, inhaled, and lowered her voice to a near-whisper. "Strike that. Sister Fabian most likely is going to rot in Hell." She pounded the soap on a stubborn food-wine-bile splotch. "And don't. Tell me. To leave. Judgment. To God." The stain lost that battle. Giulia held out her hand, and Bart gave her the next veil.

"We don't talk about it with each other, either."

Giulia slammed the soap, splashing both of them. "You didn't think this situation was important enough to break the unwritten rule of 'Keep it between yourself and your Confessor?'"

"Our Confessor is Father Ray."

The drain sucked in the edge of the veil, making it float on a thin layer of soapy water. Giulia dragged it out and beat its lower half with the soap, even though it had escaped Vivian's mess.

"I forgot. Sorry." The veil landed on top of the other wet clothes, and she inspected Vivian's habit. "How's your leg?"

Bart shied away. "It's okay. I, um, know my limit."

Giulia stopped scrubbing and just stood there, hands wrinkling in the water. Then she started to laugh. She was too exhausted to raise her voice above the sound of the water. She stopped laughing after several seconds, but didn't trust herself to look at Bart for a full minute.

"Shut up," Bart hissed. "It's not funny."

Giulia looked at her red, angry face. "It is. You're slicing yourself like some medieval doctor who believes bleeding the patient will release the evil humours. Or are you afraid to admit the truth to yourself, that the pain you can control is a cheap disguise for the pain you can't?"

Silence. Bart blinked. As though her eyelids possessed an *On* switch, tears poured down her cheeks. Giulia dropped the soap and the habit and put her arms around the sobbing Novice. Neither spoke for a while. When the sobs turned to shuddering breaths and sniffles, Giulia released her.

"Here." She took a tissue from her pocket and looked around for more. "Be right back."

When she returned from the bathroom, several lengths of toilet paper in her hand, Bart had wrung out the last habit and started on the veil. Giulia finished it and the slip while Bart blew her nose.

"Why are you cutting, Bart?"

A longer silence. "Bridget killed herself. I have to be what everyone expects all day, every day, no matter what. Some nights I can't make myself too tired to think."

"Are you this bright and helpful and energetic every day?"

"Are you asking if I act exactly the same way now as I did before the day our spiritual leaders turned us into their drug mules?" Bart shrugged. "Yes. Because everyone knows me as 'Bart Who's Always Ready to Help,' it's easy to hide things from the rest of the Community. It got harder when Vivian turned into 'Extreme Weepy Vivian Who's Keeping the Tissue Companies in Business.'"

"But those who noticed put it down to the standard Novice adjustment period."

"You bet. They see what they expect, and we keep up appearances. Bridget was always quiet, even with Sister Arnulf, but after the drug got into her, she withdrew even further. Some days she didn't talk at all except during prayers."

Giulia gave the already washed clothes an extra wringing. "How did Sister Gretchen miss this?"

"She didn't, not completely." Bart set the soap in its niche. "The merger camouflaged it. Bridget came from far away and so did Vivian. It was easy to assume Vivian's weepy fits and Bridget's silence stemmed from that."

"How convenient." Giulia restrained yet another urge to shake Bart. "I understand Fabian's threat to your vocation and how she used your fear to manipulate you. Sort of. But you're not children. Why didn't you band together and fight her? Canonical Year isn't solitary confinement—you could've gotten out to talk to someone."

Bart's shoulders un-slumped. "Look how Mr. Driscoll reacted earlier to the story. Look how you're reacting, and you're one of us. People outside the convent don't understand."

"That's not always true."

"It's true enough. How often could one of us get out to find a willing ear? No—not willing. An outsider who could understand how the vocation is the most important thing in all this. It overrides every other issue."

Giulia started to argue, but the words soured on her tongue.

"See?" Bart crossed her arms. "You almost lost yours, didn't you? How much of your year out did you spend begging God to return your vocation? How many nights did you spend on your knees pleading for Him to restore you?" She snatched the veils.

Giulia put a hand over hers. "You can't try to see inside my head without opening yours. How many nights have you spent on your knees in the little chapel?"

Bart snatched away her hand. "Sorry. I'm forgetting my place again. I'll start the washer. You can't use too much of our soap in it. Sister Beatrice did one day and the suds burst open the door. It was a disaster."

"But the floor never looked so clean?" Giulia carried the wet clothes across the room after her.

"Nah. We keep it extra-clean so if we drop something we don't have to re-wash it." She looked at Giulia with hooded eyes, but relaxed when Giulia smirked. "It left a stubborn coating, though. We finally had to do a vinegar rinse. Stunk up the place for days." She poured in a scant eighth of a cup of soap powder and took the rest of the clothes from Giulia.

"The short cycle takes fifteen minutes."

Giulia looked at the clock and cringed. "You missed the earlier refrigerator raid. Let's make another."

"At one a.m.?" Bart's stomach growled.

Giulia smiled. "Yes, at one a.m. Come on."

———

They sat on the middle of the long table, waiting for the drying cycle to end. Giulia peeled an orange while Bart devoured a ham and cheese on wheat.

"I thought for sure you'd make instant coffee," Bart said.

"Have you seen the instant they stock here? It's an abomination. Besides, my body's telling me it needs a vitamin C hit." She popped the first slice into her mouth. "What I really wanted to do was cut into one of those sheet cakes."

Bart giggled. "Sister Damien'd have a cow."

"Which is why I chose to sacrifice the pleasure and offer it up instead."

Bart chewed another bite of sandwich. "My grandparents used to say that. My folks never did, but in here we say it all the time. Is it a Catholic saying only the older generation uses?"

Giulia shook her head. "Bart, you have a knack for making me want to check for gray hair. Just like Sidney."

"Who? Oh, you mentioned him at the coffee shop."

Giulia kicked herself. "Sidney is a her. She's Mr. Driscoll's admin and incredibly young and perky."

"But you're not that old." Bart finished the sandwich and picked up her glass of grape juice.

"I'm twenty-nine, thank you. You just wait. A few more years inside, and you'll talk like your grandmother, too."

"You make it sound like jail." She stared into her glass. "That wasn't supposed to be a straight line."

Giulia sectioned more of the orange. "Frank—Mr. Driscoll—would have the right joke to follow that."

Bart looked over the rim of her glass at Giulia. "How long did you work together before you came back? That is, if you don't mind me asking."

"Why?"

Bart stared into the dregs of grape juice like she was reading tea leaves before she spoke. "Well, it just seemed, in the Shot, you know, that you and he were a little more, um, familiar than boss and employee."

"Mr. Driscoll was training me to be a private investigator, and I was training Sidney to be my replacement—I started out there as the admin."

"Weren't you afraid you'd, well, cross the line between professional and personal?" She picked a shred of ham from her plate and ate it.

"Bart, casual friendship is a far cry from an office romance. Just because I held you earlier when you were upset doesn't mean you and I are going to plunge into a Particular Friendship."

Bart's head jerked up, eyes wide. Giulia grinned.

"Saying that phrase gets the same reaction as someone in a *Harry Potter* movie saying 'Voldemort.'" When Bart smiled, Giulia continued, "I know how it gets in here. You start over-analyzing every thought, word, and action. If you don't mind a little advice from someone with more experience, don't worry about everything so much."

Bart's hand moved toward her bandaged leg, then made a feint at her now-empty plate.

Giulia didn't miss the aborted gesture. "Not tomorrow—it'll be too crazy—but the day after, you and I are going to have a talk with Sister Gretchen."

"No—no, I can't. It's too—"

"Stop the melodrama. You can and you will. I've worked with high school students who cut. It can be stopped, but you have to be ruthless." She gestured with the last slice of orange. "I don't care if you think I'm shoving my nose in where it doesn't belong, and I don't care if you never speak to me again. I'm ruthless enough for both of us."

Bart stared at her like Bambi-Bart confronted with a five-lane highway full of headlights.

Giulia scooped up her orange peels and tossed them in the trash. "How much longer do you think these'll take?" Giulia stared into the circular glass dryer opening.

"It's been twelve minutes. They might be nearly done." Bart slid off the table.

Giulia held out a square laundry basket while Bart squeezed the collar and hem of the first habit.

"A little damp, but the stains are gone, I think." She held one dress up to the light, then the next two in order, while Giulia inspected the veils and slips. "You did a great job, Sister Regina. These are practically dry. We could hang these in our rooms to finish."

Together they checked the wall clock.

"Tell me that doesn't say one-thirty." Bart covered a yawn with a sleeve of the third habit.

"I would, but lying is a venial sin." Giulia covered her own mouth. "Don't yawn. It's catchy." She waited for Bart to drape hers and Vivian's clothes over her arm, then took her own. "I've got the dishes if you'll get the lights."

Up in the kitchen, Giulia stacked their few dishes with the ones left by Sister Arnulf's friends. She and Bart moved like ghosts up the stairs. When they separated at the third floor, Bart's candy-cane nightgown vanishing up the dark stairwell reinforced Giulia's nightmares of wandering in a haunted Motherhouse.

TWENTY-EIGHT

Four hours later, Giulia slapped her alarm like it was Sister Mary Stephen's face. After taking one of the briefest showers in the history of mankind, she shoved her desk chair under the door handle and texted Frank.

Progress on drug dealers?

Her phone vibrated while she was hooking her bra.

2 long 2 txt. Can u talk?

Giulia frowned, stared at the walls, the window, the door ... the bed. She crawled under the covers, making a tent of sheet, blanket, and bedspread, and dialed Frank.

"Giulia? Where are you?"

"I'm under the covers on my bed. Can you hear me?"

"Barely. Let me turn up the volume ... say something now."

"Good morning." She tucked the sides of the blanket around her feet.

"Better. Okay. Jimmy and I've been up half the night with the Pittsburgh Task Force. Remember that employee I was checking out for Blake's company? The one who was a small-time dealer? The Pittsburgh guys recognized his name and we gave them what I had. This network's a lot bigger than either of us thought. It's got tentacles from the northeast side of Pittsburgh over to Allentown and up to Scranton. Not to mention Cottonwood, but I think that's only because our small-timer moved there when he got married."

Giulia stepped on his last word. "Darn it. I forgot to tell you this at the Shot. Captain Teddy Bear may want to check out Sister Fabian and Father Raymond as possible links in his drug chain."

"Already doing it. Made the connection from Sister Bartholomew's story last night."

"Good." Giulia pinched her temples. This frustrating phone-and-text communication merely highlighted how much she missed working directly with Frank. "Will you find something out for me? Bart said she carried white pills, but Vivian dropped an orange one yesterday. I want to know if the orange ones are stronger than the white."

"Why?" Frank made slurping noises. "Sorry. Coffee's hot."

"Because I think those two had increased Bridget's dose, and the higher levels put the idea of suicide into her head."

"Just a sec." The sound of pen on paper came through the phone. "You sure?"

"No, but something caused her to jump from addicted and depressed to addicted and suicidal. I don't know enough about this particular drug's side effects to be sure."

"If that's true, these things are like the Skittles from Hell. If I wasn't an honest, upright citizen, I could make a boatload dealing 'em."

Giulia didn't quite growl at him. "Bart and Vivian and Bridget are honest. It's Sister Fabian making the money, forcing them to be couriers. Did the police catch the alley scum we told you about?"

"Working on that. The Pittsburgh guys've been chipping away at this network for two years. They get small-timers—like Blake's man—but no luck finding the Moriarty."

"Father Raymond could be the answer to their Moriarty problem. If so, arresting him would free the Novices. That's the only thing I'm interested in."

"You are way too focused. Don't argue—it's a compliment." He yawned. "Excuse me. Crashed on a hard-as-rock couch at three. Not conducive to sleep."

"Tell me about it. I was up till two getting puked on and threatening Sister Bart."

His voice sharpened. "What?"

She sighed. "One of the Novices is dealing with it by drinking too much altar wine. Sister Bart is dealing with it…" She slapped her forehead with her free hand.

"Giulia? You still there?"

"That's what they meant. Although how I could've made the leap from crying jags and obscure hints to drug dealing, I don't know." *Stupid, stupid, stupid.*

"What are you talking about? What does it have to do with the dead Novice—sorry, Sister Bridget?"

"Everything. The police absolutely have to connect Father Raymond and Sister Fabian to this."

"Yeah, well, that's the problem. Jimmy and I had a helluva time last night—this morning—trying to convince the task force that a priest is at the top of this pyramid. I mean, come on. Just because the papers still have pedophile priest scandal stories—"

"That should make it easier for them to believe you. They're policemen. They're used to seeing the worst in people."

"That's just it. They see so much of the worst that they need someone and something to look up to." He paused. "We have another problem with that."

"Yes?"

"I told them how Sister Bartholomew described the way they transported the pills in the front part of their veils. There's two Cradle Catholics on the team, and you'd have thought I was telling them I raped their baby sisters."

"Frank."

"Sorry, but the room got cold enough for the furnace to kick in by the time I was done. You know how it is. There's some scummy priests in the world, but nuns are still nuns."

"Yes, but at least you're not treating me like one now. I can't see my watch under here. What time is it?"

He chuckled. "Are you having visions of yourself at age ten reading under the covers with a flashlight long after you were supposed to be in bed?"

"Time, please?"

"It's six twenty-two. Lighten up. That was supposed to make you think fondly of your childhood."

"I've had too many flashbacks this week to think fondly of the past, thank you. Are you telling me they don't believe the Novices were forced to courier drugs?"

"Once they got over how I shattered their pedestals, they started to." He slurped more coffee. "But that's what I was trying to tell you: they had the same reaction I did in the coffee shop. None of us understand why three reasonable adults would knuckle under like that."

Giulia started a slow burn. "I hope you're not telling me that they're blaming the victims."

"Well..."

The burn ramped up. "This is not the 1950s. Are you going to tell me that when these particular policemen respond to a sexual assault report, the first thing they ask is if the victim was wearing a miniskirt?"

"Don't go there, thanks." Frank's voice took on a slow-burn quality as well. "We're talking about free will and illegal activity. If you want to discuss the history of patriarchal chauvinism in the justice system, I'll take you out to dinner and an evening of kick-boxing—you and me, that is."

Giulia's burn dissipated. "Deal. Frank, you said that you and your brother discuss the concept of the vocation. Plus, you went through Catholic school, so you also got the annual vocation speeches."

"Yes, yes, yes. I know the drill: pray that you'll be open to God's call. God whispers to the hearts of the ones He chooses, and nothing is more precious than the vocation to the priesthood. Or Sisterhood."

"Exactly, and please don't brush it off like the latest infomercial. Every word of those speeches is true, and that is why Bart and Vivian and Bridget agreed to Fabian's blackmail."

"Right, she said Sister Fabian threatened to kick them out of the convent. Christ, the place sounds like something out of my mother's favorite soap opera." He huffed. "That's not a compliment. Sorry I cursed."

"Take my word for it. A threat to living out their vocations would make them agree to almost anything."

"You've survived just fine without it." The phone clicked. "Wait a minute, I've got another call." Silence.

Giulia gripped her temper in both hands.

Click. "I've gotta go. Keep your phone on you. I'll text you as soon as I know something more."

When the connection severed, Giulia held the phone away from her and spoke at it. "Goodbye, Frank. Nice talking to you."

She flipped the covers off and got a full-on view of her alarm clock.

"Good Lord, it's six thirty-eight and I'm still in my underwear."

She snatched pantyhose out of the dresser drawer and pulled them on, threw on her habit without bothering to find her slip, and shoved her hair any which way under the veil.

The clock, which obviously had it in for her, now read six forty.

"I hope a power surge shorts you out." She slid into her flats—and got a perfect view of the twelve-inch run on the shin of her brand-new pantyhose. "Lord, is there a purpose to these annoying little trials?" She grabbed her phone from the unmade bed. "Don't be stupid, Falcone. Of course there is. You just haven't figured it out yet."

She ran down the stairs the way she used to get in trouble for when she was a Postulant. The first floor was just as empty; the smell of bacon wafted through the hall from the refectory. The noise of nearly a hundred and fifty voices crashed into that mouth-watering aroma, and Giulia ran into the hall leading to the chapel, braking by the Saint Anthony window.

Except the back rows were packed. She hovered in the doorway, craning her neck left and right. There—three rows up on the left. She hugged the back wall as long as she could, then headed straight up the side. It worked perfectly until she squeezed into the end of the pew and bumped Sister Epiphania.

"That's Edwen's seat."

Perhaps the elderly Sister thought she was whispering, but her voice was pitched high enough to cut through the sedate response to Psalm 119. Every head in the twenty pews in front and to the right turned toward Giulia. Farther away, the Psalm continued, but the sharp decrease in volume caused more heads to turn.

"Sorry," Giulia whispered, and walked past four more rows plus the Confessional. A Sister she didn't recognize slid aside to make room in the aisle across from the tall wooden booth, saw Giulia's empty hands, and held her prayer book between them. Giulia smiled and both their voices blended into the current verse.

The rest of the Office passed without incident. Giulia allowed the well-known prayers to soothe away most of the morning's chaos. When the last prayer finished and the rest of the Community filed out for breakfast, she leaned back against the pew, eyes closed, to organize the relevant information from this morning's phone call. Something tickled her neck. She slapped at more loose hair and tucked it into the bottom edge of her veil.

"Do you enjoy drawing attention to yourself in such a spectacular manner?" Sister Mary Stephen whispered into Giulia's ear.

Giulia opened her eyes onto the shining statue of the Blessed Virgin. None of the replies that came to her mind could be allowed to pass her lips.

"You may think you have special dispensation, but you're about to be disillusioned." The whisper added a note of glee to its resentment. "I have an appointment with Sister Fabian tomorrow."

Giulia murmured, "I wish you joy of each other."

"What?"

Giulia turned in the pew and glared into Mary Stephen's malicious face. "I said, you deserve each other."

Sister Mary Stephen imitated a beached fish.

Giulia coughed to cover a laugh. "Close your mouth, Stephen. I can count your fillings." She winced at the resulting *snap*. "How about a truce? It's a feast day, everyone's worked hard to make the Sisters from other states feel welcome and have a good time. I'm more than willing to get the best of you in another word-battle, but not today."

"Arrogance is going to be your downfall, and I plan to be there to see it."

"Only you think I'm arrogant. And underhanded, a kiss-up, disobedient, and undeserving of special favors." Giulia made a show of thinking about the list she just invented. "I take it back. I do have an issue with obedience. Feel free to discuss that in detail with Sister Fabian. Right now all I want to discuss is whether or not we'll get real eggs in honor of Saint Francis Day."

She stood and left the pew, walking fast enough to thwart any reply from Mary Stephen.

The hubbub from the refectory filled the main hall, erasing Giulia's two a.m. impression of a decaying Motherhouse haunted by her and Bart. She eased into the line at the food station near the door, smiling at Sister Arnulf as they passed each other. Sister Arnulf gave Giulia the same brief nod as she had in the hall after the kitchen raid. She didn't see Sister Winifred, but she was quite prepared to wake her up if she had to.

Rows of croissants headed the choices, followed by bacon, yogurt, grapefruit sections—and imitation eggs.

Giulia set down her plate next to Sister Cynthia's. "Can I get anyone refills? I'm headed for the coffee."

"Tea, please, one sugar," Sister Eleanor said, intent on a square of beige paper.

She returned with two cups. "I suppose I shouldn't expect to get everything I hope for."

"The eggs, right?" Sister Cynthia said. "The croissants almost make up for them."

"You look like death warmed over." Sister Susan returned to the table with two glasses of grape juice. "You've got a curl falling out of the left side of your veil."

"Blast." Giulia tucked it in. "I got dressed too fast this morning. Don't look at my stockings, please."

"I have clear nail polish in my room," Sister Elizabeth said.

"She made me go into the gift shop at the airport to buy it, too." Susan buttered a piece of croissant.

"You were going in there to buy T-shirts for your nieces."

"You just didn't want the appearance of frivolous adornment to tarnish your 'perfect Sister' image." She looked at her traveling companion. "Hah. Made you blush."

"I've got it." Sister Eleanor unfolded her piece of paper. "Watch, everyone." She turned the papier-mâché Saint Francis to face the rest of the table and passed out papers to everyone. "Start by fold-ing the paper in quarters."

Giulia sliced her croissant in half and turned it into a bacon sandwich. In between bites of that and sips of coffee, she folded the paper into an origami Saint Francis along with the rest of her table-mates. When everyone made the last fold, Sister Eleanor ges-tured for them to hold up the results.

"Your head is wrong," she said to Giulia. Everyone chuckled, and after a moment, so did she. "That's not at all what I meant. You folded the top corner, but forgot the half-fold after it."

"Okay, let me redo it." Giulia unfolded her creation step by step until it lost its bulbous space-alien look. She sneaked in another bite of her sandwich.

Eleanor dipped her "eggs" in ketchup and balanced them on dry toast before eating a bite. "Cynthia, that's perfect. Do you teach art? You should."

"I did at one school when the art teacher went out on mater-nity leave. An old friend taught me Chinese brush-art painting and I passed it on." She creased Saint Francis' robe and set him next to the centerpiece.

Giulia held up her origami. "He doesn't look like an extra from *Close Encounters* now."

Susan laughed. "I think mine needs some arms."

Eleanor shook her head. "What he needs is human DNA. How did you give him two heads?"

"I'm not sure. I think I was eating when you described those folds." She drank from her juice glass and shook all the folds out of the paper. "Let me start again."

"I'll help you, if Eleanor will approve mine." Elizabeth set her paper figure on the table and demonstrated the first fold for Susan.

Susan and Elizabeth bickered and laughed over the origami folds. After another paper saint joined the row, Susan leaned toward Giulia. "You're being watched again."

Giulia didn't look. "I expected as much."

"Did you two have another fight?"

"Unfortunately, yes."

Elizabeth laced her fingers exactly like Giulia's grade-school principal used to. "Sister, I'm sure I don't have to remind you of proper decorum."

Susan said, "Elizabeth, I'm used to you, but please don't lecture strangers. No offense, Sister Regina, I didn't mean that you're strange."

"None taken."

"Susan, in the spirit of Charity I'm obliged to remind Sister Regina of our duty as Franciscans to exercise love and forgiveness to all."

"Elizabeth, you're curdling my yogurt."

"It's not possible to curdle—" Sister Elizabeth caught herself and huffed.

"I agree with you," Giulia said. "My goal had been to stay out of her way, but I haven't been too successful."

Cynthia plucked Susan's origami from her fumbling fingers and re-folded the mistakes. "We'll all be returning home by Friday. That's the pot of gold at the end of the rainbow." She made a face. "I apologize."

"You've been watching too many G-rated movies," Eleanor said.

"The principal had me screen several animated features for the day care attached to our school," Cynthia said. "One day half of my conversation came out in rhyme. My homeroom students spread the word, and by lunchtime they were answering Periodic Table questions in rhyming couplets."

"Be grateful none of them captured it on their phones and posted it to Facebook," Giulia said.

Cynthia's eyes narrowed. "That would be the moment they discovered I'm not the harmless science geek they think I am."

Eleanor winked at Giulia and mouthed, "Yes, she is."

Elizabeth picked up her dishes. "I promised my former Superior General I'd take photographs of the chapel."

"It's seven forty-five already?" Giulia stood. "I'll see you all at Mass."

Susan caught up to Giulia at the dish carts. "Please don't take this the wrong way, but Elizabeth mentioned something to me after prayers." She set her silverware in the smaller plastic bin. "You've seen how Elizabeth is. She can find an *Imitation of Christ* quote relevant to taking out the trash."

"Yes?" Giulia set her coffee cup in the sectioned drainer.

"You've been spending quite a bit of time with the two Novices."

"Yes?" She kept her voice neutral.

"Back in our day, the spectre of Particular Friendship got pounded into us on a regular basis." Susan's normally confident voice hesitated. "I realize we only met on Sunday night, but everyone's in each other's pocket here. Casual events and conversations are going to get noticed."

They walked around the emptying tables. Sister Fabian passed through the doorway, Sister Mary Stephen half a step behind. Sister

Arnulf and her two friends had pushed their chairs together in the corner farthest from the doorway and were gesturing and talking as though they were planning a tour of Pittsburgh's most exciting attractions.

When Giulia entered the crowded main hall, her only thought was how to get away from Susan so she could find Sister Winifred.

Susan stayed next to her like a shadow. Giulia paused with her hand on the main stairway banister. "What exactly are you trying to say?"

Susan's posture changed from "waffle" to "discovered her spine."

"Rumors have been flying ever since Monday after breakfast. And now this morning you and Sister Bartholomew came late to prayers. You both look like you haven't slept. Your habits are slightly awry."

Giulia's brain went *zzzt*. Susan's gaze held hers. Half a dozen Sisters passed them, throwing odd looks over their shoulders and hurrying upstairs.

When the group had passed the landing and were clomping up the next flight, Susan said, "Elizabeth couldn't sleep last night. She got out of bed to get a book from the fourth-floor library. When she saw headlights in the driveway that late, she indulged her curiosity."

Sister Gretchen not-quite-ran past them toward the chapel, violin case in her hand.

Giulia remained silent.

Susan lowered her voice. "She saw you and Sister Bartholomew coming up the driveway at eleven-thirty at night. If she hadn't pulled aside the curtains at that exact moment, if she'd looked through the window half a minute later, the natural interpretation of the tableau in the driveway would have been you and Sister Bartholomew putting in extra hours to help the late arrivals come in from the cold weather."

Giulia stared at this woman who'd been gruff and funny and kind up till this moment.

Susan reached out to Giulia's hand resting on the banister, but aborted the motion before any physical contact. "You must realize what it looks like. You've been in the world for a year, and she's new and vulnerable. In the old days we'd call it a 'near occasion of sin' and do whatever it took to avoid it."

Giulia's phone vibrated and she found her voice.

"I see that the cliché is true: self-appointed moral watchdogs really do have the filthiest minds. Tell Sister Elizabeth for me that if she thinks I'm a predator, she could use a dose of 'the world' herself. Apparently she's unfamiliar with the basic Franciscan concept of helping people in need." She returned a hard smile to Susan's open-mouthed expression. "And both of you can keep your prying eyes out of my business. Happy Saint Francis Day." She turned her back and took the stairs two at a time.

"Sister!" Susan called after her in a low voice.

Giulia pretended not to hear amidst the other voices in the hall and on the stairs. *Narrow-minded, suspicious old maids! This is my earthly reward for trying to help overworked, stressed-out Novices? Veiled sexual predator accusations, of all things. Frank'll be appalled when I tell him this one. Just wait till tomorrow when I drag Bart into Gretchen's office and get these troubles out into the open. Too bad the visitors will be gone by the weekend. For once I'd like a moment of spotlight so Elizabeth and Susan can apologize.*

If anyone from her past happened to be on the stairs, she didn't see them. *It's the hazard of one hundred fifty women living together. Nothing to do but pick at each other. No place to get some perspective—the kind that shows you how real people interact. If Susan ever took a close look at her rule-bound friend, she might discover a chink in her Armor of Righteousness. Just like that senator, congressman, whatever he was, who ranted against equal rights for gays right up until the day the paparazzi caught him coming out of a gay bar with his secret lover.*

Her phone vibrated again. She tripped over the frayed carpet where the stairs met the third floor. Four pairs of hands caught her.

"Sister, are you all right?" "Oh, dear, that's a huge run in your stockings." "I brought some spares if you need one." "Anyone have some clear nail polish?"

Giulia caught her balance and smiled into four faces she didn't know. "Thank you. I was thinking about five different things, none of which included watching where I stepped. I'm just going to change these ruined things."

She escaped into her room, making a mental list: Frank first, stockings next, Sister Winifred third.

The telephone-handset voicemail icon and the tiny-envelope text icon both appeared in the upper left corner of the display. She flipped a mental coin and dialed voicemail.

"Giulia, Pittsburgh PD owes you. They owe me, too, but getting your Novice to tell her story about smuggling illicit prescription drugs was the missing link in their investigation."

In the background, she heard his desk telephone ring.

"Damn." His voice sped up. "I'll text you."

She hit the *End* button and scrolled to the message that had buzzed during her standoff with Susan.

2 much 2 txt. Call me as soon as u get this.

She crawled under the still-mussed bedcovers. The weight of the blanket knocked her veil askew, and she pulled it off before dialing Frank's number.

"It's about time. Have you seen that priest today?"

"Hello, Frank. No, I haven't seen Father Ray. Why would I?"

"Perfect. Did you get my voicemail?" His voice had a smushed quality, like he was holding the phone between his shoulder and ear. The sound of fingers pounding a keyboard punctuated his sentences.

"Yes. Are you seriously going to tell me that Father Ray and the Novices comprise a big enough network to register on the Pittsburgh radar?"

He snorted. "That sounds like an R&B band from the Sixties."

"Stop it. They're scared young women. Need I remind you that one of them killed herself over this situation?"

"When you get out of there, I'm going to give you a crash course in modern conversation. You're talking like my grandmother again."

She stifled a growl. "Whose fault is it that I've regressed to my convent days?"

"Guilty. We'll discuss it later. Now listen. What's happening there right now?"

"Several presentations on the new, improved Community at eight. Controlled chaos on the Novices' floor. A convention of Swedish Chef impersonators across the hall. Mass at ten. And if I figure out how to change this alarm, a twenty-minute nap before that for your long-suffering partner."

The keyboard noise stopped. "Are you kidding? You can't sleep now. You've got work to do. What time does that priest arrive?"

"I have no idea."

"Use logic then. Does he show up just in time for Mass or does he hang around chatting people up beforehand? You must have seen him."

Giulia thought back to the last two mornings. "He arrives maybe five minutes early. We're all in the chapel saying the Office—morning prayers—right up till Mass time." The keyboard started up again as she talked. "He may arrive a few minutes early today because Mass is late and fancier."

"Okay, we'll work from that assumption. Here's the bones of it. Blake's employee—remember I told you more about him last night in the coffee shop—had a hell of an income dealing MS Contin."

"Dealing what? Do you mean OxyContin?"

"No I mean MS Contin. The version he's been spreading on the streets is a timed-release cousin to the well-known drug. Even though Blake's guy was one of the middlemen—and we think there are at least thirty of 'em—the priest was smart enough to give his dealers a slightly larger cut than is usual with these street networks."

"Stop. What about Sister Fabian?"

"Beats me. I don't know how he got her involved. Wait." More tapping. "When did this Community merger happen exactly?"

"Sometime during the summer of last year, when I was clawing through the last of the paperwork required to be dispensed from vows."

"Just a sec … Damn, I wish I had Sidney here. My Google-fu is not awake this morning."

"Where are you and what are you looking up?"

"I'm at the central Pittsburgh police station, of course. I told you that earlier. Been here all night. I'm looking up why those Communities merged … Not this spreadsheet … I had it last night … nonprofit reports for … Aha. Got it." A pause. "The other three Communities were either in the red or teetering on the edge of it, but the one in Pittsburgh started to pay off its arrears six months before the merger. Guess that's why it won the location lottery."

Giulia's fingers drummed the mattress. "I told you that last Friday, remember? The Communities had to merge or declare bankruptcy."

"Did you? I forgot. One to you, then. See the connection?"

"I don't …" Barely four hours of sleep had done nothing for her brain. "Wait … Sister Fabian's using illegal drug money from Father Ray to pay off the Community's debts?"

"Bingo."

"Good Heavens."

"Yeah. Boggles the good Catholic mind."

"Good Heavens."

"Pull it together. The Pittsburgh guys are letting me tag along to the priest's house when they search it. We're just waiting for a judge to issue the warrant. I'll bet my brother's collection of *Playboy*s that he's got a pile of the stuff ready to distribute, and then *wham*. We've got him. I'll call you when we've tossed his holy ass in jail."

"Please stop swearing, Frank."

"Yeah, yeah, I know. Listen. We need the layout of that place."

"What do you mean?"

"What I said. Where's the church part in relation to the main driveway where I dropped you off?"

It was easier to answer his rapid questions than to predict where he was aiming with them. She could figure that out after the call. "You go in the main door, turn left when you reach the hall, right when you reach the stained-glass window hallway—"

"Not from the inside. Think! We need to get there from outside so we don't spook the quarry."

"Quarry? You mean Fabian?"

"Who else? The guys picked up your alleyway thug and flipped him."

"They did what? You mean like a house?"

"No. They offered him a deal. He couldn't agree fast enough to give evidence against the nun and the priest."

"Oh." *There's so much I don't know yet.*

"That gave us probable cause and another warrant. So I'm hoping that Sister Fabian, being Head Nun, will have a private area all to herself. Us being men, I figured the best place for us to breach the walls will be the door the priest uses to enter so he doesn't disturb all the nuns at prayer. Where is it?"

"I see. Good Heavens. All right, when you're in the driveway facing the Motherhouse, the gardens are to your left. You'll see a flagstone path next to the building. Follow that around until you reach a set of brown-painted doors. They lead into the back hall.

Turn right and the hall takes a slight curve around the chapel. The carpeted area at the end is where Sister Fabian's rooms begin."

"Perfect. We're going to do this as quietly as possible. Everyone's going to be at this ten o'clock Mass, right?"

"Yes."

"Thought so. I'll call my brother Pat, get him to pinch-hit for your Mass. He's a Jesuit, but don't hold it against him. His first class at Carlow—he's an adjunct prof there—doesn't start till noon on Wednesdays. He'll get to your place in time."

"But Father Ray'll be there too. That'll be an awkward scene."

"No, he won't, because we're arresting your priest first, at his house, remember? We'll deposit him at the station before we head over to pick up Sister Fabian. If everything goes as planned, you'll never know we were there."

Background voices on Frank's end interrupted him.

"Gotta go. I'll call you when it's all over."

Three beeps and silence. Giulia closed and pocketed the phone. Only then did she realize she was stifling under the blanket and bedspread. She flung them backwards and sat for a long minute on the bed, staring at the imitation-wood headboard.

"She drove Bridget to suicide for money. She damaged Bart and Vivian, she caused them to sin, to redecorate her living room. Fabian, I will dance on your grave, you miserable b—" She stopped herself from swearing. "Fabian in jail. I wonder what the Vatican inspectors will have to say about that."

Crash. Thud. Yelp.

TWENTY-NINE

GIULIA JUMPED OFF THE bed and ran into the hall. A large, irregular lump of black double-knit lay half in and half out of the elevator. A four-pronged cane lay near the lump, one rubber foot caught on the long, frayed edge of the hall carpet. Giulia was halfway to the elevator when part of the lump resolved into a large rear end.

The elevator doors started to close. Giulia jumped into the cage and slammed the *Emergency Stop* button. She knelt next to the prone Sister and said over the rattling bell, "Is anything broken? Can you move?"

"Sister Regina? I'm so glad it's you. I'm all tangled up." Sister Joan of the harmless wisecracks looked up at her with one eye. Her off-kilter veil covered the other.

"Let's get you up." Giulia bent Joan's knees until her legs were free of the elevator, leaned in, and yanked the red button. The alarm stopped.

"Praise God." Sister Joan fumbled her veil out of her face. "That noise would drive the Blessed Mother herself to violence."

Giulia helped her roll onto her back, grinning. "What were you in such a hurry to get to?"

"My photo album. I have some embarrassing pictures of the upper echelon from the Pittsburgh Community back when they were Novices." She inched her left arm out from under her back. "Did I lose a shoe in this debacle?"

"You did. Let me put it on for you and help you stand." Giulia worked the nursing-style slip-on over Joan's hammertoe. "Your stockings have given up the ghost, I'm afraid."

"So have yours. Stupid things. Overpriced and too fragile for a vow of poverty." She raised herself on her elbows. "I hope Sister Fabian has a suggestion box. I'm going to place a strongly worded request to replace this rug."

"I'll second it. Are you ready? Let's try sitting up first."

Giulia took Joan by the armpits and pushed her upright. "How's that? Dizzy? Any shooting pains in your legs or your head?" She stared into Joan's eyes. "I wish I had a flashlight."

Joan batted her away. "I landed on my knees, not my head. Speaking of heads, prepare yourself for a frightening sight." She ripped off her veil, exposing dark gray hair with a rippling Bride of Frankenstein streak on the right-hand side.

Giulia gasped. "It's amazing. I know you didn't dye it, but it sure looks that way."

Joan stuck both hands into her pasted-down hair and scratched her scalp. "When I was going through the entrance process way back in 1952, the Superior General asked me if the desire to cover my hair had an undue influence on my vocation." She winked at Giulia. "It did, a little."

Giulia pretended to scowl. "You are destroying my image of the saintly life Sisters led pre–Vatican II."

Joan laughed like an asthmatic beagle. "Then I won't tell you about the time we short-sheeted the Postulant Mistress's bed." She rubbed her knees. "You know that section of poured concrete under the clotheslines? We said Rosaries on it for a month, rain and sun and wind, in full view of every Sister in the place. My knees still have phantom pain."

Giulia sat on her heels and laughed. "That beats ours. Three weeks into our Canonical year we escaped to McDonald's and bought french fries and chocolate shakes. That illicit celebration netted us a week of fasting."

"I'll bet you learned what it really means to 'offer it up.' "

"Not on the night they served liver." Giulia stood the walker next to Joan's right hand. "Ready to stand?"

"As I'll ever be. I'm a little bottom-heavy these days."

"Only underwear models care about that. One—two—three." She leveraged Joan onto her feet and steadied her for a moment.

"Thank you. It will take more than a frayed rug to tuck me into a casket." She reached for the cane. "If you'll get my veil for me, I'll make myself presentable for the Big Celebration Mass. You might want to put yours on, too."

Giulia clapped her hand to her head. "Oops." She handed Joan her veil with a smile. "Someone's grand entrance interrupted me."

Joan scrunched her nose at Giulia. "Always take responsibility for your own actions, Sister. That's what we teach our students."

"I stand corrected. Would you like an extra arm till you get to your room?"

Joan gripped her cane. "I'm all right now, thank you. When you see me in the chapel, the Bride of Frankenstein will have transformed herself into the Bride of Christ again."

"I'll go transform myself as soon as I fix the carpet." Giulia knelt in front of the elevator and ripped out several new loose threads. "I can't take care of the rest without a pair of scissors." She tucked the thicker frayed areas under the edge as best she could.

Footsteps pounded up the stairs. Giulia raised her voice. "Careful—the rug is loose."

"Sister Regina? Thank God—you're just the person I need." Sister Gretchen pushed a flailing violin string away from her face. "Where's your veil?"

"In my room. We had a fall up here."

"Anyone hurt? No? We've got to find the money to replace this antiquated rug." She pushed down the broken string again. "There's a minor crisis in the chapel. Sister Arnulf was giving the grand tour to her visitors, and one of them knocked over the table and vase on the steps near the vestry. My D string picked today of all days to break, and it's already nine o'clock. Can I beg you to help Sister Bartholomew fix it? The vase, that is, not my string."

Giulia got to her feet. "Of course. Just let me get my veil."

"You're a life saver. Thanks." She took the next flight of stairs two at a time.

Giulia slapped at her tangled sheets. Maybe if Mary Stephen decided to snoop again, she'd fix the bed. She stood before the mirror to put on her veil, shoving stray brown curls under the headband around her ears and at the back of her neck. At the same time she railed against yet another obstacle to corralling Sisters Winifred and Arnulf.

The sounds of a trumpet and flute warming up with scales reached Giulia in the chapel hallway. No one wanted to listen to warm-ups. That guaranteed an empty chapel for her and Bart.

She walked down the center aisle. Someone had put the table back in place and set the vase on it, but most of the flowers were askew on the banged-up floral foam. The palm leaves leaned every which way. At least three of the carnations were bent in half and something had decapitated one of the stargazer lilies. Mum petals sprinkled the floor like snow.

"Sweet cartwheeling Jes—"

Giulia pointed a finger to her right and behind her, and Sister Bart's voice cut off. They climbed the steps together. A wet patch littered with flakes of green foam spread in an irregular circle on the platform and down to the first step.

Bart groaned. "What a disaster. Sister Fabian's going to have a cow."

"Let's make it a small cow. I'll get the floral wire. Could you bring the roll of paper towels?"

While Bart used most of the roll soaking up the water, Giulia spread the flowers out on several towels.

"This floral foam looks like someone played baseball with it." She re-taped it to the sides of the vase. "I can save the palms ... not this leaf. Not that one ..." She wiggled the three palms so the missing leaves only showed if she looked at them from a thirty-degree left-hand angle. "That hole can be camouflaged with the mums."

The trumpet began the voluntary, hit a flat note, and started again.

Giulia wound wire around two flopping carnations and turned one mum around so the bare spot faced the back.

Bart stood with her arms full of wet paper towels. "That's pretty good."

"It's short one lily." Giulia nodded at the broken pink-and-red mess on the table. "I probably should remove one from the other arrangement."

"Oh, no—they're too pretty."

"But they're no longer symmetrical." She propped up an injured mum with the last bit of wire. "That'll have to do."

"I'll be back with the vacuum in just a second."

Giulia made a *blech* face at the floor. "I'll pick up what I can."

She wiped the vase and table with two paper towels, then used her fingernails to collect mum petals and foam bits. A flute solo replaced the trumpet voluntary. The sound of squeaking vacuum wheels clashed with the flute as the vacuum approached her.

"I've got it." Bart plugged it into the outlet near the BVM statue and drowned out the flute.

Giulia stayed on her knees, gathering the bits too heavy and wet for the vacuum's suction. Bart turned it off after a few minutes and inspected the floor with Giulia.

"Good enough?"

Bart pressed her hands onto the carpet. "Ugh. Still wet."

Giulia imitated her. "Not that bad." She looked at her watch. "Nine fifteen. It's got to be good enough."

"Already? Yike. I have to check on Vivian and get to the choir loft. Would you mind?" She turned her Bambi eyes on the vacuum, then on Giulia.

"What's wrong with Vivian?"

"A hangover direct from Hell itself. Sister Gretchen was keeping an eye on her till she had to restring her violin."

"Vivian deserves nothing less. Go ahead. I'll take care of the vacuum."

"You're the best. Thank you." Bart walked at a rapid pace off the sanctuary steps and down the center aisle.

The violin started to tune a capricious new D string to the organ. Giulia smiled at a very unladylike word from Sister Gretchen. When she pushed the vacuum through the vestry and into the back hall, its squeaking wheels echoed off the bare walls.

Her hand clung to the storage closet when she closed the door. She opened and closed her fingers, then sniffed them. "Ick. Mum and lily petals don't mix with wet foam."

She reentered the vestry and washed her hands at the sink. *I wonder if they've arrested Father Ray yet? I wonder if Frank's brother is anything like Frank?*

Something slammed into the small of her back, pinning her against the sink. An arm wrapped around her from right to left. A soaked cloth slapped over her face. She breathed in mint and harsh alcohol and something sweet. It stung her nose and eyes. She coughed, trying for a clear breath. The arm tightened around her, bending her backwards. She fought against the arm, against the mint-booze-sweet liquid filling her mouth and nose...

The world slowed. The arm didn't feel quite so tight. Her head filled with cotton candy. *I like that ... reminds me of carnivals ... my hip is buzzing ... hello, Mr. Bee ... want some cotton candy?*

Two hands led her away from the sink and toward a wardrobe. *Just like Narnia ...* The door opened and the hands pushed her inside, folded her legs in half, and closed the door in her face.

She took a deep breath of cleaner air, but the potent mint, like mediciney mouthwash, still filled her nose. She leaned her head against the back of the wardrobe, which remained solid. *Darn. I wanted to meet Aslan.*

A rectangle of light outlined the door. She took another breath, this time smelling dry-cleaned fabric and incense. Her fingers, hands, arms felt like they should float up on their own. Her hip buzzed again. *How'd a bee get in my pocket?* She fumbled her uncooperative fingers between her hip and her compressed legs. *Can't get to it. Doesn't matter anyway. Bees can't talk 'cause I'm not in Narnia…*

She closed her eyes and let enormous fluffs of cotton candy envelop her.

———

Ow … my head hurts. My back hurts. My knees hurt. She pressed fingers against her temples and opened her eyes.

Pitch black.

No. A rectangle of light. What…

She arched her (sore. Why was it sore?) neck. The back of her head clunked against something hard, with a hollow echo. Fabric brushed her arms. The thin rectangle of light resolved into the outline of a door.

I'm folded up like a pretzel and sitting in a closet?

She closed her eyes and the pounding in her head receded. A minty smell lingered in her nose. Her mouth tasted mint, too. Her ears rang.

Voices reached her through the door. Faint, but getting closer.

"You did what?" Father Ray's voice.

He shouldn't be here, I think ... why do I think that?

"I dissolved half a pill in two shots of peppermint schnapps."

Ugh. Sister Fabian.

"You can't mix them with alcohol, you stupid bitch. Did you make her drink it?"

"Of course not." Sister Fabian's voice imitated a glacier. "My intelligence quotient is quite high enough to know that. I poured it onto a washcloth and used it on her like chloroform."

"All right, I suppose ... How did she react?"

"She stopped fighting within ten seconds, just like that reprehensible website said. Really, Raymond, did you think I wouldn't research the proper way to do this?"

Something scraped against the door and the rectangle widened. White light slapped Giulia's eyes. Father Ray loomed over her and stuffed a thick, woven cord between her teeth. Before her sluggish brain could tell her mouth to cry out or her arms to fight back, he pushed her head down onto her chest and yanked the cord tight around her veil. A moment later he released her and her head bounced back; a knot in the cord shielded it from banging on the back wall.

He dragged her out of the wardrobe, long hanging garments flapping against her face. *They're albs and chasubles. I'm in the vestry. That's right, I was washing my hands.*

He sat her down hard in the bentwood chair usually kept next to the sanctuary doorway.

She had to get out of this, but her arms moved like she was swimming through molasses.

Sister Fabian wound green floral tape around and around Giulia's upper body from elbows to biceps. It snapped a few times, but

Father Ray kept his hands on Giulia's shoulders while Fabian layered more tape over the breaks. Giulia's arms refused to obey her with anything like normal speed. Her legs rebelled as well, twitching and jerking rather than kicking Fabian's legs when she came around to the front of the chair.

Giulia refused to look in Father Ray's warm brown eyes; her situation brought up images of a mouse before a cobra. *Not good. Fabian's not even rushing. How out of it do I look? What did she force me to inhale? I swallowed a little too, I think.* She jerked her head left and right. *You're talking ... thinking ... drivel. Dribble ... something's dribbling down my neck.*

She wiggled her ears; nothing. Her eyelids, her nose; the same. At last she narrowed the sensation down to the cord in her mouth. Now that she had something to focus on, she identified what was causing the tickles: saliva had soaked the cord and was dripping from the corners of her mouth down into her collar.

As the spit trails thinned in the vestry's chill air, goosebumps erupted all over her upper body. Her brain shook off the cotton-candy shroud. She struggled for real against the floral tape. It gave, but not much.

Her de-fogged ears heard pews creaking from out in the chapel. If they were starting to come in for Mass, it had to be close to ten o'clock. She couldn't have been loopy in the wardrobe for more than a few minutes.

Father Ray's hands banged on the top rail of Giulia's chair and she jumped, as much as her green mummy wrapping let her.

"Sister Regina Coelis. I hope you enjoyed your brief mental journey." His "I'm everyone's friend" smile turned darker with each word.

"You disgusting predator." That's what she tried to say, but around the cord in her mouth it sounded more like "Goo guh-guh'n chl-eh-eh."

Off to Giulia's left, the pews continued to creak and kneelers banged down onto the floor.

Father Ray's smile became genial again. "My cincture seems to be interfering with your speech. I beg your pardon." He reached behind her and unknotted the cord.

She shoved at it with her tongue. He stepped back, still smiling, and watched her fight until the thick, woven gold cord plopped onto her lap, discolored in the center from her saliva. Her dry mouth tasted like thread and mint and bitter medicine.

"I said you're a disgusting predator." Her tongue felt too thick.

Sister Fabian came into Giulia's line of vision. "It's half-full out there."

Father Ray kept his eyes on Giulia. "Then we'll be quiet. There's plenty of time." He chucked her chin, just like he'd done to Vivian that first day. "It's unfortunate that my dear Fabian chose for her investigation the one Sister she couldn't browbeat into submission."

"Your dear Fabian is a criminal and you're her accomplice." Her head fuzzed for a moment and she shook it clear. "What did you drug me with?"

"I'm 'her' accomplice?" Father Ray gave a subdued laugh. "I feel quite disrespected."

"Stop wasting time, Raymond." Fabian shouldered him aside. "I drugged you, you interfering bitch. You knew what I expected of you. All you needed to do was agree with my official report and you would've been out of my hair for good."

"If you remembered anything about me, you should've known I wouldn't roll over for you." She started to cough.

Fabian tilted Giulia's head back and poured water in her mouth. Giulia spluttered and sneezed.

"Don't think calling for help will solve your problem." Father Ray dangled a purificator in Giulia's face. "I know how to silence uncooperative Sisters."

Giulia stared at the pure white linen meant to wipe the chalice after Communion. "You make me sick. How do you say Mass with a clean conscience?"

"You should have paid more attention to Church history, Sister. I am following the excellent path laid out by certain Holy Fathers."

Giulia stopped her surreptitious bicep-flexing and deep breathing, intended to stretch the floral-tape wrappings. "What path?" She knew copious amounts of Church history. No document about the right era opened amidst the trails of cotton candy still gumming up her brain.

"Raymond, finish this." Fabian glanced through the doorway. "Three-quarters full."

Father Ray sneered at Sister Fabian. "Relax. You'll live longer. I have a little pill that would do wonders for you."

Fabian left the doorway and joined Father Ray in front of Giulia. "Take your own counsel. If you had kept to one vice we wouldn't be in this situation."

He shook his head. "Fabian, Fabian. Why don't you just admit you want to claw the eyes out of every succulent young Novice you bring to me?"

Giulia pushed her elbows out. The tape stretched a little more.

"If we didn't need the money—"

"Exactly." Father Ray hooked his right arm around Fabian's neck and dragged her into a hard kiss.

Giulia made a disgusted noise to get their attention. "Is he your Confessor? Has he given you permanent dispensation from your vow of chastity?"

Fabian pushed Raymond away. "Not here. What are you thinking?"

"I'm thinking that you've lost focus." He gestured to Giulia, exaggerated forbearance on his face. "She said she was willing to do whatever it took to preserve the Community."

"I still am. I trapped her for you, didn't I?"

"True." This time when he faced Giulia, his face was filled with mad-scientist-like glee. "Your detective boss and his Keystone Kops missed me this morning. You have one of the Sisters to thank for that."

"Stop playing with her." Fabian straightened her already perfect feast-day corsage. "Sister Mary Stephen came to me before Office this morning."

"Oh, for crying out loud." Giulia slumped, expanding her chest and pushing out her arms at the same time. "Did she tell you she's raided my room twice? That she played with my underwear?"

In the chapel, Sister Gretchen's violin played the high, sweet opening to "O Sanctissima."

Father Ray laughed. "Did she really? I'm intrigued. What are you wearing today?" He picked up her skirt.

Sister Fabian slapped away his hand. "Control yourself." She said to Giulia, "Sister Mary Stephen brought me an extensive list of grievances against you. I had no trouble pretending to take her seriously. Her pride has always made her easy to manipulate."

"If Mary Stephen had known anything, she would've thrown it in my face."

"Her festering jealousy of you caused her to make hurried copies of everything in your room, including the pages in your daily organizer."

Father Ray's smile widened. Giulia wondered how she ever thought he was charming.

The tape at Giulia's left elbow gave way. To cover the sound, she said, "I'm not surprised. At either of you."

"Give the snitch to me," Father Ray said. "I'll enjoy breaking her, even if she's too much like you to enjoy any other part of it."

Sister Fabian stood rock-still for a long moment. Giulia heard more kneelers hit the floor as the choir took a breath between measures. In that beat of silence, Giulia's phone chose to vibrate, buzzing against the wooden chair like a swarm of hornets.

Father Ray dug into her pocket. "You have a text message, Sister. Let me read it for you." He pressed buttons and gave the phone a dirty look. "I dislike text-speak. It makes me feel my age. 'Missed priest at house. May be coming to your place. Be careful.' " He aimed the phone at the wall, but Fabian stopped him.

"No noise," she whispered.

Giulia reached for her phone without thinking of the mummy wrappings. She popped several strands, but not enough to escape the chair.

Father Ray held the phone out of her reach. "You miserable, sneaking, disobedient bitch. You've destroyed my business. Six years' work, gone in two weeks." He turned the smile on Fabian. "Although technically, I could divide the blame equally between both of you."

"Me?" Fabian glanced at the doorway and lowered her voice. "If you'd kept your hands off the Novices we wouldn't be in this situation."

"I beg to differ. We had an excellent business plan until you pushed for more frequent deliveries."

"We had to have money. You promised you'd keep them compliant."

Giulia ripped more of the damaged wrappings free while Fabian and Ray weren't looking at her. Every cell in her brain wished for a hidden recording device.

"No, you became greedy. You and your big celebration plans. I knew that Bridget was unstable from the move and that the drugs heightened it." He clamped his hand on Giulia's almost-free arm. "Don't assume I'm distracted, Sister."

The organ began Pachelbel's "Canon."

Father Ray gave Fabian a disgusted look. "I despise that song."

"It's not your Motherhouse. And she was fine even after we upped the concentration."

Giulia said, "I knew it. Didn't you consider the side effects? What you did sent her into a suicidal tailspin."

Ray glanced at her, a scrap of admiration on his face, before he said to Fabian, "No, you desiccated nag, she was not fine. Even your intended puppet here figured that out. You would've seen it if you hadn't been so obsessed with your Motherhouse. Did you enjoy watching her vomit bleach and blood and stomach lining there on the laundry room floor? Did you even consider calling 9-1-1?"

"What?" Giulia's voice pierced the muted, peaceful song. Fabian shoved her hand over Giulia's mouth.

"Of course not. She was collateral damage. Ow—" She jerked away her hand, red teeth-shaped dents in two fingers.

"And now it's all ruined." Father Ray gave her a deliberate once-over. "I needed those Novices as an antidote to you. Remembering how good it is to fuck their sweet young bodies is what sustains me when you demand to be serviced." He looked down at Giulia. "You didn't know the Novices were my personal harem?" He jerked his head toward Fabian. "She convinced them to give themselves to me, you know. Anything it took to keep the Community in the black." He laughed. "I wish I had a camera right now. Your face is comical. Oh, wait—I do." He flipped open Giulia's phone. "I'll keep this to remember you by, before I deliver you to my dealers. I promised them compensation for their interrupted income."

Sister Fabian leapt at him, nails raking his face. Father Ray crashed onto the floor, a foot shy of the sanctuary doorway.

"You bastard! I ruined myself for you—you said I was beautiful—you said—"

Father Ray heaved her off and punched her. Fabian gasped and kneed his stomach. Giulia ripped away layers of tape with her free hand as the chair fell on its side from her struggles.

Father Ray gripped Fabian's throat. "You frigid, greedy bitch! I could've lived for years on my Contin money and enjoyed a new crop of Novices every year on top of it."

Giulia threw off the chair. It crashed into Father Ray and he thumped onto the floor, his rear end over the threshold.

The organ and violin notes clashed and stopped.

"You lying pig!" Sister Fabian grabbed his ears and banged the back of his head against the door frame.

He clamped his hands over her wrists and yanked. "You dried-up whore!"

Giulia pried Sister Fabian's fingernails out of Father Ray's scalp. "Have some respect for the house of God!"

The door to the hallway slammed open. Two men in suits ran in. Father Ray's hand dived into his cassock and came out with a weenie black pistol. For a surreal instant, Giulia thought it was a cigarette lighter. The suits both pulled guns that looked one hundred percent real.

BOOM.

THIRTY

Giulia touched her cheek and looked at the blood on her hand. Her ears rang. Dust and smoke filled the vestry. She blinked, took a breath, and coughed.

Three men ran around her. She heard their voices through the noise in her head, distorted at first, but slowly clearing up.

"Fire and EMTs on their way."

"I need to stop this bleeding. Tony, find a towel."

"Small fire on the other side of this wall. We've got to evacuate."

Giulia raised herself on one elbow in time to see Sister Theresa run in from the supply hall with a fire extinguisher. The pin at its top dropped to the sanctuary rug as she braced herself against the altar and sprayed powdery chemicals at the wainscoting.

"Good job, Sister." One of the suits followed her into the sanctuary. "That's got it. I'd use another one to make sure."

"Here comes the one from the vestibule and we're bringing two more from the kitchen."

Another pop and hiss.

Giulia could hear those noises now. She tried to sit up straighter.

"To your left…there you go. The fire department will be here any minute to check the walls."

Giulia looked around the crowded vestry. Father Ray lay face down on the floor, unconscious. His shredded cassock exposed several gashes from the small of his back to his knees.

"I could've lived without seeing your naked butt," she muttered.

Sister Fabian also sprawled unconscious on the floor with her head in Sister Beatrice's lap. Blood soaked Fabian's veil as Sister Beatrice shrieked for a bandage. One of the suits handed her the purificator Father Ray had been holding, and she wadded it onto Sister Fabian's injury.

A multitude of female voices reached through the minor chaos in the vestry. They babbled and exclaimed and overlapped each other until the suit checking Father Ray's butt injuries had to yell into his cell phone. One of the other suits stood in the ruined doorway making calming gestures.

Frank appeared out of the chaos and knelt in front of her. "Giulia, are you all right?"

"I think so." Her voice echoed in her head a trifle. "Where did you come from? Who got shot?"

"Nobody. Tony says it was a pipe bomb."

A deep male voice cut through the shrieks and chattering. "Ladies—Sisters—please don't touch anything. Who's in charge?"

"Sister Fabian." Several voices.

"Could someone bring her here, please?"

More voices overlapped each other.

"She's on the floor in the vestry." "What happened to her?" "What exploded?" "Is the fire all out?"

The suit looked over his shoulder at Frank. "Can your partner control this?"

"Give her a minute." Frank stared into Giulia's eyes. "You're not dilated. Can you stand up? The crowd out there's headed for hysterics."

Sister Gretchen's voice rose above the commotion. "Sisters, please give the authorities room to work. Sister Florence, Sister Catherine, could you usher them back to the pews? Sisters Dorothea and Helen, our elderly Sisters need a little help down the steps. Thank you so much." She raised her voice to a near-shout. "Sisters, the firefighters are in the hallway. Please clear the aisle for them."

The suit in the shredded doorway turned back to Frank. "She's good. Reminds me of my high school principal."

Two firemen invaded the vestry from the chapel side, Sisters Gretchen and Bart following. Two more came into the vestry through the door from the hallway, a fire hose unrolling behind them.

Frank peeled ragged floral tape from Giulia's sleeves. "What's with this stuff?"

She ripped away the pieces clinging to her crucifix. "Frank, Fabian forced the Novices to have sex with him." She made a movement toward Ray's unconscious body. "If he was awake I'd make sure he'd need surgery just to be able to pee again."

Frank snorted.

"He taunted Fabian with her looks and she went postal. She was sleeping with him, too."

Frank whistled. "This'll be an interesting court case."

"That's your reaction?"

"Sorry." He gave her a once-over. "You've got a bump on your head, too."

A pair of EMTs squeezed into the vestry. One knelt next to Ray, the other by the Beatrice-Fabian Pietà.

Giulia touched her hairline below her skewed veil. "Must've been from when the chair fell over." She plucked a remnant of tape. "Fabian forced me to inhale some of their drug and they taped me to the chair. Ray said we'd ruined his income and he was going to let his dealers take it out on me. I got out of it when they were catfighting." Her veil fell across one eye. "I should've let them beat the crap out of each other."

Frank grabbed both sides of her face and kissed her hard.

Two horrified gasps sounded over their heads.

When Frank broke the kiss, Giulia said, "What was that for?"

"For brilliant undercover work. And maybe I wanted to see what it was like to kiss a nun."

Giulia tried to scowl, but couldn't hold it. They both laughed.

One of the suits squatted next to them. "Excuse me, Ms.—Falcone, right? Can we get your help out here? This little old nun's translator says she insists on talking to you."

"Sister Arnulf. Frank, would you give me a hand up?"

A brief wave of dizziness hit Giulia. She leaned on him for a moment. "Okay now."

To their left, Bart and Gretchen stared at Giulia. Bart's face was a picture of horror, but Gretchen looked like she wanted to snatch Giulia's ring and crucifix and boot her out the door.

Giulia smiled. "Let me introduce myself. I'm Giulia Falcone, working undercover here to investigate Bridget's death. I haven't been Sister Regina Coelis for a year and a half."

The air around them thawed. Bart's face morphed from horror to surprise. Gretchen lost her Vengeance Is Mine attitude, but one of the suits took her aside before she could reply.

Giulia and Frank passed through the dripping, frayed doorway into the sanctuary. One firefighter was checking the wall, but the others were packing up. The air smelled of smoke and chemicals and burned insecticide.

Their feet squelched across the rug and ground in the remnants of the flower arrangements. Most of the Sisters still crowded the pews, talking and rubbernecking at the train wreck that had replaced the Feast Day Mass. The suits—detectives Frank came with—went from pew to pew, writing in what Giulia hoped was rapid shorthand. No fewer than three Sisters spoke to them at any one time.

Sister Arnulf stood by the Communion rail, back straight, mouth compressed, a mixture of triumph and frustration in her eyes. Her friends from Sweden stood next to her, looking like her personal guard. Sister Theresa ran to Giulia, Sister Winifred hovering by the other three.

"Sister Regina, I don't know what to tell you. I never expected anything like this. Never. If we had only looked into their luggage last night, but how could we have imagined anything like this? What is the Vatican committee going to say about Sisters in jail?"

Giulia stopped her. "What? What are you talking about?"

Sister Arnulf stepped forward. "Jag stoppade honom för Bridgets skull."

Sister Winifred translated. "She did it for Bridget. Those poor girls were too afraid to say anything, but Bridget told her what that priest did to them. Bridget thought it was safe because no one else understood Sister Arnulf."

Sister Arnulf poked Giulia's arm and resumed speaking.

Sister Winifred translated: "When I realized you came here to find the truth, I showed you. I drew a picture of his mole for you. That should have pointed you in the right direction."

"Why would a mole have done that?" Giulia said.

Sister Winifred translated question and answer.

"Don't they teach young girls anything? His mole location means 'treachery.' How much more of a hint could I give you? You tried to learn my language, but there was no time. Besides, Sister Fabian attached that one to spy on me." She pointed to Sister Theresa. "I knew I had to act before little Bartholomew gave up."

Sister Theresa's mouth fell open. "What does she mean?"

Giulia said, "Sister Fabian and Father Ray addicted the Novices to drugs and used them as their personal delivery service. She also forced them to have sex with Ray to keep them controlled."

Horrified exclamations from the English-speaking Sisters, including four who were hovering near the Communion rail.

"I'm sorry to spring it on you like that, but since Sister Arnulf knew about the situation, I can see why she'd be suspicious of anyone appointed by Fabian." Giulia said to Sister Arnulf, "I'm sorry I didn't understand you."

Sister Arnulf shrugged when Sister Winifred translated this. "I knew what I had to do. That man—" Arnulf said it with a spitting motion— "was as bad as the Nazi who raped and killed my mother. He even looks like him. As we knew then, so we knew now it was time when God uses His people to mete out His justice. So I emailed Peregrin and Georgia. They contacted one of our American friends from the Resistance. She procured the supplies." Sister Arnulf smiled. "When you picked up that hockey bag, I thought Peregrin would have a heart attack."

"Hockey bag? Right—the one in the trunk of the car last night." Giulia looked at the three visitors. "What did you do?"

Sister Winifred said, "They made a pipe bomb."

The firefighters carried the used extinguishers out through the opening in the Communion rail.

Giulia stared at the three innocuous elderly women, shaking her head. "We underestimated you."

Sister Arnulf said one word and the others repeated it, like a secret handshake.

"I had no idea," Winifred said. "I thought the hockey bag had souvenirs in it. Apparently they haven't forgotten what they learned in the war. They made the bomb in Peregrin's room last night. This morning, when the 'Canon' began and we heard loud voices from the vestry, she left her seat and walked up to the Communion rail. When Father Ray's behind crossed the threshold, she pulled the pipe from the folds of her skirt, lit the fuse, and threw it." Sister Winifred shook her head. "She blocked it from everyone's view until the last minute. From a tactical standpoint, it was perfect."

One of the detectives trotted down the steps to them.

"They've got the priest stabilized and are taking him to the hospital. The nun doesn't need it."

"Thanks, Tony," Frank said.

Sister Winifred translated for Sister Arnulf and refused to reveal to the group the first part of her reply. Sister Arnulf kept talking.

"She's angry because her arm isn't what it used to be. When she was sixteen, the bomb would've landed square in the middle of Father Ray's back."

"*Dia naofa.*"

Giulia elbowed Frank.

"You don't even know what I said." He gestured toward the Swedish line of defense. "Tony, this is Sister Arnulf. She's responsible for the pipe bomb."

Tony stared at Frank, then at Sister Arnulf, whose posture radiated the opposite of remorse. "Driscoll, you're not telling me I have to arrest a nun old enough to be my grandmother."

"I'm afraid I am. Correct, Sisters?"

Sister Winifred opened her mouth, but Sister Arnulf spoke first.

Winifred sighed. "She says she can tell you're a policeman, and she is quite ready to go to prison for stopping that … I won't translate the rest."

"It's bad enough we're arresting a nun and a priest in there. How the hell am I going to explain this in Confession on Saturday?"

Giulia thought at Winifred: *Think of something! Every idea I'm coming up with to prevent that sweet old nun being taken to jail is either lame or ridiculous.*

Winifred stepped between Arnulf and Tony. "Gentlemen, I understand that you have a duty to perform. However, Sister Arnulf is a citizen of Sweden and also under the protection of the Vatican." Her eyes never wavered from Tony's face. "She also has several health problems in addition to her advanced age."

Tony returned her steady gaze. "So she isn't a flight risk."

Winifred gave him a wide-eyed look. "If you're reaching that conclusion as a representative of the law, it's not my place to argue with you."

"Right, Sister. Let me see what I can do." He hit the *Call* button on his cell phone. "Ann? It's Tony. Give me the captain."

He walked away, still inside the Communion rail, staring at the statue of Saint Joseph while he talked.

Frank touched Giulia's shoulder. "You want to keep her out of jail, too, don't you?"

"Absolutely."

"You're wrong. I don't care how sweet you think she is. She tried to murder that priest."

Giulia turned on him. "She blew up arms depots during World War Two. Criminals died because of that. He's a criminal. How is this different?"

"Simple. It's against the law. Besides, innocent till proven guilty, remember?"

"He admitted it to my face. If I'd known Sister Arnulf's plans, I might not have stopped her."

"Will you listen to yourself? You once said you were all about Franciscan ideals: peace and forgiveness and all that. What happened in three days to make you toss it in the garbage?"

She opened her mouth and closed it again. A cold breeze hit her face; to her left came the sound of a stretcher bumping over the vestry threshold and out the garden door.

"Well?" Frank said, looking in the same direction.

"If I'm honest with myself I think I wish her arm had been what it was in the war." She sat on the top step. "What does that say about me?"

Sister Bart came out of the vestry and picked up the least-trampled carnations. "They're not symmetrical anymore."

"No one's going to have a cow about that now."

"Yeah." Her smile lost its guilty air. "They're both gone now. They're not coming back, right?"

Giulia looked up at Frank.

"Yes, Sister. You'll be called on to make a statement and testify at their trials."

Bart nodded. "Good. Vivian will too. Sister Gretchen will take care of it." She sat next to Giulia. "When you two kissed each other back there, it was like watching your hero crumble to bits." She ducked her head. "I kind of started to look up to you this week. You've got balls." She slapped her hand over her mouth. "Sister Gretchen will kill me."

Frank studied the painted ceiling.

Giulia laughed. "Thank you for the compliment. I'm sorry I had to lie to you, but it goes with the job."

"Bridget will stop haunting the laundry now."

Sister Gretchen came over to them. "I want to corral everyone into the refectory. It's early, but coffee and tea will give them something to occupy themselves. They need to get out of this insanity."

Bart stood. "I'll start with the Blessed Virgin side." One step down, she turned back to Giulia. "You're going, aren't you?"

"Yes. I have paperwork to fill out." She struck a pose. "My work is finished here."

Bart wrinkled her nose. "That sounds like a line from a corny Western."

"It made you smile."

"Cheater." She held out her hand. "Thanks."

Giulia stood and clasped it. "Bridget wasn't haunting the laundry."

Bart looked skeptical, but turned her attention to the milling, gesturing groups in the nave.

Giulia said to Frank, "That's why I may not have stopped Sister Arnulf from throwing that pipe bomb. When I get back to the world, I'll get my head on straight. You got the psychiatric rider on the insurance, right?"

Tony beckoned to them. "Sister—Gretchen, is it? Thanks to some fast talking, our no-longer-retired bomber is under house arrest. A female officer will be stationed outside her door for the next few days."

Gretchen visibly exhaled. "Thank you, Officer. I'll be available to help sort things out whenever you require me."

Frank said, "I'll drive Giulia to the station and we'll get the process started."

"Good. It's going to be a long day." Tony went back into the vestry.

"Where did you park?" Giulia adjusted her veil.

"In the driveway. When we missed the priest at his house, we came over here in a hurry. Why is that thing still on your head?"

"Because I have to go upstairs to pack my clothes, and I don't want to be delayed by a lot of questions." She smoothed her habit. "See? Just another Sister dealing with the Saint Francis Day Scandal. I'll meet you outside in ten minutes."

She weaved through the stragglers in the hallway and main hall. No one stopped her. She stuffed her clothes in her old black suitcase any which way. "Out of here," she practically sang to herself. "Home. Free. The Novices safe. The scum locked away." Desk drawer emptied. Dresser drawer emptied. Toiletries, spare habit, pantyhose both pristine and wrecked. Her Godzilla slippers. "Huh. Never took them out of the wardrobe."

A last look around the room with her hand on the doorknob. "Goodbye and good riddance, cell. Never again."

As soon as she'd closed the door behind her, Sister Mary Stephen launched herself from across the hall.

"Regina, what horrible scandal have you involved the Community in?"

Giulia set down her suitcase and held out her hand.

"Allow me to introduce myself, Sister Mary Stephen. I'm Giulia Falcone. I've been working undercover here for the past few days, and now I'm going home."

Mary Stephen took Giulia's hand with an automatic motion, but simply stared without returning the handshake.

Giulia squeezed and released the limp hand. "The Community may be saying good things about me again. I'm afraid you've been sucking up to the wrong people."

She walked away, open raincoat flapping against her suitcase.

"Regina?"

"Offer it up, Mary Stephen. Offer it up."

The din from the chapel seemed twice as loud now that it was trapped inside the refectory.

Poor Sister Gretchen. Now that she's taken temporary charge, the ten-ton weight from Fabian and Ray's sins will get dropped on her shoulders.

Giulia reached the hall. She didn't detect any smoke odor this far from the chapel, but muddy bootprints discolored the rug. Scuff marks marred the paint in the foyer and dirtied the floor.

Of course—firemen aren't interested in the floor polish when they're trying to save your house. Fabian would have a cow if she could see it.

She turned the door handle. *And what Fabian wants doesn't matter anymore.* Her grin stretched her cheeks so wide, her veil popped off the tops of her ears.

Frank's Camry idled in the same spot the Convent Clown Car had parked the night before.

Giulia paused in the doorway and took a huge breath of cold fall air. Then she ran down the steps.

THIRTY-ONE

At ten o'clock the next morning, Giulia rang the Motherhouse doorbell—the habits, veils, crucifix, and wedding ring in their box under her arm. Her rented Kia Soul—she couldn't resist—was parked on the street behind the wall.

Sister Alphonsus answered, her smile more mechanical than sincere.

"Good morning, miss. May I help you?"

"Good morning, Sister. I have a package for Sister Gretchen. She's expecting me."

"I see. I'm glad it wasn't with Sister Fabian—oh. Oh, dear, please don't mind me. We're all discombobulated today. Let me find Sister Bartholomew."

Bart walked into the foyer at that moment.

"Sister, what perfect timing. This young lady is here to see Sister Gretchen."

Bart looked from Giulia to the doorkeeper and back again. Giulia shook her head slightly, and Bart put on her cheerful smile.

"Good morning, I'm Sister Bartholomew. Just follow me."

When they were on the first flight of stairs, Bart said, "She didn't recognize you?"

"Everyone looks different without the veil. How are the troops holding up?"

"The older ones are handling it better than the middle-aged ones. Vivian had to be sedated. The Postulants called home, and they're both leaving."

Giulia's stride broke. "I didn't think about them. Were they forced into dealing too?"

"No. He waited for vows."

"To add to the guilt and pressure. Bastard. Oops." She glanced around, but no one else was on that flight of stairs.

Bart laughed.

Giulia said, "If you'll forgive a cliché, you look like a different person."

Bart's smile dimmed, but not for long. "We're free. I didn't realize the weight of it all till the ambulance took them both away. The cops were amazing. They let Sister Gretchen stay with me when I told them everything. I felt kind of bad for her, because there was some stuff I didn't get a chance to tell her in all the craziness."

"Frank and I were with them for a good three hours after the Mass that didn't happen."

They reached the fifth-floor landing.

"Where is everybody?" Giulia said. "I counted maybe ten people in the halls."

"Lots of them are in the chapel, praying. Most of the visiting ones hit the road right after breakfast. Sister Gretchen's been huddled with the Superiors from the other Communities off and on, working out a stopgap plan to run the place."

When they reached the Novices' living room, Bart took Giulia by the shoulders. "You look so different. It's not just the pants and sweater and makeup. You look, I don't know, bouncier."

Giulia smiled. "I'm free again. Leaving here—for real—was the hardest thing I ever had to do. Coming back and pretending to belong, and lying, and searching out a murderer, well…let's say I looked for premature gray hair in my mirror last night."

"I'm staying, you know." Bart held her head high when she said it. "Sister Gretchen and I talked till some ungodly hour this morning. I didn't expect to reach that decision, but when I said it out loud, I knew it was right."

"Good for you. If God's talking to you, then you have to listen."

Sister Gretchen's door opened. "Sister Regina? No, wait. I'm sorry. I've forgotten your name. It's been crazy here."

"No problem. It's Giulia."

The Novice Mistress closed her sitting room door and pulled out two chairs at a small round table.

Giulia set the box on top of the table. "Everything's in there. Two habits, two veils, crucifix and wedding band."

Sister Gretchen placed one hand on the box. "Bart told me what you've been doing here this week. She insists that the situation is not my fault, but I disagree. I'm responsible for them, body and soul, for a year and a day. I should have noticed that there was more to everything than the standard adjustment period."

"You didn't get invested with psychic powers when Fabian promoted you. Don't beat yourself up over this. Ray had been dealing for six years after he took over his father's ten-year business."

"Oh, my Lord."

"There's a sad story behind his father's fall, but I have no sympathy to spare for Ray. He's a criminal and a predator, and if I had my way I'd slice his junk off with a serrated knife and feed it to him." Giulia's fists clenched and then relaxed. "I'm glad Bart's content with her decision to stay. I know I don't have to ask if she and Vivian will be getting counseling."

"Their first appointments are tomorrow." Sister Gretchen rubbed her temples. "I know about the box of razor blades, too. Now that the danger is gone, Bart told me everything. The police assured me that she and Vivian won't be prosecuted."

Giulia sighed with relief. "There is justice in the world. I wish there was some kind of deal the Community could make for Sister Arnulf."

Sister Gretchen looked down at the tabletop. "You don't have to worry about that."

"Really? Why?"

"They're gone."

Giulia's forehead wrinkled. "I'm sorry?"

Sister Gretchen bit her cheek. "Sister Winifred was on the phone for hours yesterday with the Swedish consulate and the Diocesan office. We all thought she was arranging lawyers and more interpreters and giving them the details of what the three of them had done. The police officer sent to guard them arrived before noon. She stayed in the hall outside their doors, followed them down to the refectory, went everywhere with them except the bathroom."

"How did that affect the general morale?"

"Everyone was numb by then. Even the most gossip-ready hardly gave her a glance."

"But you said the three Sisters are gone."

Sister Gretchen looked like she was making an effort to appear ashamed. "Even police officers have to use the facilities. Sister Theresa volunteered to take her place in the hallway for those times." A pause. "After Compline, when she was in the bathroom, Sister Winifred spirited them out and to the airport. By this time, they're back home."

"What? They set off a homemade bomb. That's an act of terrorism. Homeland Security will—"

"Actually, there's a ninety-five percent chance they won't. The Church has more power than I imagined, even in this modern day. A few years back a diocese in Arizona had a priest accused of pedophilia. His bishop put him on a two a.m. flight out of the country before an arrest warrant was issued. The priest made it to Ireland, and the Justice Department decided it wasn't worth fighting the might of the Church to extradite him."

"You'll forgive me for saying this, but I hope someone took care of him in a dark alley the same day he landed."

Sister Gretchen didn't blink. "I confess to hoping the same when I heard about it. But the precedent helps our situation."

Giulia nodded. "It's a good bet that they won't want to fight the Church to extradite three eighty-year-old nuns who took out a criminal like Father Ray."

"That's what we're hoping. I should be appalled at myself for allowing this to happen." She met Giulia's gaze. "But I'm not. I wanted them to go free, and I want Raymond to end up in a prison that doesn't take kindly to priests who—rape—young nuns." Her jaw clenched.

"We'll do our best to see that it happens. And we'll keep telling ourselves that we're fighting for justice, not vengeance."

Sister Gretchen unclenched. "You too? I'll pray for you if you'll pray for me."

"Deal." Giulia stood. "I have to get back to work. I couldn't count all the emails waiting for me. And I have an admin who's going to burst if I don't tell her what the convent is like."

Sister Gretchen opened the door. "Bart will escort you down. Now that you're 'you,' it would raise a few eyebrows if you walked around by yourself."

Bart didn't say anything until they reached the front door. "Giulia, would you, um, write to me occasionally? I'm going to miss you."

"Of course I will." She gave Bart a crushing hug.

"Are you going to marry the detective who kissed you?"

Giulia gaped, then laughed. "One kiss does not a proposal make. Besides, he has issues with dating a former nun. Sometimes I think he sees a phantom veil on my head."

"And you've been wearing a real one again."

She grimaced. "I know. We've regressed to the days when I first talked to him. It's tough to uproot the indoctrination in some Cradle Catholics, but I'll work at it."

Sister Alphonsus opened the door and they stepped out onto the porch.

"Get inside before you catch your death. What do you think this is, a midnight coffee run?"

Bart laughed and returned to the foyer. The door closed. Giulia took another deep, wonderful breath and jogged to her car. While she waited for the heat to kick in, she drove two blocks to the Double Shot.

"A large pumpkin cappuccino, please." The barista did a double-take, then shook his head and brewed her coffee.

She took the first sip inside the car just as her phone rang.

Frank started talking as soon as she opened the phone. "Where are you?"

"Hello, Frank. I'm in the car about to come back to the office."

"Good. Sidney says she's getting pizza for lunch in honor of your triumphant return, and she promises it won't have too much tofu."

"Despite the threat of tofu, I'll be there in twenty minutes."

"Wait. Are you ready for this? The Diocese of Pittsburgh just called. They're so happy with the way we kept the scandal out of the news that they want to talk about putting us on retainer. Can you imagine? The Church! My grandmother is step-dancing in Heaven right now."

Giulia turned the heat up. "That's great, Frank, but fair warning. If we get any more convent jobs, you're going undercover in drag."

THE END

© D. Steven Hodge

ABOUT THE AUTHOR

Alice Loweecey is a former nun who went from the convent to playing prostitutes on stage to accepting her husband's marriage proposal on the second date. A contributor to BuddyHollywood .com, she is a member of Mystery Writers of America and Sisters in Crime. She lives with her family in Western New York. *Force of Habit* was her first novel.

Please visit Alice's website, at www.aliceloweecey.net.

ACKNOWLEDGMENTS

Thanks are due to several people who helped with Giulia's personal wormhole journey.

To my editor, Terri Bischoff, and my production editor, Brett Fechheimer. You two make me look good.

To my friends and fellow writers who graciously allowed me to turn them into nuns for this book. I'll keep your true identities a secret: enjoy pointing out your new self to your friends! To my beta readers, Julia Austin and Sue Laybourn. To the people who graciously shared their knowledge with me: Amy Bai for the correct way to smudge, Susan Owens for her medical knowledge, Joe Richardson for police information, Max Quaye and K. A. Stewart for correcting my Swedish. To the many brilliant and creative people at Absolute Write, without whom these books wouldn't be shelfworthy.

And always to Purgatory, home of the best friends and writers on the planet. /bootay shakes and *vamp dust* for all of you. Purgatory Will Rule the Publishing World!

www.MidnightInkBooks.com

From the gritty streets of New York City to sacred tombs in the Middle East, it's always midnight somewhere. Join us online at any hour for fresh new voices in mystery fiction.

At midnightinkbooks.com you'll also find our author blog, new and upcoming books, events, book club questions, excerpts, mystery resources, and more.

TM
MIDNIGHT
INK

MIDNIGHT INK ORDERING INFORMATION

Order Online:
- Visit our website www.midnightinkbooks.com, select your books, and order them on our secure server.

Order by Phone:
- Call toll-free within the U.S. and Canada at 1-888-NITE-INK (1-888-648-3465)
- We accept VISA, MasterCard, and American Express

Order by Mail:
Send the full price of your order (MN residents add 6.875% sales tax) in U.S. funds, plus postage & handling to:

> Midnight Ink
> 2143 Wooddale Drive
> Woodbury, MN 55125-2989

Postage & Handling:

Standard (U.S. & Canada). If your order is:
> $25.00 and under, add $4.00
> $25.01 and over, FREE STANDARD SHIPPING

AK, HI, PR: $16.00 for one book plus $2.00 for each additional book.

International Orders (airmail only):
> $16.00 for one book plus $3.00 for each additional book

Orders are processed within 12 business days. Please allow for normal shipping time. Postage and handling rates subject to change.

ALSO BY ALICE LOWEECEY